ACROSS THE ENCHANTED BORDER

What Reviewers Say About Crin Claxton's Work

The Haunting of Oak Springs

"This is a very well written and engaging mystery with a protagonist who can communicate with ghosts. ...Despite being the third book in the series, it works fine as a standalone. The author is quite adept at providing the necessary backstory without info-dumping. Four stars. Strong narrative, good pacing, very disturbing in places."
—*Nonstop Reader*

The Supernatural Detective—*Foreward Review Winner*

"This was an extremely tense, but amazing thriller with an amazing touch of comedy that helped lift it from being too dark and twisted. That formula made the story so enjoyable and a lot of fun to read. The paranormal and thriller genre can be quite scary, but I loved how this provided some relief and made it a story that anyone could enjoy. The humour didn't detract from the depth and excitement of getting caught up in the intense drama this story provided, but it was brilliantly executed to only attract the reader more and offer personal connection to the characters. A great story that I highly recommend."—*LESBIreviewed*

"*The Supernatural Detective* is a sexy, supernatural thriller. A perfect read for the beach."—*Diva Magazine*

Scarlet Thirst

"*Scarlet Thirst* is a book for those who like their erotica to be a little more subtle but still sexy—a la Anne Rice or Mary Renault. Surely a fangtastic read for fans of Buffy, Willow, and Tara!"—*Gay Voice*

"Claxton's descriptions of Granada are sensuous and entirely in keeping with her characters. Claxton manages to pull the disparate threads together with prose and plotting that is never overwritten or superfluous. Claxton has created an entirely believable other world. *Scarlet Thirst* is a great big fun, sexy, smart novel. Look out for it."—*Rainbow Network*

Death's Doorway—*Rainbow Awards Honorable Mention*

"I loved this one. I like the flow and writing style of the author. The story is packed full of twists and turns and keeps the reader engaged. The characters mesh well together! Really enjoyed it—the setting in London England, the main characters were entertaining, the suspense and the humor were spot-on."—*Elisa Reviews*

"There was enough action to keep me excited and enough twists and turns to keep me wondering, through the final thrill. All in all, this was a fun read, with interesting characters and an intriguing story. I recommend it to lovers of diversity, paranormal mysteries that involve ghosts and private investigators, and romantic stories with realistic issues."—*Butterfly-o-Meter*

Visit us at www.boldstrokesbooks.com

By the Author

The Supernatural Detective Series:

The Supernatural Detective

Death's Doorway

The Haunting of Oak Springs

Scarlet Thirst

Across the Enchanted Border

ACROSS THE ENCHANTED BORDER

by

Crin Claxton

2025

ISBN 13: 978-1-63679-804-2

This Trade Paperback Original Is Published By
Bold Strokes Books, Inc.
P.O. Box 249
Valley Falls, NY 12185

First Edition: March 2025

Credits
Editor: Cindy Cresap
Production Design: Susan Ramundo
Cover Design By Inkspiral Design

Acknowledgments

There are many people who lend their skills to this work. My beta readers, who give their time, support, and insightfulness. Thank you, Evren D, Hiraani Himona, Kate May, Sarah Purdue, Semsem Kuherhi, and Susan Purdue; your contributions are beyond measure. The novel would be much the poorer without my editor, Cindy Cresap. Your craft raises my work to the next level. Thank you, Sandy Lowe and all at Bold Strokes Books for your helpfulness and all you do.

Thank you to Rita Hirani, and again to Semsem, for your encouragement.

Thank you to readers who message me and to readers who take the time to write reviews.

Dedication

For Deni and Luca, of course. And Smudge.

And for gender warriors everywhere.

CHAPTER ONE

The canteen was crowded with butch warriors ending night duty and returning from morning drill.

Lieutenant Skylar Larkrye rarely neglected her dawn routine of exercise, combat, and sword practice. She screened out the clatter, intent on the bowl of porridge before her. The barley grains sweetened with the last of the season's honey and enriched with the morning's creamy milk were the fuel her body needed.

She picked up her spoon, mulling over the swordmaster's request for her to tutor sword skills. It was an honor that spoke to her proficiency with the sword, and it *had* been a quiet spring at the warrior training compound. Thale was her home, and she would be proud to repay her community. But Skylar was ready for missions, honed to answer requests for aid. She was not yet ready to tutor cadets.

She dipped her spoon into the porridge and winced. Someone at the doorway screamed her name. She looked over to find a flustered cadet running Skylar's name through zir mind as ze searched the room. A telempath, Skylar sensed feelings more strongly than thoughts and rarely recognized actual words, but this pup's mind was wide open.

The telepath opposite Skylar ground her teeth. "Deal with it, Larkrye, in the name of all that's holy."

Skylar obliged. "Over here, cadet."

"Thank you," Skylar's comrade muttered. "Cadets from the isolated regions should be taught to shield before they walk through Thale's gates."

The training ground took its name from Thale, a dry plains district in eastern Gaea. The land had once been known as Alba's wilderness. Now, it was a country in its own right, albeit a secret one hidden behind the enchanted border.

The cadet bounded to Skylar's table, bursting with the importance of zir task. Unacquainted with the cadet, Skylar naturally used the Gaean neutral ze and zir pronouns.

"Captain Noro wishes to see you," ze said gravely.

Skylar glanced down at her porridge. "Immediately? No time for breakfast?"

The cadet bit zir lip, awash with confusion and embarrassment.

Skylar's comrade grimaced. "Lieutenant, go and see Captain Noro before my head boils from this pup's shouting."

Skylar sighed. "Cadet, you might care to put shielding high on your training schedule." She scooped spoonfuls of porridge into her mouth as she rose to her feet.

In the dirt-packed yard, the cherry trees bore clumps of blushing pale berries. The green leaves fanned out to veil the cloudless blue sky. It had been a quiet season thus far. Maybe this call to duty was the change Skylar had been thirsting for.

The day was already warm. A scant breeze carried the sweet hay scent from the grasses in the plains beyond the compound. The abundance of air was a joke amongst warriors. There was so much of it, far from anywhere.

Skylar had completed her training over ten years ago. Like many, she elected to live on at Thale. Some were without family. Others stayed simply because they were butch and liked the company of their gender. The regular life at the compound with occasional missions suited Skylar. Or it had. This season, she found herself yearning for something more.

Skylar mounted the steps to the clerical building and swung open the door.

Captain Noro looked up, pen in hand. Noro was a seasoned butch warrior with pale skin, short-cropped, light hair, and intense blue eyes that drilled into many a frightened cadet on the parade ground. Ze must be at least forty but was as fit and fierce as any of the young recruits. Skylar read both seriousness and urgency behind Noro's expression. She was glad she had not dallied.

"I need you to travel to the southwestern region. Your telempathy could aid the search for displaced people."

There had been an earthquake on the other side of the country some weeks previously. Here was Skylar's chance to help. She nodded vigorously. Even if Skylar had not wanted to go, she could not have refused. A warrior understood that their superiors would fit them to appropriate tasks. There was no reason to challenge orders in Gaea, where democracy and egalitarianism were prized. The land was created by refugees fleeing from oppression. The military was respected and well-maintained. Even though the enchanted border protected them, the tyranny of Alba remained a threat Gaeans could not ignore. The new leader promised to increase recruits to all the regiments. There had been much talk of improving the founding values of Gaea in her campaign.

"You will travel by boat, shortening the journey by many days. There are wildlands in the south so close to the border. Bandits roam there. You will need to act with caution. Your exemplary sword skills should see you through. It is time you took on a solitary mission."

"I am to travel alone, Captain?"

"Indeed. You will assess the area and report back. There are warriors from the general regiments posted there already. Skylar, there will be many wounded and dead. People will be unaccounted for, and their families will be desperate. There will undoubtedly be lawlessness, and you must act quickly and sensitively. You will cooperate with the local platoons."

Skylar met Noro's eyes. She was keen to rise to zir expectations.

"Pack for a round trip of three weeks. Ride out as soon as you are ready. You will stay in the river inn and sail at first light." Noro stood, extending zir hand.

Skylar returned the Amazon clasp, wrapping her hand firmly around Noro's. The time-honored gesture of greeting and leave-taking was a sign of respect and an acknowledgment of orders received and bargains made. It had been created by the sisterhood in the days when Gaea was a young land. Now adopted by others, it had special meaning for butch warriors wherever they found themselves and each other.

Noro handed Skylar a rolled bundle of papers wrapped in an oiled cloth. "Here is a map and a docket for food and medicine. The supplies will await you at the store near the inn."

Skylar took the bundle and left immediately. She had much to do.

❖

Bhaltair was the butch warrior in charge of the stables. Young for a stable lead, he had an affinity with horses and tended them well. Skylar waited outside the stalls, pack on back, trying to curb her irritation at Bhaltair's provocative tone.

"I have not been sent word that I am to release one of my horses, let alone one of my best. Come back with a docket, Lieutenant, and I will consider your request."

Skylar stared impassively at Bhaltair. The butch was handsome and tall. He wore his long hair in a ponytail. The black color contrasted with his light brown skin and chestnut eyes. His body was taut with muscle. When he was not in the stables, Bhaltair exercised and practiced archery and swordsmanship to the point of exhaustion. Bhaltair had many admirers drawn to his power, his combat skills, and his gentleness with horses. Skylar was not one of them. Two academy years her junior, Bhaltair had focused on Skylar from the beginning as the one to best. The only score Skylar was interested in beating was her own. Still, Bhaltair was competitive and adversarial to the point of stubbornness.

Skylar stepped to the stall before her, where a black mare called Midnight chewed from a feed bucket. Skylar scratched the mare behind her ear. "You are right," she said evenly. "I will go back and ask for a docket. I am headed for the earthquake zone and was fetched from my breakfast in haste. Still, Captain Noro will undoubtedly appreciate your dedication to protocol."

Bhaltair straightened. "Captain Noro's orders, is it? I see. How far do you travel?"

"Just to the river inn. I take a boat from there. The horse will be returned to the compound with the next supply load."

Bhaltair nodded briskly. "Then, you'd best take Midnight. She is rested and will serve you well."

Skylar smiled genuinely. She liked Midnight. And she valued Bhaltair's decision-making. However difficult he could be, he was a worthy ostler. "Thank you."

The stable door opened, drawing in a breeze from the dusty plains. Skylar grinned and strode quickly across the hay-strewn floor to greet her sometime lover. Efren was short and wiry. She excelled at hand-to-hand combat, where her strength belied her physique, taking opponents by surprise. Efren and Skylar had trained together. They had become fast friends and then lovers. Theirs was an uncomplicated, open relationship. Skylar was content to spend the occasional night with Efren while Efren had several relationships. The most serious of them was with Bhaltair.

"You have received orders?" Efren asked.

"Yes, I am packed and leave as soon as my horse is ready."

Efren stepped close, pulling Skylar in for a kiss. "May the Goddess travel with you," she murmured.

"Thank you." Hooves clip-clopped sharply toward them. Skylar opened her eyes.

Midnight was prepped with saddle and bags and pulling away from the reins held rigidly in Bhaltair's clenched fist. Even without telempathy, Skylar would have sensed Bhaltair's anger. She took the reins from Bhaltair with a polite "Thank you" and led Midnight out of the stable into the sunshine, as eager as the horse to be away.

But she managed just one foot in the stirrup before Captain Noro marched briskly across the compound.

"An urgent message came with the mail," Noro said. "Dismount, Lieutenant."

Skylar did as asked, prickling with foreboding.

Skylar opened the letter. It was a request from Skylar's mother, Hera, to join a healing circle. Skylar sighed. Her mother was a healer with a highly sensitive nature. Excruciatingly empathetic, when it all got too much, Hera self-medicated. Skylar had been nine the first time she had joined a healing circle for her mother. This request would be the sixth. Perhaps this time, Hera would cleanse herself of the sedatives she drank like water. If so, she must do it without Skylar's help.

Skylar handed the letter back to Captain Noro. "I have already accepted my orders."

"We can send another warrior, Lieutenant." The captain's expression was kind.

Skylar knew zir intention was honorable, but the captain did not understand. Noro was not empathic and had not experienced Skylar's childhood.

Skylar swung up into Midnight's saddle. "Merry part, Captain."

Noro straightened at once. "Merry meet again, Lieutenant."

Skylar turned Midnight around and rode through the main gates into the vast, dry, ripening grasslands. Rippled by the wind, great bronze waves undulated either side of the trail. Skylar rode at an easy pace, thinking of Hera. It was hard to keep faith with someone intent on destroying themselves. Even if that someone was your mother.

Skylar concentrated on the wind on her face, the hay scent of the grasses, the clip of Midnight's hooves, and the sunshine on her skin until the compound was far behind her. Looking only forward, she fixed her thoughts on her task alone.

❖

The sun was warm and high. A cooling breeze brushed Skylar's face with each turn of the oar, making the journey pleasant. Birds chattered in the trees lining the river. The air was tangy with the scent of river weed and all the life teeming below the surface. The boat's hull was in excellent condition, offering scant resistance to Skylar's strokes as she cut through the water. Skylar welcomed the upper body exercise and the solitude. She relaxed into the rhythmic movement as her eyes skimmed the open vista ahead.

She would need to find a place to camp overnight, but the sun had not yet reached its noon-day position. There were hours of rowing before she would need to halt. Supplies for the journey and the earthquake zone were packed under oiled cloth tied down with rope at the rear end of the craft.

She let the boat drift while she took a long swig from her canteen. The occasional cloud skimmed across the broad, blue sky. She knew to stay as close to the right bank as possible because the border with Alba fell roughly in the middle of the river. Some of the overhanging trees posed a challenge, but the river was easily wide enough to accommodate the small craft without leading her into danger.

Skylar strung the canteen around her neck and bent to pick up the oars.

The cry of an animal in distress pierced her mind.

Skylar listened. The only sounds were the wind, the birds, and the water lapping against the hull. Then, she felt it again, a terrified whimper flooded with pain and frustration. It came from somewhere close to the left bank.

Skylar hesitated. Crossing the border was forbidden.

Every Gaean knew the enchanted border kept the Gaea safe. Alba was a brutal, dangerous country ruled by people with strange ideas. People were assigned male and female genders at birth based on genitalia. The males were considered superior to everyone else, and rulers were exclusively recruited from this group. Albans believed there were only two genders and that attraction between those genders was the only accepted bond.

Many years ago, Alba and Gaea were one country. Rulers came to power preaching hate and restriction. The first warriors, the founders, had fought the rising tyranny. Many had died. The rest had evacuated north in the thousands. The southern rulers attempted to wipe them out with terrible weapons. Witches and mages enchanted the boundary land to create the hidden border. It was unknown if the present Alban rulers knew the border existed. It was safer for Gaea if they did not.

Warriors were trained in the enchantments to cross, but doing so without explicit orders was against the code. Skylar sat in the boat, hesitating while the craft drifted closer to the middle of the river as if deciding for her.

The terrible cry came again. The animal was a vultrix, a sapient fox. Telepathic, intelligent, sensitive, and rare, it was a creature of such beauty and magic that meeting one was considered a blessing. The male vultrix's life force reached out to Skylar. He was strong and young, but his energy was fading. Vultrix were seldom seen in Gaea. Skylar had not known there were any in Alba. As far as she knew, they had been hunted to death there.

Breathing softly and bending the force of the border enchantment, Skylar scanned the area beyond, searching for humans.

She found none, but as her mind reached out, her connection with the vultrix soared. His hind leg was caught in a metal trap. She felt the bite of the teeth into his flesh and winced at his pain. He had been trying to release himself for some time but had only succeeded in deepening his injuries. Skylar smelled the iron scent of his blood and the sharp smell of the grass crushed beneath his body as he lay exhausted and panting. She felt his terror. He was weakening.

She could not deny his call.

❖

Vigilant to any trace of human, Skylar crept silently through the long grass, following the vultrix's rapid, short breaths.

He lay beside an ancient oak. He was young, just a year from being a cub. His coat was the deep clay red of sapient foxes with a sand-colored bib that ran all the way to his black snout. His orange eyes gazed sadly at her. His expression was of one worn down with pain.

I am here to help, she told him, unsure if he would understand the words but hopeful he would sense their meaning.

The light in the forest dimmed. A quick glance at the sky revealed thick, dark clouds covering the sun. Skylar took it as a sign from the Goddess to hurry.

Skylar felt the fox's misgivings when she stepped closer. He longed for help, but she was human, and he knew humans could not be trusted.

He blinked when she crouched next to him. "I am going to force the trap open. This may hurt." Moving carefully, she placed her hands on the levers on each side of the powerful metal jaws.

The vultrix shrank from her. "It is okay," she murmured, keeping her voice soft, trying to reassure him as she pressed down.

He whimpered but held still, his eyes fixed on hers. The jaws inched slowly apart. Skylar took a breath and pressed harder. With a quick yelp, the vultrix snatched his bloody paw from the trap.

They watched each other, the vultrix licking his wound without taking his fiery eyes from hers. His thanks flowed through her mind as a warm breeze.

"I am not from here," she said quickly. "I am from a land where these do not exist." She tipped her head toward the trap with disgust. "You can come with me if you choose. You will be safe there."

The vultrix blinked slowly. Then he stood, testing the ground and sniffing the air. Skylar rose, too. She said nothing more and began quietly retracing her steps.

Her boat was pulled up onto the riverbank where she had left it. When she pushed it back into the water, she glanced over her shoulder.

The vultrix stood a few steps away, his wounded paw raised from the ground. He eyed the boat warily. His tail twitched. He looked at the river. Skylar felt his mind soar and stretch across what looked from this side of the border to be the world's edge.

Mind made up, he limped down the slope of the grassy bank and leaped gracefully into the rowing boat.

Skylar stepped in after him, thankful to have accomplished her task. In a few short strokes, they would both be safely back in Gaea.

❖

As they sailed from the riverbank, the clouds thickened, and it grew dark as night. A whirling mass of wind rushed across the water. It surrounded the boat, rocking it. Torrential rain burst from the sky.

Skylar dropped the oars into the bottom of the boat and crawled to the cloth covering the supplies. Struggling against the wind, she lifted the fabric high enough for the little vultrix to slip under. At least one of them could shelter.

Skylar fastened her cloak tightly around her and scrambled back to the oars. If she could get them back across the border, they could wait out the storm safely.

Rain blurred her vision. The wind tore at the oars. She gripped on tightly, but when she tried to row, one was ripped from her hand.

She paddled as best she could with one oar, dipping it on one side and then the other. But the boat spun in the vortex, and she struggled to make headway. A thunderclap boomed violently overhead.

Lightning zig-zagged across the water. Skylar screwed her eyes shut from the scorching flash.

And heard a tremendous crack astern. She peered over her shoulder.

To see a branch crashing toward her. She had but a moment to throw her arms over her head and pray.

Before the world went dim.

❖

Darkness…water…cold…and then warm…the wind blowing softly across her skin. Pale green leaves on a branch overhead. The sky spinning. And then darkness again.

❖

Water flowed over her fingers. It lapped rhythmically against the boat. The sound was peaceful, as was the gentle rocking beneath her. Skylar blinked, opened her eyes, and winced at the sun's glare as her head pounded violently and her stomach roiled. She gulped air as her training kicked in. She pushed back the pain as best she could because she had no idea where she was or what dangers were near.

She reached out beyond her immediate surroundings, searching for signs of life. She sensed birds in the woods, fish swam near the boat, and an animal was nearby, but no humans.

Skylar took several long, deep breaths, then cautiously sat up. She stretched to test her limbs. They felt okay. After a quick examination, apart from the sick headache, she did not appear to be ill or injured. That was something. But where, by the Goddess, was she?

The boat was pinned between rocks at the edge of a stream scarcely wider than the craft. Shallow water ran swiftly over stony bedrock. A mossy bank rose on either side. A forest flanked one side. The other led to a road.

She turned her attention to the boat. There was no sign of the oars. She remembered then that one had been lost in the storm. The other was missing now, too. The oiled cloth was still pegged save for one loose corner. Moving her limbs gingerly, Skylar checked under it. The supplies were there, and to her delight, so was the vultrix, curled asleep. He opened his eyes and yawned. Skylar slowly put her hand out to his nose. He sniffed it and blinked at her.

How is your hind leg?

The vultrix stretched. Scabs had formed over the wound, and it was clean. Skylar tried to guess how many days had passed, but she had no idea how quickly foxes heal. Even trying to think about it hurt.

Skylar stepped out of the boat into freezing water. The cold settled her sick stomach. The hull was in a bad state. Something had ripped into it, perhaps when it had become meshed with the rocks. She could not sail the boat like that, and she was not carrying materials for repair.

Keeping alert for any approaching humans, Skylar sat on one of the rocks and pulled her compass out of her pocket. She tried to stay calm, but her instincts screamed that she was still in Alba.

The stream ran north to south. The area due north was flat, and even when standing on the rock, she could not see or hear the great river. From the sun's position in the sky, she judged it was mid-morning. She had almost certainly drifted deeper into Alba. That was not good.

Skylar had trained for hostile environments. In Gaea, that meant extreme weather conditions, natural disasters, and the occasional band of bandits. She thought about everything she had heard about Alba and tried not to panic. She was alone. Her only means of transport was damaged.

Skylar sucked air in through her nose and pushed it slowly out again. She must stay calm. Panic was not her friend. She concentrated on what she did have available to her. She was in good shape, and her combat skills were strong. Her telempathy would help her pass as a binary male. All she had to do was repair the boat and sail back to Gaea, meeting as few Albans as possible.

She surveyed the area around the stream for a supply cache. Then she remembered that it was not an Alban custom to leave supplies for travelers. Everything in Alba was traded. Luckily, she had some gold.

First, she examined her head. It was not sticky, and there were no scabs. She winced when she found a tender area. She opened the small med kit from her pack and mixed a pain-relieving powder with water.

The road beside the bank was wide enough for a cart and looked well-traveled. Skylar added some food to her pack. She strapped the cloth over the rest of the supplies in case it rained and filled her water canteen from the stream. She checked her knife was still at her belt before strapping on her sword and short staff. Finally, she slipped her bow and quiver over her shoulder. She turned to the vultrix. *Stay safe, little one, till I return.*

The vultrix blinked back at her.

Skylar set off along the road. Hopefully, habitation was near, the locals were friendly, and she would soon be sailing back to safety.

❖

By the time Skylar reached the outskirts of a quiet hamlet, the sun had risen to its noon position. Crops grew in fields bordering the road. The hamlet was a farming community. It was a good sign.

Her head had cleared, and a portion of trail bread had settled her stomach.

Skylar passed a small dwelling with no one apparently at home, and then she saw a rough carving of a basket hanging from a wooden house ahead. In Gaea, this was the sign for a general store. She hoped it was the same here and quickened her step.

The shutters were raised, indicating the shop was open. A man sat on a stool at the back of the dim interior, tacking a new sole onto a leather boot. Against the walls were sacks of grain and dried foods, a bolt of cloth, various tools, and a small row of apothecary bottles.

Skylar calmed her nerves and cleared her throat, projecting an enhanced image of maleness about herself. She wore a shirt, jerkin, and trousers in the butch warrior colors of grain tan, the color itself named for the plains surrounding the butch compound. From a glance, her clothes were a different color but otherwise similar to the merchant's. The man put down his repair and stood, running a wary eye over her from top to toe. Waves of suspicion flowed from him. The shopkeeper was a tall, broad fellow with a heavy beard that obscured the lower part of his face. His brow was furrowed. Though his face was closed, his mind was wide open. With relief, Skylar sensed he took her for an Alban male. But she also read that he did not trust outsiders and disliked trading with them.

He walked unsmiling to the front of the store and dropped one of the shutters to waist height. The shutter was transformed into a trading counter, creating a physical barrier between them.

"What brings you to this quiet outpost, stranger?" he asked.

Skylar projected an aura of confidence, strength, and peaceful intent. She lowered the pitch of her voice. "I am passing through the area and was caught in the storm. My boat has been damaged. I am looking for materials to repair the hull."

The shopkeeper's suspicion deepened. "It is not easy to travel by boat around here. Water's too shallow, and the stream bed is plagued with rocks."

"As I found," Skylar replied evenly. She sensed his fear of the great river and decided not to reveal she'd been sailing it. If he thought the river was the end of the world, he would take her for a rogue or even a demon.

"Passing through, you say?"

Skylar nodded.

He stood waiting for Skylar to elaborate. When she did not, he frowned then turned away, scratching his beard. He walked to the corner of the store, which housed a small array of tools, scraps of wood, and items Skylar could not identify in the gloom. He sifted through them.

He returned to Skylar with a small rectangular item wrapped in cloth. When he pulled the fabric back, Skylar was pleased to see a block of pitch resin. At the boat, she could shave off what she needed, heat water, and create repairs strong enough to get her back to Gaea, in calm waters at least. Skylar nodded and smiled, immediately regretting the smile when she felt greed surge within the shopkeeper.

"What kind of boatsman travels without pitch?" he asked.

Skylar ignored the attempt to goad her and kept her voice calm. "What is the price, sir?"

"Do you have something to trade?"

"I have gold."

The shopkeeper placed the resin on the counter. "Five discs."

The sum was extortionate. Skylar did not need to know the local trading values because the man's spirit screamed his avarice and his certainty that she was without choices.

"It seems high." Skylar's pride outrode her nerves. And her instincts told her a show of strength was necessary with this fellow.

The shopkeeper merely smiled. "You can get a better price northwest of here in Freymar if you can spare the four days to walk there."

Skylar blinked at him.

His smile deepened. "It's quicker by horse, of course. I would be happy to sell you one for fifteen discs."

Skylar swallowed her rage. She was in no position to bargain, and the merchant knew it. She had not considered carrying resin. In Gaea, supply caches were scattered everywhere. River caches would hold the essentials for boat repairs. If not, most citizens would gladly help, and should a merchant insist on payment, a fair price would be asked.

But this was not Gaea. Skylar fished five discs from her coin purse. The shopkeeper tested each between his teeth while Skylar stared at him impassively. At last, he pushed the block of resin toward her.

She turned without taking her leave, unable to bring herself even to thank him.

His laughter followed her along the trail.

❖

It was late afternoon by the time Skylar arrived back at the stream.

She stopped at the place where she had left the boat and frowned. She looked up and down as her heart began to race.

The boat had disappeared.

She was sure it was the right spot. This was the only section of the road that ran so close to the stream, and she had carefully retraced her steps.

She ran down to the rocks at the edge of the water. Ahead was the slight bend. On the other side of the stream was the start of the dense forest.

Even though she knew she was right, for a moment, Skylar doubted her senses. She had taken a blow to the head during the storm, after all. Was it possible she had not walked far enough? Was the boat still a-ways hence?

Something lying between the rocks caught her eye. A fragment of wood was trapped between two great boulders. Skylar waded in, reached down, and prised it out.

It was a piece of the hull.

Skylar walked slowly along the bank beside the stream. There were crushed blades of grass and boot marks. And where the road began, now that she was looking for them, Skylar found horse tracks, wheel ruts, and gouges in the packed dirt. Someone had hitched the boat behind a cart and driven off with it.

Skylar was stunned. Everything was gone: bedroll, tent, provisions, cooking pots, and the medical supplies so badly needed in the earthquake zone.

Without a boat, she could not get back to the part of the border she had crossed. She was stranded. Without transport, the country felt more dangerous than before. If discovered, her chosen way of dressing and behaving would be seen as impersonating a man. A crime punishable by death. She could hide her sexuality, perhaps, but her body could betray her if she were injured or arrested. The founders' tales of Alba warned how a country had turned to tyranny.

And she had been stupid enough to sail blithely across the border.

She sat down on a rock, completely at a loss.

Water trickled by, unperturbed by her predicament.

But then she took control of herself. She straightened her shoulders.

She was an adult, a trained butch warrior. She had already passed as an Alban male. She must hold her nerve, that's all.

Calmer now, she took stock. Not everything was gone. She had weapons, her flint and compass, a small quantity of food, her water canteen, the small med kit, and some gold. And a costly block of pitch resin.

The border ran the entire length of Gaea's southern edge from Thale in the east, across mountains, through the great river, and finally along the western marshland. None of the land was easy going on foot.

The odious shopkeeper had spoken of a town, Freymar, to the northwest. It would be sensible to head there and stock up with essentials. With a map, Skylar could quietly make her way to the border, avoiding habitation. Prices should be more reasonable in Freymar, and with luck, she could afford to purchase a horse.

The road to the hamlet had branched a short distance hence. One branch had run west, likely toward Freymar. She must walk to the town, buy essentials, head north, and get back across the border to Gaea. The most sensible place to cross was northwest over the marshlands. The mountain way would take too long. She could not afford a boat, and she still hoped to be of use in the earthquake zone, so heading northeast back to Thale was a pointless waste of time.

Not such a daunting task, perhaps.

Warriors did not give way to fear. And Skylar was a warrior.

She shouldered her pack, lifted her head, and set off.

Skylar had taken but a few steps when she saw a flash of red in the trees. The vultrix emerged from the forest and stopped on the path ahead.

Skylar reached out with kind thoughts. After a moment, he came cautiously over and sniffed at her boots.

Well, my friend. I was worried for you. Did you have the sense to leave the boat before it was stolen? I am still going to Gaea and will gladly take you with me.

The vultrix looked up and bobbed his head as if to say "yes." When Skylar walked on, he walked with her, limping a little.

It was a sign from the Goddess, surely? Skylar's spirits lifted. The journey was daunting, but less so, at least with a friend at her side.

Chapter Two

By noon of the fourth day, the road to Freymar grew busy with riders, carts, and hikers on foot. The little vultrix slipped away. Skylar felt him moving silently through the undergrowth. He kept pace with her, and she was glad of his quiet, steady touch at the edges of her mind. The increase in travelers must mean that Skylar was nearing the town. She was nervous at first. But, to her relief, no one tried to engage her in conversation. She sensed no threat, only a wariness. As more people walked the road, Skylar observed that this behavior was not directed solely at her. People did not strike up conversations with strangers.

By the middle of the afternoon, Skylar was more relaxed. The additional people provided a welcome anonymity. Even though she reached out constantly, scouring for signs of danger, it seemed this trip to Freymar might not be as perilous as she'd feared. Skylar had a surge of confidence that she could soon accomplish this unsolicited mission and get back to safety.

Ahead, the wayfarers slowed. Wooden barriers narrowed the road, funneling travelers through a gap one or two at a time. Five men that Skylar assumed were guards were dressed in charcoal gray shirts, trousers, and boots. They bore swords, carried long staffs, and were positioned around the barriers.

A thin guard of medium height and the unfortunate look of a ferret scrutinized the approaching travelers. He nodded at a group of four before Skylar and waved them through without comment.

But when Skylar went to follow, he stepped in her way. He looked her over without speaking. His eyes rested on her sword and short staff before flicking to her face.

"What is your business in Freymar?"

Skylar's pulse quickened. She stifled a burst of irritation at the guard's imperious tone. "I am going to buy provisions."

She tried to read the guard and found him strangely neutral. She wondered if he were a telepath or empath. From her limited knowledge of Alban customs, Skylar knew the skills were feared and discouraged. But that did not mean individuals did not use them. She did not feel anything from him and had to rely on his facial expressions and body language. His eyes bore into hers, and the scrutiny made her nervous. She straightened up, matching his self-assured stance.

"You are very clean-shaven," he said, unswayed by the mumbled complaints from the growing crowd behind them.

Skylar squared her shoulders. "The men of my family are naturally smooth-faced." She pursed her lips, projecting that she was offended. Her growing anger at the fellow's arrogance made the projection easy.

His eyes bore into hers. He had taken a dislike to her.

"What ho, gentlemen," someone cried out in a voice slurred with drink. "Come, sirs, what is the delay? We are eager to sample your taverns."

Laughter rang out, and a second fellow called, "Indeed. My flagon of ale is as dry as my throat. I need replenishment."

The guard's eyes narrowed, and he walked smartly toward the voices. The other guards looked over the heads of the crowd at three horsemen so inebriated they were in danger of slipping from their mounts.

Skylar took advantage of the guards' distraction to slip through the barrier and walk quickly to a cobbled road. No challenge pursued her. After a few steps, she felt heartened again. If the road had been prepared with such care, Freymar must be near.

❖

Skylar smelled, heard, and sensed Freymar before she caught sight of the high stone walls surrounding the town. Its presence was vibrant, diverse, and loud, with merchants calling from stalls and hawkers wandering through the crowd, even outside the walls. Skylar fleetingly wondered if she would need to go inside the walls, but then she realized the produce here was exclusively edible.

Skylar stood a few steps from the crowds, moving toward the town gates. The smell of bread and sweet rolls drifted from one stall and savory pies from another. Skylar's provisions had run out a day and a half since, and her stomach protested the fact. An older man with shoulder-length gray hair was standing behind the pie stall. His spirit was gentle and open.

He saw her and called over. "Is there something I can get you, traveler?"

On an impulse, Skylar went to his stall, her mouth watering at the smells rising from small, round pies crimped at the edges and baked until their crusts were golden. "How much for one?" Skylar asked. If the price were ridiculous, she would move on. There should be plenty of choice inside the town.

"Three pennies for vegetables. Four for meat."

Skylar had no Alban coin. "I only have gold."

The man leaned forward. "Best to keep your voice down, young sir, if you carry gold. I am sorry to say pickpockets and thieves work the market crowds, even here outside the walls. If you are going into the town, you should keep your purse in a safe place and not allow anyone to stand close. And I'm sorry, but I cannot exchange a gold disc. They are worth a hundred pennies in Freymar. Do not let anyone give you less."

Skylar smiled. "You are kind."

"And you look hungry," the man said. "Here." He handed a pie to Skylar.

She tried to refuse, but he placed it firmly into her hands.

"Come back and pay me when you have change."

"I will," Skylar promised. "Can you please tell me where I should head for? I need provisions for several days, a tent and bedroll, a map, and possibly a horse."

"The traders will be packing up soon, traveler." The stall holder looked up.

Skylar followed his gaze and saw the sun had dropped almost to the horizon.

"You should make your way to the central market. It is the biggest and best. The trader with a stall in front of the guild hall gives fair prices, and his wares can be trusted. He will not be the cheapest, mind. But you'll thank me when you lie on your bedroll or if the heavens open above your tent."

Skylar smiled, pleased that she had stopped at the elder's stall. "Thank you. I appreciate your honesty and your advice."

The stall holder clasped her hand firmly. "Kindness costs nothing."

"It cost you a pie." Skylar broke into a grin that was returned.

"And gladly given. Go safely, traveler."

Skylar took her leave and headed for the city gates, warmed by the elder's generosity.

❖

Skylar hurried along narrow, cobbled streets, making her way to the center of Freymar. She barely took in her surroundings, so keen was she on reaching the market before all the stalls and hawkers closed for the day. Everyone seemed to be coming in the opposite direction, ambling with little purpose. Some had stopped to converse, blocking the way further.

Skylar tried not to show her frustration as she was forced practically into a pile of horse droppings to traverse a group of three men talking excitedly about their day's trading.

Intent on avoiding the manure, she brushed past a fellow on the opposite pavement.

"Watch where you walk," he snapped. He smelt strongly of ale and was belligerent. His hand flew to the knife at his belt.

Skylar put up both hands in a pacifying gesture. "My apologies, sire. I was in haste and did not see you."

"You rustics should not come to the city if you do not know how to behave here." The stranger glowered at Skylar. He took her for a rural man ignorant of city ways. She felt him deliberate whether to strike her. His hand left the hilt of his knife. "Damn haystack," he said and shoved her rudely aside.

Skylar looked after the fellow. She could easily floor him, but fighting in the streets of a strange city would be foolish. She was alone and knew practically nothing about Alba and even less about Freymar. She shook her head and walked quickly on.

The sunlight had turned golden. The merchant houses in the street were shut, and the inns were lively. Skylar swallowed. All shops would close soon. She must hurry.

At last, she turned a corner and found herself in a great square bordered by stores and wooden stalls. Unfortunately, it was empty of people. She was too late. The market was done for the day. Still, she hurried to the corner described by the food seller and, to her relief, saw the shutters had not yet been drawn down on the trail goods store that the pie man had recommended.

As she approached, a middle-aged man with a weather-worn complexion and deep frown lines etched alongside his down-turned mouth went to the rope that manipulated the shutters.

"Sir, sir," she called out. I am glad I caught you. Can you please sell me a tent and a bed roll? I'll take some trail cooking equipment, too, if you have it."

The man stared at her, cross and weary. "The market is over. My store is closed. Come back tomorrow."

Skylar looked at the store's contents, trying to see if there was anything she could point to, but the goods were stacked in a heap or covered.

The man followed her eyes. "Everything is packed away. Tomorrow, you can examine at your leisure and pick the goods for your needs."

"Please, sir, a fellow recommended I come—"

"It is the festival night. I am tired, and my family expects me." The merchant lowered the left-hand shutter abruptly. "I open again in the morning."

Skylar sighed, not relishing another cold, uncomfortable night. "Can you not sell me a bed roll at least?" she asked in desperation.

The merchant studied her. "You do not have a room for the night?"

Skylar shook her head.

"And you will not find one. The town is full for midsummer festival." The merchant turned away and searched beneath a large cloth. To Skylar's relief, he appeared a few moments later with a bed roll and a blanket. She noticed he had pulled out a sheaf of what looked like maps in his search.

"Are those maps of the region?" She pointed to where the sheaf lay.

"Yes."

"I will take one, please. You have my gratitude, sir." Skylar smiled. She dug out a gold disc.

The merchant counted out her change in Alban pennies from a large purse tied tightly to his leather belt and then resumed closing his store.

The sun had set by the time Skylar walked away from the deserted market square. A stiff wind blew spent straw, torn sacking, and other debris of the day across the cobbles.

The bustling mood of the town changed as the night drew in. There were plenty of people on the streets, and many were already merry with ale or wine. Music, laughter, and the occasional argument came from the inns that, indeed, looked full to bursting.

But fellows lurked in the shadows of empty doorways, watching passers-by with too much interest for Skylar's comfort. She sensed they were waiting for an easy mark to cross their path.

Skylar did not want to enter the brightly lit taverns and risk attracting attention. Neither did she wish to jostle amidst the crowds who celebrated on the streets.

She set off away from the center, seeking a quieter area to buy a meal and bed down.

❖

As Skylar walked north, it became quieter and considerably poorer. Houses were small. There were no shops, traders, or inns. The deep sunset would turn to twilight soon, yet no one lit public torches. Now that she looked closely, there were no sconces on any wall. This area must grow very dark.

The road narrowed, and the cobbles disappeared until Skylar walked along a hard-packed dirt track. Houses were pressed close together with no land for gardens front or back. How did they feed themselves or their livestock? There were tiny alleys threaded between some of the dwellings. Skylar had wanted somewhere quiet to bed down, but she did not relish venturing into any of the dim and ominously quiet passages. They were a good hiding place for pickpockets and cutthroats. Besides, the wind carried the odor of human and animal waste. Skylar shuddered at the thought of sleeping there.

It did not seem like a festival night. Perhaps families were feasting together behind their shuttered windows and doors.

On the summer solstice in Gaea, people celebrated together on the streets or in green places. There was a solemn sunrise ritual followed by a joyous, raucous evening feast with food, wine, music, and dancing.

Three women talked softly in the tiny space between a front door and the street. The conversation stopped when Skylar approached. They watched her. She waved and nodded, but none responded. Distrust followed her. Skylar sensed they were scared and wary of strangers. Odd behavior for townsfolk who must be used to travelers, surely?

Raised voices put Skylar on guard. She sensed several hostile people and someone alone. Someone in trouble. Skylar moved quickly toward the sounds.

A short distance ahead was a group of boys. They trailed behind a child, calling out with taunting voices.

Skylar stepped into the shadows to get the measure of the situation.

The child walked on, ignoring the youths. Zir shoulders were slumped, and zir head bent as if trying to make zirself smaller. Ze had beautiful, long brown hair that fell in ringlets down zir back. From zir height, Skylar judged zir to be about twelve or thirteen years old.

One of the older boys, a tall, wiry youth probably in his late teens, shouted after the child, "Stop, creature. I want to talk to you."

The child hunched further and walked faster.

The same youth glanced at his fellows with a sinister smile. "Why do you wear a girl's clothes when you are not a girl?"

Skylar's hackles rose protectively. She did not know if this child was what some would call a boy, defined by genitals alone. She guessed so from the way the child's eyes were resolutely fixed on the ground.

Emboldened, a second young male, also older, followed the child. "You are ugly and disgusting. Come here. You should be wearing these." He waved a pair of breeches in the air and grinned at his friend, puffed up and pleased with himself. The two laughed together, and then the whole group joined in. The pack's laughter was cold and malicious. Rage coursed through Skylar.

She could not stand by. Her desire to pass unnoticed through Alba was nothing to her need to defend this child.

"Stop this at once," she called. "This is no way to behave. Go about your business somewhere other than here."

The group of boys stopped dead, looking for the owner of the voice.

Skylar breathed evenly, projecting herself taller and stockier than she was. She deepened her maleness, standing squarely. She pulled her staff free.

Before she could step from the shadows, the wiry youth ran to block the child's path. One of the others lifted a catapult, about to let loose a stone.

Skylar was across the street and on him before he got the chance, her fingers gripping his wrist. The youth cried out in pain and surprise. She twisted his arm until he dropped the weapon.

"How dare you torment a child this way." She held his arm still, coldly furious.

The youth yelped. "You should not defend him. He pretends to be a girl, but he is a boy. It is not permitted. It is deviant."

Skylar itched to twist the ignorant youth's arm further, but she was his elder and a trained warrior. She released his arm. "Get away from here, all of you."

The group looked to the tallest youth, the one who had spoken first. His lips curled. "Who are you to give orders? You are nothing to me, stranger. *You* go away. We live here."

Skylar straightened to meet the youth's defiant stare.

The youth glowered at her, but he began to walk away. The others followed churlishly.

The child stood uncertainly by the side of the street, looking down at the ground.

"Where are you heading? I will walk with you," Skylar offered.

The child's eyes darted to hers and quickly away.

Skylar lowered her voice. "It is okay. I am a soldier."

Horror flooded the child's face.

Skylar was shocked. "I mean, I am a warrior. My job is to protect and aid."

The child ran. For a moment, Skylar hesitated. She did not want to terrify the child, but the youths had congregated outside one of the small alleyways and were watching them.

Skylar set off behind the child at a quick pace. It sickened her to feel the young person's terror. Terror she had unwittingly induced. But she also felt the violent intent of the youths.

Skylar would aid any who needed her. And this was both a child and a gender ally. She would not let the child face this alone.

❖

Skylar kept twenty paces or so behind the child, all the while feeling the steady presence of the tormentor group trailing not even the same distance behind her.

The houses gave way to wasteland, and Skylar grew more uneasy still. The footsteps behind quickened. Here, in the open, there was no one to see or judge or intervene. The youths were young, but some were tall and athletic. They might not have Skylar's battle training, but they had strength, aggression, the benefit of numbers, and were armed.

A stone landed a few steps to Skylar's left. She stopped and turned. Three of the youths had slings, and all five advanced swiftly.

Skylar drew her staff. She did not want to fire an arrow at the youngsters. If only she had a shield, but it was with the rest of her stolen belongings.

The three with catapults each fired a stone. One landed an inch from her foot.

But she held her ground, wanting the child to get away. The eldest youth ran at her with a cudgel. As Skylar met the stick with her staff, a stone smashed into her brow. She staggered, disorientated, blocking the blows raining down on her by instinct and training. She felt sick. But she poured her energy into her staff, and the youth crumpled.

She kicked his cudgel away. Other youths ran past. The child tried to escape, but two youths gained, laughing and taunting as their longer legs ate the distance between them.

Then, a snarling dog ran into the fray. No, not a dog. The magical fox that Skylar had last seen at the city gates ran between the child and the youths.

The vultrix was magnificently frightening. He growled at the youths, revealing long, sharp canines. They stopped where they stood, terrified.

The vultrix's shoulders were pure muscle. His ears were back and pointed. His amber eyes were narrowed and fixed on the two boys. His snarl warned what would come should any of them dare make a move.

The youths fled.

The leader stumbled to his feet, groaning. He looked after his companions. Then, at the child, vultrix, and Skylar.

He backed away slowly, shoulders sagging and face pale. He dared not take his eyes from the vultrix.

The fox yipped. Skylar shivered at the cry that was somewhere between a bark and a howl.

The youth turned and ran back toward the town.

❖

"My name is Florian," the child said.

Skylar pulled a rag from her pocket and mopped at the blood trailing down one side of her face.

"Thank you." Florian looked shaken but unharmed. "What is that animal?"

"A friend of mine."

The vultrix whined softly. He came to Skylar and sniffed her hand. And then he slipped away into the undergrowth. She felt his loyalty and was filled with gratitude. Skylar did not help anyone for recompense. Her aid or protection was freely given. This beautiful vultrix, however, had repaid her kindness in full.

I will still take you over the border if you wish it, she told him as he disappeared into a thicket.

Skylar gingerly touched her temple and winced. She should clean the wound but had drained her canteen dry on the walk from the center. "Is there somewhere I can get water?"

"Yes. Follow me."

Florian walked across wasteland, which led nowhere. Twilight was upon them now, and Skylar had to trust that Florian was taking her to a dwelling.

"He looked like a fox. Was he a fox?" Florian peered out to the edge of the field in the direction the vultrix had gone. The child was interested in animals.

"A kind of fox, yes." Skylar felt somewhat dizzy. It might have been from a lack of food and water. It could have been the blow to her head.

Then, to her relief, lights flickered, and small buildings appeared on the horizon.

As they grew closer, she saw the dwellings were roughly assembled from branches and sacking. Some were pasted with mud or straw, while others were little more than poles strung with cloth. The air was pungent with smoke that rose from holes in the few straw roofs or, more often, from fires in front of the shacks. Cooking smells triggered a sharp hunger in Skylar, and no wonder. She had eaten nothing but the small pie all day. Well, it was no good. She saw no stall or hawker selling food.

The small settlement was busy. People walked along narrow trails between the huts or sat tending the fires. Florian waved to some of them. They were dressed in poor clothing. The few weapons she saw were mainly wooden. Some had daggers at their belts. Dogs and cats trailed through the pathways. Most were shooed away from the huts, but an elder sat with four thin cats nestled around her low stool. Skylar smiled as they passed, and the elder nodded back kindly.

It appeared that no one in Alba shielded their thoughts. The makeshift settlement was alive with concern, fear, love, desire, and hope. The onslaught of feelings wearied Skylar further. This was a place people had come to in desperation and made a community. Despite the poverty, it felt safer than the houses Skylar had passed earlier. Perhaps there would be somewhere she could bed down.

Florian stopped at an old ale barrel with the top removed. It served as a makeshift well for the shanty village.

"This is okay to drink?" she asked.

Florian passed her a clay cup tied to the barrel by a string through the handle. Skylar drained it in a moment.

"Is it all right to take another?" she asked.

Florian nodded and then pointed toward the west. "The stream is in that direction, but it is a distance away."

The water had the faintest taint of ale, but it was cold and sweet to Skylar's parched throat. It helped dispel her nausea.

"I do not think you *are* a soldier," Florian said.

Skylar paused her drinking. "Why is that?"

"You do not behave like a soldier. Why did you help me?"

"Because it was the right thing to do."

Florian glanced at the bedroll and blanket under Skylar's arm. "Are you looking for a place to sleep?"

Skylar nodded.

Florian studied Skylar. "Your wound looks sore. Come with me. My mama can look at your head and tell you where is safe for you to rest."

Florian's kindness touched Skylar. "Thank you."

Florian set off along a small pathway.

Skylar followed, curious about the person who allowed her son to express zir chosen gender in this dangerous land.

❖

Another evening of noise, heat, and longing in Freymar's notorious shanty town. Calida had wanted more for Florian. Actually, in rash moments like this, she wanted more for herself. A stew containing vegetables of doubtful quality and dubious origin bubbled over the hearth, seasoned with spices from her personal blend. The hearth was a makeshift affair with a clay pipe chimney that sucked smoke up from the fire and out through the straw roof. It was effective enough.

Calida sat on her favorite stool, knife in one hand, grinding stone in the other. The stool was her favorite merely because it shed no splinters. Her knives, though, each one was treasured. They were her only wealth and the only things she cared about besides her child, Florian.

He should be home by now. She tested the blade's edge with a piece of twine. Satisfied, she placed it in its sheath in the lining of her long coat. It housed six per side. She kept a pair of short stiletto knives in her boots. But wore no weapon at her waist. It would not do for the public to see a poor woman armed. She could be hauled to gaol simply for appearing to be dangerous.

Beginning to worry, Calida got up and walked to the doorway. It did not take many steps even though their small dwelling was better appointed than most. It was a one-roomed hut with a bed against one wall, a rough table made from a plank resting on lumps of wood, the hearth, and a wicker basket containing their garments.

Florian was thirteen. He would be an adult in nine moons. He wanted to go out alone, and she must let him. Besides, his job brought in precious pennies.

Florian pushed aside the rough cloth curtain just as she reached it, calling, "Mama! I bring a friend."

Calida stepped back to allow him passage. A male stood behind Florian.

"Good evening," she said courteously, for Florian had said "friend," but she was instantly on guard. Calida appraised the stranger.

He was a beardless youth of medium height and build, though muscular, and he looked strong. He wore a matching tan tunic and trousers, a calico shirt, and dusty brown boots. A sword and a staff hung at his belt, and a bow was strung over his shoulder. He had the posture of a soldier or someone used to fighting. That did not endear him to her. He was handsome, Calida supposed, with short, dark hair, olive skin, and intense chestnut eyes. She did like his nose. It leaned to one side, possibly from being broken at some time. It gave him character. He gazed at her without even replying to her greeting. She looked harder, intrigued, and smiled. For this was no youth. Unless Calida was very mistaken, Florian's new friend was a virago, likely of thirty years or so. The pleasant surprise coursed through her veins. Where had Florian found her? No wonder she had the look of someone used to combat.

"I am Calida, Florian's mother," Calida said. "Won't you come inside?"

"My name is Skylar," the stranger spoke haltingly. When she turned, Calida saw a nasty cut on her right temple and dried blood along her cheek.

"What happened?" Calida looked at Florian with concern.

"Those boys. They came after me again. Skylar drove them from me."

Calida rushed to Florian. They were the reason she would never let Florian from her side if she could. If that course of action would protect him. It would not, of course. She had worried every day since one of those malicious, snooping boys had seen Florian washing in the stream. It took all her resolve not to battle the knaves herself, but that would bring the wrath of the townsfolk upon the settlement. He avoided them most nights. They would have to think of another way now.

"Are you all right? Did they hurt you?"

Florian leaned into her, trembling. "I am fine, Mama. Please, will you look at Skylar's wound?"

Calida turned to Skylar and examined the cut. She dipped a cloth into the wash bowl and dabbed at it. Skylar winced.

"Sit." Calida pushed Skylar down onto the empty stool. "I need to clean it properly. You helped Florian?"

"Of course. They were unpleasant youths who wished Florian harm." Skylar closed her eyes when Calida dripped water onto the wound. "I abhor bullies."

"So do I," Calida murmured. She pressed some ointment gently onto the area. "It is not too deep. The wound is already clotting."

Skylar opened her eyes and met Calida's. Calida stepped away, walking to the hearth to stir the stew. "Can I offer you a meal? It is good, hearty fare."

Skylar's stomach groaned. She looked embarrassed. "It seems my stomach is answering for me. Yes, please, Calida. If you have enough to spare, I would be grateful."

Calida began to ladle the stew into rough bowls.

"Mama, Skylar is a soldier, but don't worry, he is a good one."

Calida froze. Was the virago completely mad? "You work for the King?"

"No," Skylar said, her brow furrowed.

"Are you a guard or not?" Calida calculated how many steps it would take to reach her coat of knives.

Skylar seemed to sense her unease. She unstrapped her sword and laid it down. "I am a protector."

Calida let out a breath. She had never heard of such a thing. "I do not know what that is."

"I am a warrior. I protect, and I help."

Calida stared at Skylar for several long moments. Who was this person? She passed as a man and spoke strangely. Calida did and did not trust her all at the same time, and that fact alone concerned her greatly.

But the shanty settlement was full of folk with dangerous secrets, and it was still safer than the streets around them. She resumed ladling stew into the bowl and passed it to Skylar. She filled two other bowls and went to sit with Florian on the bed.

They ate in silence, Skylar as if she had not seen food for some time. The spoon in her hand raced between mouth and bowl. It was good to see her eat so heartily. The virago certainly did not let manners get in the way of a good meal. Sounds of shanty life continued outside with snatches of fiddle, flute, and song, and the call and chatter between neighbors. There was little privacy here. Calida tolerated it, but she yearned for a quieter place like the cottage she had grown up in, far from the city.

One of the orphan brothers, Petro, bobbed through the curtain. The two boys occupied a tiny shack on the next "street." Calida gave them errands when she could afford to pay a copper or two. All of seven years old, Petro was the older and more serious boy.

"Here is your washing, Aunty." He carried five shirts, two pairs of female breeches, and a tunic, all neatly folded. He looked for somewhere to lay them down, staring curiously at Skylar. Calida put her bowl down and took the laundry. She fished in her coin purse for a copper penny.

Petro thanked her. "I scrubbed, but not too hard, as you instructed, and I ensured they were properly dry before folding."

Calida smiled. She was particular about her laundry. It was necessary living the way they did.

Petro's eyes were all over the stew in her bowl, but he did not ask.

Calida sighed. The rest of the stew was to have been breakfast. But these boys had no one to care for them, and they were so little.

"Is Raoul with you?"

"Yes, Aunty." Raoul jumped through the doorway on hearing his name, full of the excitement of his five years.

Calida laughed. "Come in then. You can both eat from our last bowl."

"You are kind, Aunty." Petro rewarded her with a beautiful smile.

The boys settled onto the floor, delighted at receiving a meal they were not expecting.

Calida turned and found Skylar gazing at her with a soft expression. It disappeared the instant her eyes met Calida's.

What a curious person this Skylar was, but there was no point in indulging any interest in her. Skylar was likely passing through, and not every virago was a lover of women. Who she loved was Calida's secret. And it was a secret far too dangerous to reveal.

❖

Florian's mother walked ahead of Skylar in the narrow alleyway between the dwellings. Calida was powerful and feminine. It was a deadly combination. One that had been the undoing of Skylar on more than one occasion. It was all the more heady following Skylar's secluded and very butch life at Thale.

Calida had eyes the color of dark leather, skin the brown of bear pelts, and long raven feather hair that she wore tied back with a braid. She was shorter than Skylar by a head, taut with muscle and lithe. Skylar had already seen how generous she was with what little food she possessed and guessed that was why she was slight. Skylar tingled from head to toe in her presence, but it would not do. The feeling, strong as it was, must be suppressed.

Calida stopped before a tiny ramshackle hut.

"It is not much, considering poor Khazud lived here for three years or more." Calida pulled back a frayed cloth covering a doorway between rough plank walls. She pinned the fabric onto a tack, left proud, and entered the one-roomed dwelling.

Calida's candle stub threw out enough light to see the straw roof had several large holes in it. There was nothing inside the shack. Not a pot. Not a pan. And nothing on the floor but packed dirt and a few rotted strands of what might have once been a rush mat.

"People have already made use of what little Khazud had," Calida said. She shrugged. Skylar gleaned that this was the way things were here.

"You can bed down safely and keep dry, Skylar." Florian smiled. He appeared delighted that Skylar was to spend the night in the settlement. "Keep your pack near you, though."

"The settlement folk will not harm you. One or two may be tempted by your belongings," Calida explained.

Florian's warmth toward her made Skylar wish she could get to know him. It would have been satisfying and interesting to become acquainted with them both.

Calida looked at the roof doubtfully. "Let's hope it does not rain." A gust of wind blew through the many gaps in the walls. "It is better than being out in the open. Probably."

Skylar liked Calida. She used her wits and had a keen mind. She must be tough to survive in the settlement in a town like Freymar. Skylar liked Florian, too. The child was extremely brave. Despite the persecution Skylar had witnessed, Florian was welcoming to her and kind. "Thank you both," she said.

"Good night then, Skylar." Calida smiled. She handed Skylar a nub of candle and left. Florian gave Skylar a quick, shy hug and then ran after his mother.

Skylar stuck the candle onto a stone already covered with hardened drips of wax. Then, she dropped her pack onto the floor. She untied the bedroll, spread it out on the flattest-looking stretch of dirt, and lay down on it.

It was wonderful. So blissfully soft after the nights on the hard, sometimes damp ground. Using her pack for a pillow, she turned onto her side. Where was the little vultrix? Hunting? Finding shelter himself? Hopefully, he would appear when she resumed her journey tomorrow.

The thump in her head had subsided following the meal and several cups of water. How generous Calida and Florian had been. She checked the cut, remembering Calida's touch on her temple. The ointment had numbed the skin. It felt much improved already.

She drifted off to sleep, thinking about the unexpected pleasure of the meal with Calida and Florian and the community she sensed. Perhaps she was clinging to the first friendly faces she had encountered. It was a shame, but she was clear what she must do. There was no question of doing anything but returning to Gaea as quickly as possible.

Though she found herself strangely sad to be moving on.

❖

Skylar awoke, knowing something was wrong. She smelled smoke. There was wild shouting and heart-wrenching screams.

Footsteps came running. Skylar jumped into a combat stance.

"We must leave. The settlement is under attack." Calida panted at the doorway, her hair awry. She wore a long, dark, hooded coat. Florian hovered behind her.

Skylar grabbed her backpack and bent to the bedroll.

"No time," Calida grunted, tugging Skylar's sleeve roughly. "Unless you want to burn alive."

Thick black smoke filled the higgledy path between the shacks and lean-tos. Skylar breathed shallowly, struggling not to cough.

Calida ran swiftly along the uneven ground. Screams rang out streets away. Skylar stopped.

Calida stopped, too. She reached for Florian's hand and pulled him close.

"I have to help them," Skylar said, wrenched by both the screams and the waves of pain and distress coming from the heart of the settlement.

"Do what you must." Calida's voice was flat. She turned from the hellish sounds and ran forward.

But two figures stepped from the shadows at the other end of the path. Flames flickered from the torches in their hands, throwing a ghoulish light on their faces. Skylar recognized them as two of the youths who had tormented Florian.

Skylar pulled the sword and staff from her belt and marched forward. Her rage built as she advanced. Such hate poured from them. Then Calida sped past her.

Calida leaped at one of the youths and spun. She kicked out, and the youth dropped to the ground.

The second youth leered at Calida. He thrust his torch toward her hair.

Skylar swung her staff and felled the boy before he could turn in her direction. She kicked away his torch and booted him in the stomach. He was younger and weaker than her, but the taint of his deadly night's work rose from him. The psychic stench of him fouled her mind.

The screams in the heart of the settlement were no more. Skylar swallowed her distress. When Calida set off with Florian at a run, Skylar followed.

❖

The choking smell of smoke was everywhere, and it thickened the moonless night. Skylar kept close to Florian. He and Calida knew the way.

Rows of homes were ablaze. They ran past a tin-walled shelter barely big enough for one person. Flames licked at the door.

A terrible cry clawed at Skylar's mind. Someone was inside the tiny hut, curled into a corner. Ze was shaking and scared. A second small body lay on the floor, too, barely conscious. They were familiar.

Skylar kicked the door away. Heat rushed at her, but she went straight for the two children huddled in the far corner. It was Petro and Raoul. She tucked her staff into her belt and lifted them under each arm. There was no weight to them, but she choked on scalding air. The walls shook, glowing red hot. The roof was about to collapse.

She scrambled through the flaming doorway.

Outside, she gulped great lungfuls of clean air. Pain seared her throat and chest, but she ignored it.

Calida grabbed her shoulder. "How did you know they were in there?"

Skylar did not answer. Instead, she thrust Raoul at Calida.

At the end of the path, Calida turned onto a wider track. Then, she slipped through a gate into a small, worn patch of grass and stopped before a cart. It was old but looked sturdy. The box at the back had tall sides, and there was a seat for the driver behind a yoke large enough for two horses. A brown and cream stallion and a dark brown mare whickered at their approach and pulled at their reins. They looked as old and rugged as the cart. They were agitated by the shouting and frightened by the blaze.

"They were Khazud's," Calida said, untying the stallion from a post.

Skylar untied the mare and led her to the cart, soothing her as best she could. Her hands trembled from shock. They were burnt. Her face also felt sore, but there was no time for anything except their escape. She focused on her task.

Great plumes of smoke thickened the air. The crackle and pop of burning buildings drowned out distant shouts. People hurried past the paddock, clasping their belongings. Some had gotten away, thank the Goddess. Skylar hoped most had, but her senses thrummed with the terrible knowledge that many were dead.

Florian helped Petro and Raoul jump into the back of the cart, and Skylar pulled the sacking over all three. When Skylar climbed onto the seat, Calida pushed the reins into her hands.

Skylar tried to push them back. "Surely you should drive. I need both hands for my weapons."

Calida's mouth twisted into an expression sour enough to curdle milk. She flipped open her coat. Inside, knife after knife was tucked into sheathes sewn into the cloth. Skylar gaped at the steel that glinted wickedly in the firelight.

"Who is better to protect us, Skylar, you or me?" Calida asked with one eyebrow raised and a challenge in her eyes. It may have been a question, but Skylar knew she wanted no answer.

Skylar took up the reins and winced as her hands protested. She pushed the pain away.

A shout came from the other end of the path, and then a figure ran through the smoke toward them, brandishing a long staff and a flaming torch. Skylar called to the horses and tugged the reins, but the cart moved slowly in the rutted ground. By the time it had rumbled onto the track, the fellow was steps away.

Calida's arm flicked back. With a swish and a thud, the attacker crumpled.

Skylar jerked the reins more urgently. The horses broke into a trot.

"Keep moving." Calida leaped from the cart, running to the body on the ground.

Moments later, she was back on the seat. "No point in wasting a good knife," she said, cleaning the weapon on her trousers. "Metal is a terrible price."

❖

By dawn, they were beyond the outskirts of Freymar and into the countryside. The reins drooped as she listened to the steady clip-clop of the horses' hooves on the quiet road. The pain in her hands had settled into a dull throb. Her eyelids started to close, and she pulled up with a start. Skylar drew the cart to a halt by an expanse of grassland with a small stream.

Calida pushed a strand of hair from her face. She was alert but looked pale and weary.

"I do not know how far the horses can travel," Skylar said.

"Do you have travel papers?" Calida's voice was flat.

"No." Skylar had no idea what they were or why they were needed.

"Then we cannot camp, at least not yet. The city guards ride out this close to Freymar. When there has been a disturbance like tonight, they will look for displaced settlement dwellers."

"Why?"

Skylar felt Calida's emotions stir, but she could not pinpoint any particular feeling.

"If you ask that question, you have never lived in a settlement. Lucky you," Calida said wryly. "Unauthorized temporary shelters are forbidden. Camping is forbidden. Traveling without papers is forbidden. But still, people are driven from their homes through no fault of their own. In the city, the guards mostly let us be. But God forbid we should sully the countryside. And heaven help us if they find us doing so."

"Oh." Skylar stared at the reins, not knowing what to say. The horses bent their heads as well. They were tired and hungry. "We must let the horses drink and graze, if only for a short time."

"Agreed. Even guards cannot deny us that."

Skylar jumped down from the cart and stretched. Her hands complained, but she ignored them. She unhitched the horses and led them over to the brook. Skylar pondered the situation as the horses drank enthusiastically. They had traveled in the direction of Gaea thus far, but that could change at any time if Calida and the children were to go in another direction.

Skylar filled her water canteen. Calida was bent amongst the long grasses, cutting pieces from a fat-stemmed plant. She walked to the back of the cart, stripping away the outer layer from the pieces. She was a strong and resourceful warrior. The femme regiment would be proud to claim her. It was a foolish thought. Skylar dismissed it.

She returned with the horses and hitched them loosely to the yoke so they could graze. They nipped happily at fresh spring shoots in the pasture.

"Let me tend to your face, Skylar." Calida came to her, her hands covered in thick yellow sap. She dotted her fingertips across Skylar's cheeks.

Skylar winced and then relaxed when the cool gel met her skin. It eased the burns in just a few moments. "What is this preparation?" she asked, tentatively touching the sticky gel on her face.

Calida brushed Skylar's fingers away. "Your cheeks are burnt. If you do not keep the area clean, it will become infected. Now give me your hands."

The two small boys slept in the back of the cart. Their hands and faces were yellow with the sap. "You're a healer?" Skylar asked Calida.

Calida shook her head. "I know plant lore, enough to survive, that's all."

"Are the little ones in pain? I have pain-relieving powder in my pack."

"Do you indeed? Are *you* a healer?"

"No," Skylar said more fiercely than she'd intended. Her mother had wanted Skylar to become her apprentice. It was the last thing she had wanted.

Calida arched an eyebrow. "I do not know if they are in pain. They are asleep. Their burns are not life-threatening, thanks to you." Calida studied Skylar. "You said you were traveling north. Is that still your plan?"

"Yes, I must. What about you? Will you return to Freymar?"

Florian sat up, rubbing his eyes. "I do not want to go back, Mama." He had been listening to their conversation. At that moment, he sounded older than his tender years.

Calida smiled. She leaned over the side of the cart to stroke his hair. "Are you sure, darling?"

Florian nodded.

"Then, we will not return. We will find some other place."

"Where will you go?" Skylar asked.

"Why don't we go with Skylar, Mama?" Florian spoke to his mother, but his eyes were on Skylar, his expression hesitant and shy. "Could we? Can we?"

Calida glanced at Skylar. "I have a cousin in the north. He lives in a small hamlet called Bareglen."

"Can we visit him? Can we, Mama?" Florian brightened considerably.

Calida lowered her voice, speaking to Skylar. "You have plans already. You may prefer to travel alone."

Skylar took a breath. "It would be safer to keep together." She did not know if that were true, but if they were prepared to travel north, she could at least help Calida care for the three children. It was in Skylar's nature and her training. She was a butch warrior, after all, sworn to aid and protect.

"The horses have grazed enough..." Calida stopped mid-sentence at a twitch in the sacking on the cart. A little red face with a black snout snuffled out from under the cloth. Florian jumped away with a yell. Calida whipped a knife from her coat, advancing on the rear corner.

"It is okay." Skylar put her hand gently on Calida's shoulder, sensing who it was under the cloth. "Trust me, he is a friend."

Skylar lifted the cloth and found the vultrix peering up at her. His gaze was serious but gentle, too. How wonderful that he had come through their ordeal unscathed.

"Were you scared, friend?" She stroked the tender area behind his ears. "In that horrible fire?"

"That is no ordinary fox," Calida whispered.

"You are right. He's a vultrix."

Calida stiffened. "A witch fox."

"The children are in no danger," Skylar said. "I know this vultrix. I freed him from a trap."

"Is that why his leg looks sore?" Florian asked.

The wound was healing well, but the jagged outline of the trap's teeth was visible, marked by a browning, scabbed-over line circling the vultrix's rear leg. Skylar was impressed with Florian's perception. Perhaps he had some animal empathy. The vultrix did not mind him.

Skylar put her arm over the vultrix. He nuzzled into her. "Yes. This leg was trapped. It was lucky I found him when I did. He is sapient. Do you know what that means?"

Florian shook his head.

"He can sense your emotions. Let him get your scent. I am sure he will feel your gentleness."

"Will he bite me?" Florian eyed the vultrix with a mixture of compassion and fear.

"Not if he gets the scent of you first and you make no sudden movements toward him. Hold out your hand and let him come to you."

Florian moved his hand slowly toward the vultrix. The vultrix blinked, sniffed Florian's hand, and finally, he licked him.

Florian laughed. "His tongue is rough."

"Well," Calida said, still eyeing the vultrix with suspicion. "Is this beast to travel with us as well then?"

"The vultrix will defend us. He has already protected Florian. In Freymar, he attacked one of the youths."

"Did you, little red witch fox? Then you are welcome, indeed." Calida tipped her head in the vultrix's direction, and he gazed up at her, assessing her. Calida turned to Skylar. "I think we should move out. We are chancing our luck not to meet with a patrol. The horses will be fed, watered, and rested enough by now."

Skylar nodded. She jumped into the driving seat, reaching for the reins, but Calida was lighter and quicker.

"Your hands are healing. Let me drive."

Skylar thought to protest, but in truth, she was exhausted. She leaned back against the railing of the box, already nodding off.

As she slipped into sleep, Skylar felt the vultrix turn around and around and settle into the space behind her, snuggling into the protection of Skylar's back.

❖

It was late afternoon before Calida felt they were far enough from village or town to risk making camp without a permit. They had driven the cart into a fragrant meadow bordered by a broad and gurgling brook.

The two little boys slept by the fire, wrapped in the sacking cloth lifted from the cart. The vultrix nestled into Florian. Skylar built the flames, hoping their warmth would see them through until first light.

"This little fox should have a name," Florian said. "I wondered, can we call him Kit?"

Skylar sat beside the vultrix, feeling the warmth of his spirit. *Do you have a name, my friend?*

The vultrix stared back at her and shook his whiskers.

"Do you mind if we call you Kit?" Skylar asked.

The vultrix rested his head on Florian's lap with a sigh.

"I think that is a yes." Skylar patted Kit, who groaned happily. Skylar returned to the stack of logs by the fire.

"Here." Calida held out the last handful of bitter leaves she had picked before the sun set, making further foraging impossible.

Skylar's stomach growled, but even so, she did not relish chewing the sharp, bitter assortment of stems and leaves. She plucked a long, yellow-green, notched dandelion leaf from the pile. "This is enough for me. You finish the rest."

Calida nodded without comment. She gazed idly into the flames and chewed leisurely. She did not seem to mind even the peculiar, sprawling, hairy stem that had clung relentlessly to the inside of Skylar's mouth, releasing a grassy flavor.

Florian yawned and clambered up into the cart. He snuggled down under the sacking with Petro and Raoul.

Skylar studied the map in her hands, trying to estimate how far they had traveled along it. It was hard to read by firelight alone, but the distance to the northern border looked ominously far. "We will need provisions."

Calida edged closer, scrutinizing the map. She traced a line with her finger. Skylar focused on the lines drawn on the paper in her hands rather than the warm body next to hers.

"Galamoor has a market tomorrow," Calida said. "We can reach it by midmorning. But I have nothing to trade and just two pennies in my purse."

Skylar reached into the purse tied to her belt. She pulled out one of the pieces. It glinted in the firelight.

Calida raised her eyebrows. "You carry a lot for one with so little, Skylar."

It was Captain Noro who should be thanked. "We need food, some bedding, water carriers, and perhaps cloaks for the children."

"You do not mind buying for everyone? That is generous."

"We are in this together. At least while we are traveling the same road."

Calida's face softened. "We had to leave what little we had. But I can supply us with knives." The corners of her mouth twitched.

Skylar thought back to the previous night. "I recognized some of the attackers in Freymar. They were the youths who taunted Florian the night we met."

Calida took a swig of water from their now-shared canteen. "I am not surprised."

Skylar expressed a worry that had been gnawing away at her all day. "People died last night. All those homes were lost. If I had not involved myself, intimidating them, do you think they would have left you all alone? Was it my fault?"

Calida stared at her in disbelief. "Does the sun rise just for you, Skylar? Do waves turn on the shore because you command them?"

Skylar frowned and then could not help but chuckle. Calida was as direct as an arrow.

"The attack was going to happen," Calida said a shade more gently. "If not that night, another. Those youths were never going to tolerate us. What is more interesting to me is why you make yourself responsible." Her eyes sought Skylar's. They were lovely eyes. Her black pupils were made tiny by the fire. Reflected flames danced within her brown irises. Calida gazed back intently. Skylar swallowed. And then Skylar realized Calida was studying her cheek.

"The burn is healing. That is good. Here, you should treat it." Calida held out a crushed stem that oozed the yellow sap. Skylar felt Calida's laughter. Skylar's reaction had not gone unnoticed.

Abashed, Skylar shifted away, gingerly covering her burns with the cold, sticky plant juice. It soothed instantly. She had been raised to appreciate the efficacy of plant medicine, and she admired Calida's knowledge. It was vital in such a perilous situation.

She banked the fire and settled on the ground, wrapping her cloak around her and reflecting on wasted opportunities.

Skylar had had plenty of chances to gain a grounding in plant lore. The good reasons why she had not lay leaden in her heart.

❖

Gaea, twenty-one years previously

Skylar opened the door carefully. Mama should be treating patients now, listening to their problems, and making up their herbs and tinctures. But this morning, Mama had been agitated and fearful. Badly so. Skylar had not wanted to take herself and Cora to school. One glance at Mama's wide, frightened eyes, and she knew she should not leave her alone, not when her hands shook and her lower lip bled from biting. But Mama had pushed her out the door.

Skylar could not concentrate in class. She loved her teacher, and lessons were usually fun, but her mother's mood had trailed behind her. It had seeped into her mind, insistent that all was not well at home.

At break time, Skylar ran through the gate and along the streets until she reached the corner house that was both Mama's clinic and their home.

She knew to go around the back. Only patients were allowed at the front when the clinic was open. She would be quick. Peek through the kitchen to the sick room, see for herself that Mama was fine, and then run straight back to school. Maybe no one would even notice she'd been gone. Perhaps she would not get into trouble at all.

Skylar took off her shoes inside the door as always, but her socks stuck to the tiles, and she gasped when something cut into her foot. The floor was covered with shards of glass and a creamy, congealing stream that pooled toward a broken beaker. The smell of roots and bark and dirt and bitter pepper hit her, and her thumping heart sank. The mess underfoot was her mother's nervine mix. The medicine Mama took to slow and numb and escape to a place Skylar and Cora could not reach her.

Skylar pulled the glass out of her foot and ran on, not caring about the blood on her socks. She found Mama in their sitting room. She was slumped in a chair, her head flung back, eyes closed, and mouth open. Drool traced a line to her chin. Her normally olive skin was the color of ash. Skylar pulled an eyelid back. Mama's pupil was tiny. She pressed her fingers against her neck. The pulse was faint and slow.

Skylar wanted to scream. Instead, she ran across the street to their neighbor. Madam Reed stopped a carriage in the street and paid them to take Mama to the infirmary.

Afterward, she sat Skylar down with a glass of milk and put her arms around her.

Skylar and Cora stayed with Madam Reed for twenty days. Then came the healing circle, and Mama swore she would never take the nervine again. That was the first and the last healing circle for Cora. But not for Skylar. For Skylar, it was the first of many.

Chapter Three

S kylar woke soaking wet. She threw aside her cloak, bathed in sweat. She opened her eyes to a pale dawn under a blanket of heavy clouds that released a fine drizzle. It was unbearably humid, but the campfire burnt brightly.

Skylar groaned. She rolled away from the oppressive heat of the fire and tried to slip back into sleep.

A crash at the fireside put an end to that idea. Through half-closed lids, she watched Calida pull stout branches from a fresh bundle and build the fire up further.

"By the Goddess, this is a sweaty country," she grumbled. There would be no chance of sleep with that great heat roaring.

Calida froze. "You are a goddess worshiper?"

Skylar sat up, shock bolting through her as she remembered that Albans worshipped a single male deity. All other religions were forbidden. She cursed herself for the foolish mistake committed while half-asleep. She stood quickly. "I must wash," she mumbled, already striding toward the stream.

Recounting her words, Skylar realized she had said, "sweaty country." It was a ridiculous thing to say. It was not humid everywhere in Alba. Parts of the south were as dry as the Gaean plains.

Well, it was out of her mouth now. Hopefully, Calida had been too distracted by her mention of the Goddess to notice the rest of Skylar's blundering words.

The children were already at the stream. They did not seem to mind the humidity and drizzle. Raoul and Petro tended a horse apiece, letting them drink their fill. There was plenty of water, at least. They had traveled for two days through a wilderness with no one to trade with and nothing to hunt, fish, or forage. Skylar's stomach ached from gnawing at itself. How lucky she was to have never known such consistent hunger. If she needed food badly, how must those half-starved children be faring?

Florian sat on the bank, his eyes on Kit. The vultrix stood delicately on pebbles at the shallow edge of the stream. His attention was fixed on the water trickling past him. The stream's rhythmic gurgle was soothing. The air felt fresher here, scented as it was with the sharpness of pine from branches that reached toward the water. Tiny brown fish flickered and turned just beneath the surface. One would barely be a mouthful for Kit, but it was his energy to expend. The vultrix threw Skylar a look of disdain as he picked the thought from her head. Then he snapped, neatly and quickly, and snapped again. Two thin tails hung between his lips briefly before he swallowed and crouched to hunt again.

Skylar dipped her hands into the water and splashed her face. It was deliciously cold and chased the sleep away. If only she could strip off and bathe.

"Are you strong?" Florian looked at her inquisitively. He seemed happier this morning, and Skylar was glad.

"I would say averagely so," Skylar replied.

"And you can fight?"

Raoul and Petro had turned to listen. They observed her quietly.

Skylar tapped the weapon at her belt. There was no point in false modesty. "I am better than most with a sword. I perform well hand-to-hand and with a staff. I am a fair archer, although I prefer to use my bow for hunting."

"Will you teach me?" Petro's expression was serious. Skylar felt the yearning within him to protect himself.

"If we have time along the way, yes." Skylar wiped her hands dry on her trousers.

Petro stepped closer to his brother, still holding tight to his horse's reins with one hand. With the other, he took hold of Raoul's. Skylar felt how much the little boys longed for a safe place to settle.

And beneath that grand demand, Petro had not dampened his desire to be loved.

"And me?" Florian came to stand by Skylar. He reached out and tentatively touched Skylar's sword. "Is it very sharp?"

"Of course. A swordsperson must keep their weapon keen enough to cut through a blade of grass with one swipe."

Florian straightened. "I can throw knives already. And Mama has shown me some combat skills. I can defend myself with anything nearby, such as some yarn or a bowl perhaps, or, if we were here in the woods, a stick. Or just with my fingers."

Calida is a clever woman. What a shame the children had already learned the need to protect themselves. "Well, I will show you young ones what sword skills I know."

Florian smiled at Skylar. "I like traveling with you. I feel safe with you and Mama. I do not mind that we have left that place. I like to be in the open among trees and water, with nice people."

Skylar nodded. "Me too. Although, towns can be good places to live when you are welcome there."

"Where are those towns?" Florian asked quickly.

Skylar could not answer. "I do not know. That is, I do not know this area," she answered honestly.

Florian looked disappointed.

"Your mama will find you somewhere safe," Skylar said and then included the little boys. "We will find you all a good place to stay."

A whistle came from the camp. "Come, you four. If we are to reach the market town today, we must make haste." Hands on hips, Calida frowned at them.

Skylar's stomach growled as she and the children hurriedly complied with Calida's demand. Galamoor market had things to buy, and the thing she most wanted was something to curb her nagging hunger.

❖

Galamoor Square was teeming with traders and customers gathered for the weekly market. There was not much to Galamoor beyond the market. Narrow cobblestoned streets ran between timber houses. There was a blacksmith, a great house, an inn, a well, and a temple to the Alban god. The temple was the biggest building. Skylar studied the walls built from great slabs of stone, the craggy winged creatures that frowned down from the eaves, and the elaborately carved timber doors, and she wondered how much time and taxes the building had cost the working folk of the district.

The cherry trees planted in front of the temple had shed their fruit. High summer had passed here. Skylar looked at the dry leaves, already turning to flame, and felt sad. The trees would still be plump with deep red cherries in Gaea.

But today was not a day for regrets. The sun shone benevolently through a layer of wispy clouds that cooled its heat. A light breeze teased Skylar's hair, and scents bombarded her nostrils in an exciting mixture of known and unknown aromas. There was the dry husky smell of animal feed, the pungence of the animals themselves, scented oils, crisp swathes of linen and sacking, and, most exciting of all, a myriad of savory and sweet scents from the cookshop bordering the square.

The mood was carefree. Traders cried their wares from the merchant's shops built on all sides of the marketplace and from every stall. They called in a loud, easy-going fashion. People smiled as they passed Skylar's little group. Skylar sensed no fear, distrust, or threat from the folk around them. Galamoor was a friendly town, relaxed in itself and open to visitors.

Perhaps it was the lack of guards throwing their weight around.

The little boys darted excitedly from stall to stall until Calida took one of their hands apiece and crouched down to warn them against getting lost. They stayed close then, and Skylar was glad because the crowd thickened as the morning wore on. She was happy that the children seemed unbothered by their burns. Their skin looked much better, as were Skylar's face and hands. Yellow and sticky, it may be, but Calida's plant sap was a miracle healer.

"Beef ribs here and many a pie," a singsong voice carried above the chatter and laughter of customers and the cries of the other vendors. Skylar inhaled a rich, savory scent. She could practically taste the gravy.

"Shall we eat?" she asked Calida.

Calida stepped close, keeping her voice low. "We should buy the bedding and other provisions first. Your gold piece will be too much on display in the crowd around the cookshop. I saw a store on the south side of the market that looked to have what we need."

Too much on display? Was Calida concerned about thieves? The town seemed so jovial and safe. But Calida was Alban and must be wise to its ways. Skylar nodded in agreement.

They passed the livestock enclosures. Raoul and Petro rushed to the pig pen and stood cooing at the pink and black beasts.

"We kept a pig," Petro said. "When we had a home."

Florian put a hand on each of their shoulders, and Skylar sensed the comfort they took from the simple gesture. She wondered if Florian was compassionate or whether he was empathic. The vultrix was especially comfortable with him, as were the horses.

Skylar looked enviously at the palfreys on sale. The fast-riding horses did not have the muscle and shoulders of the cart horses or the sturdiness of the pack horses, but after the slow progress of the last days, being on one of their backs would be like flying. How wonderful it would be to push down into the stirrups and rise over the horse's gallop, to feel the wind rush past and the power beneath. She could be at the border in no time.

But the traders were asking more than she had in her purse. It would also mean saying good-bye to Calida and the children. It was surprisingly easy to walk away from the palfreys.

The cloth, pottery, and metal merchant's shop was a good size. Clay pots, tin pans, blankets, bedding, and cooking utensils were displayed on tables or hung from hooks and bundles of rope. The shop was situated just off the square, and the narrow cobbled street was pleasant after the noise and press of the market. The merchant smiled from behind his counter as they approached.

"How can I help you, good folk?" he asked.

Calida listed the items they needed. The merchant brought various pieces to the counter, directing every comment to Skylar.

She gleaned that he believed Skylar to be an Alban male. As Skylar tried to direct him toward Calida, his respect for Skylar dwindled while Calida's rage simmered. Frustratingly, the merchant spoke only to Skylar even when Skylar kept silent.

"See the quality of the cloth, sir." The merchant pressed the edge of a blanket into Skylar's hand.

Skylar stepped away from the counter. "My friend is the expert. I defer to her." Skylar put her hand on Calida's arm. "Perhaps there is another store?"

"Mistress, forgive me. I meant no disrespect." Alarmed at the prospect of losing a sale, the merchant suddenly found he could conduct business with an Alban female.

"The blanket is not soft nor strong enough. Not for that price," Calida said coldly.

He whisked it away and returned with a blanket twice the thickness.

Calida brushed her fingers along the cloth. "For the same price?"

The merchant looked pained but forced a "Yes" from his lips.

Calida nodded. "We will take five. Now show me bedding rolls of medium thickness."

The merchant brightened as the purchases mounted, but Calida continued to test him. She prodded, squished, and even sniffed the bedding, discarding several before she found rolls that met her standards. And when the merchant showed her a metal cooking pan, to his and Skylar's horror, she banged it against the counter.

Before he could speak, Calida stopped him with a look. "I have seen pans painted to hide low-quality tin. Tin as thin as air. I am sure you have heard of such things. Those pans melt on the cooking fire."

The merchant opened and closed his mouth several times before regaining control. "I assure you, good woman, you will find no trickery here. Traveling hawkers may get away with selling those pans, but I have been trading here for twelve seasons. I would be hauled to the stocks."

Calida relented. "You make a good point, sir," she murmured.

Skylar watched Calida manage the merchant and smiled inwardly. Calida was quite the woman. *In Gaea, she would be popular with many and thought very attractive.* Skylar suppressed the unruly thought. Calida was a temporary traveling companion. And she was from a country that abhorred lesbians. Calida thought Skylar was an Alban male, though she had shown no fear when sleeping beside her last night. Calida had yet to show fear about anything, perhaps because she carried twelve knives concealed within her coat.

Calida turned, her eyes bright with the joy of successful barter. "It is time to settle up, Skylar." She stepped closer. "It is a good price, but it is almost a full gold piece. Is that acceptable?"

Skylar shrugged agreeably. The merchant took the piece and bit it. When Calida did not raise a hair, Skylar had to assume merchants did that in Alba. Back home, it would be insulting. But then, apart from bandits and the occasional fraud or trickster, theft was rare and shocking.

The children ran eagerly ahead, shouting to each other all the foods they had smelled or seen. Calida carried the pots wrapped inside a blanket. Skylar walked beside her with the bedding.

"You are very kind." Calida glanced at Skylar. "And generous."

"We need these things, do we not? How far north will you travel?"

"Bareglen is in the center of the northern district," Calida said. "There is a market town within walking distance of my cousin's small holding. I should be able to find work there."

"Should we buy flour for biscuits, a little hard cheese, and some salted meat and vegetables, then? I have business in the far north, and I am already much delayed. It would be better for me to keep on the road rather than to stop in the towns along the way."

"Of course. I understand."

Skylar sensed Calida's curiosity, but she did not voice it.

The cook was too busy to cry her wares. It was high noon, and townsfolk and visitors alike were pressed around the shop, drawn by the smells of rich gravy, freshly baked bread, and hot, sweet fritters.

They took their place in a fast-moving queue. Calida jiggled a purse that she pulled from a pocket. She peered inside without untying it from wherever it was fastened to. "I will buy the food."

"There is no need," Skylar said gently.

"But, Skylar."

"It is my pleasure," Skylar insisted. "You helped me yesterday when I had need." She sensed Calida's discomfort, but her desire to look after Florian outweighed it.

"Just this once, then."

Skylar smiled. "Just this once."

"Fritters, fritters," Petro and Raoul chorused when their group reached the counter.

Florian looked at his mother hopefully.

"A pie will be best, a large one. Vegetable," Calida said firmly.

"How about a meat and vegetable pie?" Skylar suggested.

All the children turned to Calida.

"Skylar is treating us," she said. "I will leave it up to him."

"What will you have?" the cook asked. She was a light-skinned woman with rosy cheeks. Her hair covering and face were dusted with flour, while her apron bore the stains of gravy and batter.

Skylar turned to Calida. "Will we take a pie for the road as well?"

Calida looked surprised. "If we can afford it," she said tentatively. "A vegetable pie would be best for traveling."

"A large meat pie and a vegetable pie also, a loaf, please, and three sweet fritters. How about you, Calida? Would you care for a fritter?" Skylar's voice could barely be heard over the noise of the children's whoops of delight.

Calida shook her head. "Thank you, Skylar. No." She stared at Skylar, and Skylar felt that she was confused and uncomfortable.

Skylar handed over three pennies, and they moved away. Skylar took a moment to tuck the loaf and the smaller pie into her pack. By the time she had done so, the children were already licking honey from their fingers, the fritters having vanished.

They found a space on a patch of grass at the square's edge to sit and eat. Calida divided the pie and handed each person a portion.

The children consumed their pieces of pie almost as quickly as the sweet fritters. Skylar used a hard-baked crust wedge to scoop out chunks of potatoes, carrots, turnips, and lumps of meat she could not identify.

"What kind of meat is it?" she asked.

Calida smiled wryly. "It was not just the cost that made me suggest buying a vegetable pie. It could be rabbit or pig. It might be mutton if we are lucky."

"And if we are unlucky?"

"It would be better not to know." Calida sniffed a chunk of meat. "It is fit to eat, whatever it is. And the cookshop is permanent, like the merchant we traded with, so it is unlikely to be foul meat intentionally hidden in a pie."

Skylar almost choked on her mouthful. By the Goddess, was this something they did in Alba? She had never heard of such a thing. She finished the rest of her portion hesitantly, chewing carefully.

Calida chuckled. "Eat, Skylar, fill your belly. The pie is fine, I promise you. I have a nose for these things." She batted Skylar's arm playfully and then stood and walked to the nearby inn. She returned a few moments later with a flagon of ale and passed it to Skylar.

"Here, you take the first drink. The sun is warm, our bellies are full, and we have ale. Maybe this is as good as life gets." She sat, her eyes bright with laughter.

The ale was clean and crisp, malty and a tad bitter. It slipped easily down. Skylar passed back the flagon and relaxed. It was impossible not to, with the children so happy and Calida smiling at her. The sun teased out glossy blue highlights in Calida's night-dark hair, and in the fullness of day, her dark complexion was the color of barley bread. She was a remarkably beautiful woman.

Raoul yelled in delight as he ran past, playing a game of chase with Florian. Petro was more interested in their purchases. "This is a proper bed, a real bed, isn't it?" He squeezed one of the bedrolls, grinning from ear to ear.

"Well..." Skylar didn't know whether to explain about wooden beds. Petro seemed so delighted with the stuffed cloth tightly rolled and bound with string.

Before she could decide how to answer him, the sounds of a pipe and the sweet strumming of a lute drifted over to their patch of ground. The children ran to the edge of a small crowd gathered around two minstrels. Skylar followed them, balancing their purchases while Calida returned the flagon. The lute player had a pleasing voice. He sang a tale of romance that began slow and mournful, but when the character's luck changed, and his love was requited, the tune picked up. It became fast and merry, and the second minstrel called for the crowd to join them in dancing.

The steps were easy. The children picked them up straight away. Skylar held on to the bedrolls and moved her feet as best she could without dropping everything. Calida managed a graceful jig, even clutching the blanket of pans. They must have looked a funny sight as the dancers weaved about them. If they had not been carrying their purchases, Skylar wondered if she would have asked Calida to dance with her. The crowd pressed together, separating again when couples began to twirl.

At the tune's end, the crowd yelled their appreciation, and the minstrels rattled their hats, calling for coin.

Skylar balanced the bedrolls in one arm as she reached for her purse. She fumbled for several moments before she realized the purse was not there.

Her joy vanished. She looked down, and sure enough, the purse string still hung to her belt. The other end had been cut cleanly away.

❖

Skylar leaned toward the horses as they clip-clopped along the trail, willing the leagues to pass. It was not long past first light. The morning was cool, damp, and misty. The previous day's sunshine had disappeared, along with Skylar's lightness of spirit.

When they had returned from the market late the previous day, they had all bedded in the back of the cart except Kit, who had gone hunting. Skylar had woken before dawn, tended to the horses, whistled to Kit, and had them on the road again before the sky had fully lightened.

She would take none of the vegetable pie. Calida eyed her dubiously, shaking her head. "Why were you carrying all your coin and gold in the same place? That is what boots, head coverings, and tunic pockets are for."

Skylar sighed deeply. She had relaxed with the pleasure of the day, lost in the children's joy and her senseless attraction to Calida. This was not how she had been trained.

She had displayed remarkable naivety. She would not be so hard on herself if her foolishness had only affected her, but now they had no easy way to feed the children.

"You are somewhat of a mystery," Calida said. "You are skilled in combat, and yet you do not seem very learned in the rules of the road."

Skylar ground her teeth in frustration. Indeed, the events of the previous day had been an education in Alba's ways. Fortunately, Skylar was a quick study. It would not happen again.

"No matter," Calida said quietly. She handed the reins to Skylar and fiddled in her breeches pocket. "I have tuppence."

Assessing resources was a good idea. Skylar returned the reins and began to search through her pack for items that could be traded. It was still a long way to the border, and there were five mouths to feed.

"We will have to live off the land. It will slow us down, but we will survive. What is that?" Calida pointed to the block of resin that Skylar had plonked onto her knee.

"It is used for boat mending."

Calida waved a hand at the expanse of meadows they traversed. "Well, I can see why it's so valuable on the road that you would save it from a raging fire."

Skylar smiled wryly. "It was the pack I was saving. The resin was already in it." Now that the contents of her pack were laid out at her feet, she saw it was only the small, expensive block that could be traded. "It is wise to be prepared." Skylar replaced the resin and shouldered her pack.

The wind picked up.

Calida glanced at the dark clouds above. "Perhaps we should coat ourselves with it. Before the heavens discharge a river upon our heads."

Skylar gave a wry smile. "Our hoods will serve us better."

There was no point in dwelling on mistakes. Skylar had trained for many moons and completed scores of missions. Setbacks were commonplace.

"I'll take the reins for a while so you can rest." Skylar leaned against the box, straightening her back.

Her mind was clear again. Moving forward was what mattered.

❖

Skylar was so tired, so deep in sleep that, for a moment, she could not fathom what had woken her.

And then a dry leaf cracked underfoot. It was a soft footstep, but it was at the edge of their camp, and it was human. Skylar's telempathy flared. She quickly found Calida on the ground next to her and Florian and the boys in the cart. All asleep. She could not place Kit. Four human males were advancing on the camp from different directions and a fifth farther back in the trees.

She nudged Calida awake and unsheathed her sword. Greed emanated from all five men. They would take everything they had. Skylar scrambled to her feet, ready for combat.

"Hold," she cried. "I am a trained warrior, and I am armed. Go about your business, and I will not pursue you."

Laughter came from the four, all now a step inside the camp. One was by the cart, one near the horses, a third circled in from the left, and the fourth to the right, near Skylar and Calida. He laughed the loudest.

"A warrior, maybe." He was bearded, bulky, and sure of himself. "But you are one man, a small one at that, with three children and a wench. Thank you for the warning, but I will take my chances." He gave an elaborate, mocking bow to the amusement of his friends. Then, he advanced, his long sword glinting in the firelight.

He took but one step before a knife whistled past Skylar and sunk deep into his chest. He had time to clutch at his heart, his mouth gaping and eyes wide with shock before he toppled to the ground.

Skylar turned to the wagon, but a thin, reedy bandit approached her. She faced him, raising her sword.

"Drop your weapons." A third bandit stood over the children, his eyes cold and thick with menace. He pointed his sword at Raoul.

Florian pulled Raoul behind him and his brother, too. Florian trembled but glared bravely at the bandits.

"Got some of your mother's fire, girl, eh?" the bandit said.

Skylar plucked from his mind the idea that he could get good coin for Florian. Nausea rose in her throat.

Skylar's mind raced for solutions. The bandits were cruel, greedy men, and they were angry that one of their own lay dead. They would kill Skylar and Calida and sell the children for labor or worse. She was reluctant to give up her sword. If she had to, she had a knife in her belt and one in her boot.

"I have already loosed my weapon," Calida lied.

"Come here, wench, so I can check you," said the thin fellow a sword's length from them. His smile was menacing and lewd.

The bandit at the cart wrenched Raoul from Florian's grasp. He sheathed his sword and took a knife from his belt. "Drop your weapon, man, or I will slit this babe's throat."

Skylar felt Calida's rage beside him and sensed her moving for another knife. But there was no time, surely, for her knife to hit the man before he killed the child?

"All right, all right," Skylar spoke urgently. She held her sword away and bent to lay it down.

Something darted from the forest. With a blood-chilling growl, Kit flung himself at the bandit holding Raoul.

The man screamed as Kit bit down on his arm. Blood splurted in an arc, and Kit held on, savaging his flesh.

Skylar grabbed her sword and sprung at the man beside them, but he was pale as a ghost. He backed off slowly, then ran out of the camp and away, crashing through the woods. The fourth fellow had also vanished.

But on the edge of the woods, the fifth man still crept toward the horses. Skylar ran to intercept him, reaching the trees before he broke out of them. He was fiery-haired, bearded, a tall fellow and strong, and carried a broad sword. A fellow of his size could detach an arm with one stroke. His muscles rippled as he raised the weapon.

Skylar took her chance. She jabbed fast and deep into his stomach, then jumped back immediately. He vomited the air from his lungs, but the weapon swung down still. It missed Skylar by a hair. He went to raise it again but sank instead to his knees. He looked up at her in surprise.

Skylar swallowed and forced herself to look into his eyes as his life drained away. At last, he slumped, and he breathed no more.

The camp was silent. Skylar stared at the man she had killed. It was the first life she had taken. No training had prepared her for this feeling of great remorse.

She stepped back, wrenching her eyes from the corpse. It was a terrible night. Skylar knew it would stay with her all her days.

❖

Calida held the reins. She looked resolutely ahead and had not spoken since they had broken camp. The children were huddled together with Kit in the cart. Skylar was left to her thoughts, and they were not pretty. She had been trained to kill if necessary. But she had not been trained on how to deal with the aftermath.

Skylar considered, in the gray pre-dawn light, the fellow she had sent to his maker. She did not harbor guilt. He had intended to murder them all. Still, it was a horrible thing to take a life. She had not wished nor set out to kill. She could not shake from her mind the moment he let out his last breath, and the light disappeared from his eyes.

Skylar had witnessed Calida kill twice to protect Florian. The attacker in Freymar had been full of hate, but had he always been so? And both bandits, one dead at Calida's hand, one at Skylar's, had they been children once, full of joy, full of dreams?

There had been no alternative. It was a fight to the death. It had been necessary, but it did not sit well in the pit of her stomach. The man breathed no more because of her.

She shook the moment of the bandit's death away and remembered instead Florian cradling the two young children to him. He should not have had to do that. No child should be a protector at the age of thirteen. That was the job of adults.

She knew too painfully well why children should not have that responsibility.

That day had also been a terrible one.

❖

Gaea, nineteen years previously

Skylar wanted to find the wild ponies and ask them for a ride. They did not always agree. Skylar was getting to know them better with the growing of her telempathic abilities. The little brown one was kindest. She called him Fast Wind because when they connected, the pony sent a feeling of galloping so fast the streaming air was a torrent. Mama was not happy with Skylar's burgeoning skills and would not allow her to seek a tutor. Mama's empathy wore her down to a nub of herself. She had moved them out of the town, away from the crowds and the emotions that lacerated her nerves. Away from Madam Reed.

Mama still worked as a healer, and patients came, but their new house was on the edge of a great forest. It had vast open spaces, woodlands aplenty, lots of air, food growing straight out of the Mother's green earth, and the village of Elderwell close enough to walk to. It had everything Mama needed. There was no piped sanitation. They had a dug-out latrine at the cabin and a well in the village.

It was the height of summer, and Skylar wanted to play with the horses, but Mama said she must go to the well and take Cora with her. Skylar knew better than to argue. She did not mind playing with Cora. Skylar's little sister was sweet and funny, and headstrong. But she never did what she was told. How was Skylar supposed to draw the water and keep an eye on Cora? Skylar soothed her irritation as quickly as it flashed up inside her. Mama felt everything, even more so out here, with no other humans around. Skylar and Cora tried hard to have no emotions around her. They practiced on each other in the meadows and the woods. Cora showed early signs of empathy. Mama was worried that soon she would have no peace. Empaths did not seek each other out, she said. The feelings were too much to bear. But Skylar loved the ebb and flow with her sister. Cora was close to Fast Wind. When he carried her, she was the hair on his mane.

"Go now and take Cora with you. I need to lie down."

Skylar blinked at her mother and did not argue. She took the bucket and went after Cora. Her sister was already on the track to Elderwell running full out. "Slow down. You'll wear yourself out," Skylar shouted, but she wasted her energy. Cora never listened to anyone.

Villagers stared at Skylar as she ran past covered in dust, her throat raw and her heart about to burst. Cora should have tired leagues earlier, but she was still ahead of Skylar with no signs of slowing.

Skylar started to worry Cora would never stop. They had to go to the well. Where was Cora running to? She pushed her aching legs harder.

Skylar could not move any faster. The bucket banged against her legs. The breath came ragged in her throat. They were nearly at the well. "Cora," she gasped out. "We've got to get water."

Cora ran like Fast Wind. The well came into view. Skylar had no idea what to do if Cora tore past it.

But it was okay. Cora bounded up to the well. She leaped onto the wall and turned, laughing. A shaft of sunlight caught her face, and her smile was dazzling. Skylar was just behind her now. Near enough to see Cora blink.

Mama would not like Cora standing up there. Skylar reached out her hand.

Cora inched away. The step and her foot were so small it should not have mattered, but she tipped backward and vanished.

Skylar felt Cora's surprise and a rush as she flew down. Skylar heard the splash.

At the well's edge, Skylar peered past the gray stones tinged with moss, past the rope down and down into blackness. *She'll be at the bottom in the bucket, she'll be in the well bucket, she'll be okay.*

Skylar frantically cranked the handle. The bucket rose full of water. Beneath it was a horrible emptiness. Skylar reached out with her mind. She searched through the water and found a small, solid form but no emotions, no thoughts, no laughter, no spark of life.

That's when she started to scream.

Villagers arrived. There was shouting and running and lots of fuss. Then, everyone spoke in quiet voices. After some time, a warrior climbed down and brought Cora up. But when they did, her face was swollen as if she had drunk the well water through the pores of her skin, and her head lay at a strange angle in the warrior's arms. Skylar looked for a rise and fall on Cora's chest. She searched, she begged Cora's eyes to open.

Mama took to her bed. She could not help Skylar with her guilt or her grief. Skylar spent all her time outside in the woods and the meadows. Fast Wind and the herd grew to know her like one of their own. The birds and animals of the forest accepted her, too, and Skylar spent many nights sleeping in the forest.

By the time she was accepted into the butch warrior regiment, her bushcraft skills were exemplary. And Skylar relied on no one, no one but herself.

Chapter Four

Three days and nights, it rained. It was not cold, but there was no let up from it and no chance for their clothing to dry out. The wet seeped inside Skylar's cloak. The children were huddled together at the back of the cart under the oiled cloth, the vultrix beside them. Four sad, gaunt faces peeked at Skylar when she glanced behind. They were hungry. The same hunger gnawed at Skylar, but she was a butch warrior with a warrior's duty to survive. She no longer second-guessed herself or berated any of her choices. She accepted the responsibility for taking a life, and she would live with it.

None of the children had asked for food, even though Skylar sensed the pain in their bellies. Each of them had gone without, she realized, on so many occasions it was commonplace. What kind of society allowed children to go hungry? It would be unthinkable in Gaea.

The pie was long gone, and the wet weather made for poor hunting as creatures hunkered down to avoid it. Skylar had scoured boggy grassland and sodden forest and sensed no movement. If even Kit had been unsuccessful in the hunt, what chance did a mere butch have? The group had barely rested since the bandit attack. At first, both Calida and Skylar wanted to get many leagues between them and the dead robbers. As the days wore on, Skylar had been reluctant to make camp, citing unsuitable ground or the poor weather. But really, the bandits' wicked intent had unnerved her.

Calida had not spoken since they'd creaked to a weary start in the gray light of dawn. They had passed no one. No ordinary, kindly person they could trade with or beseech, and Skylar was weary enough to beseech strangers at this point, if only for the children's sake. They were covering a reasonable distance, at least. The horses were steady and true. There was plenty of rich grass for their needs, and the children brushed them down and rubbed them dry at the end of each long day.

Skylar wished she could do more. If they passed a town and there was work to be had, she would seek it to get food for the children. And, hell, for the vultrix too. Every night, Kit curled up into the crook of Skylar's bent legs. Skylar liked to feel him there. His presence soothed her enough to fall asleep, at least for a while. If seeking work meant a day longer in Alba, so be it. Skylar had trained to be a protector. Though, she had learned to be that person many seasons before she had pledged herself to the butch regiment.

"We'll need to make camp tonight," Calida broke into Skylar's thoughts. "No matter how rough, open, or sodden the ground may be. The horses must have proper rest." She scowled at the dark clouds over their heads.

"Surely we'll reach a village or a town soon," Skylar said as much to convince herself as Calida.

Calida glanced at Skylar. "This is a long stretch of nowhere. It will be a day or two more, I think."

Calida said something more, but Skylar sat upright, her attention fixed on the sound of hooves thundering toward them on the wet road. Calida snatched a knife from inside her coat as Skylar unsheathed her sword.

A single white horse came through the drizzle, a streak of lightning in the gloom. It was bridled but riderless and galloping fast.

It swerved to pass them on Skylar's side. She dropped her sword and jumped to a crouch. She turned sideways, keeping one eye on the runaway horse.

The mare's eyes were wide. Sweat glistened on its matted coat. Skylar felt the rapid beating of its heart. It was running from someone malicious, and it was terrified.

Its hooves sent up clods of mud. The mare was powerful, muscular, and strong. Her teeth were bared as they clamped onto her bit. Skylar imagined those teeth biting down on her hands. She pushed that thought quickly aside.

Skylar knew she had only one chance. She leaped as the mare drew alongside. She landed on the horse's bare back, but there was no saddle, and her coat was slippery with rain and sweat. Skylar scrabbled for the harness at the horse's neck. The mare bucked. Skylar rose with the horse and landed with a hard jolt. Desperately, she twisted her fingers under the leather. The wind rushed past her face, a cruel reminder of the mare's speed. The rain beat into Skylar's eyes, clouding her vision. The mare bucked again, and Skylar was thrown to the left, half-hanging over the horse's side. Several terrible moments passed, with Skylar staring at the hooves that beat like hammers onto the road's surface. Her fingers strained near to breaking as she gripped hard onto the harness. If she did not calm the mare, Skylar would be thrown and trampled beneath those powerful hooves.

It's okay. It is okay. You are safe. I will not hurt you.

The horse slackened her pace a fraction. Skylar inched herself up and blended her thoughts with the mare's.

There is grass and a nice rest for you if you will stop.

The mare's ears prickled. Her breathing slowed. For a time, she galloped on but did not attempt to throw Skylar from her back. Skylar leaned into her neck. *Please slow down. I'll not harm you. You are safe with me.*

Skylar was able to sit up as the mare responded and finally trotted to a stop.

They were a league or more from the wagon. Skylar continued to comfort the horse with kindly thoughts and gentle murmurings. "What have you been subjected to, friend?"

The mare shuddered. Skylar linked with her and felt the memory of a whip striking the horse from behind. She winced as the thin leather strap bit into the horse's back, and the horse reared onto her hind legs. There was a loud crack as the horse broke away from the cart.

"Well, my brave one. I do not blame you for running from such treatment." Skylar gently rubbed the mare's neck and caressed her mane. "Come back with me to our cart, and we will tend to you. I promised you grass. You shall have your fill of it. Let's see if we can find you water also."

The mare turned around at Skylar's bidding. They trotted back to the wagon to find all three children staring at Skylar in awe. Even Calida looked impressed.

"I've never seen anything like it." Florian leaped onto the road, then hesitated a step from the horse. "May I stroke her?"

"Absolutely not," Calida said.

Skylar jumped down and led the runaway horse to a meadow at the side of the road. "Florian, you must do as your mother says."

Calida told the children to stay in the back of the cart and then came to Skylar. "There's more to you than meets the eye. You're an acrobat? I took you for a mercenary."

Skylar turned from rubbing down the mare, careful to avoid the spot where the whip had landed. Mercenary was not a bad guess. Skylar had said nothing of where she came from or her business. "Acrobat? No." Suddenly, she did not want to lie even if she could not tell Calida the truth. "Physical skill is part of my training."

Calida searched Skylar's face but asked nothing further, and Skylar was glad. She did not want to sully the tentative warmth stretching between them.

The mare bent her head to the grass, eating leisurely. Skylar gleaned that the horse was not especially hungry and did not need much rest. Skylar continued to gently rub the horse down, sending waves of calm to soothe the mare's fractured nerves.

"Can I help?" Soft footsteps behind her alerted Skylar to Florian's presence.

Skylar turned and held out the damp rag. "She is quiet now. I think she feels safe. You could wipe down her flank, but leave her shoulders be."

Florian reached for the rag, but Calida stepped in front of him.

"I do not think she is a nervous or dangerous horse." Skylar tipped her head toward the horse's shoulders, where three welts were raised above the snow-white hair. "I think she was mistreated."

Calida's face flushed with anger. Florian stepped cautiously up to the horse, murmuring in a gentle voice. The mare responded instantly. Within moments, they were firm friends. The child did have empathy, especially with animals. In Gaea, Florian would be encouraged into training and work where his skills would benefit both humans and beasts. Indeed, in time, his mind skills might develop further. Telepaths and empaths were strongest after puberty. Skylar wondered how he would fare in Alba. Skylar had been taught telepathy and empathy were feared, even ostracized. What a waste of talent!

"The horse seems fresh despite her adventure," Calida remarked. She eyed the sky, dark with advancing clouds. "I think we should find a better place to camp than this."

There was no running water despite the rain still dripping onto their heads. Skylar tied the runaway horse to the back of the cart. "Let us hope we do not have to travel far to find suitable shelter."

Calida nodded. "Indeed."

❖

The rain continued to fall as a fine drizzle. After the excitement had faded, Skylar became increasingly impatient with the journey. She was wet and worn out and wanted the day to be over. But they had yet to find a stream or other source of drinking water.

"You could get under cover with the children," Skylar suggested to Calida. "There is no sense in both of us being soaked to the bone."

Calida gripped the reins fiercely. "With bandits in the area? My place is here."

"With your speed and skills, I would not have thought a simple oiled cloth would diminish a scrap of your deadliness." Skylar dared to grin at Calida.

She hmphed and turned back to the road. "Indeed!"

Skylar snuck a look and found Calida smiling.

They had only traveled a league when Skylar saw someone ahead, walking hunched over by the side of the road. Calida pulled a knife from inside her coat.

Skylar unsheathed her sword and laid it across her lap.

As they drew closer, it seemed the man was alone. He turned at the clop-clop of hooves.

Calida surveyed him quickly and then glanced over the empty meadows on either side of the road. Skylar did the same. There were no hedgerows or ditches, and the only trees were far away. She began to slow the cart. Calida put her hand on Skylar's arm.

"Be careful. This could be a trap. There may be others lying in wait. Although, I am not sure where they would be hiding."

Skylar took up her sword and sent a message to the vultrix.

Assent came back instantly, reassuring Skylar that the fox was awake and ready.

The man stopped walking as the wagon approached. He looked forlorn and bedraggled. A long, pale face peered out at them from under a brimmed brown cloth hat. He wore a brown shirt, jacket, and trousers, all soaked through. Even his hat dripped. He had the watery eyes of a river under storm clouds, and his face was lined with worry.

"Good folks, you find me distressed," he began, but then he spotted the runaway mare, and his mouth dropped open. He straightened sharply, staring at Skylar. "That's my horse you have tied to your cart." He went straight to the mare. She relaxed and whinnied into his hand.

Calida jumped down from the cart. "I see she knows you. She was galloping along the road as if from a fire."

Skylar climbed down to join Calida. "I managed to calm her."

The man nodded absently, still stroking the mare. "I am amazed you were able to. She is a willful horse. Strong and brave. There's not much that would scare her enough to bolt." He noticed the welts then and ran a finger lightly alongside one. "Ill-treatment, though. That would do it." He rounded on Skylar, his face closed again and angry.

Skylar stepped back and held up her hands in a gesture of peace. "We do not beat horses, sir. Those welts are fresh but were not inflicted by us."

The man gave a long sigh. "I can guess who it was then. They got more than they bargained for if they tried to whip Willow." He examined the harness. "She must have broken free."

"What happened to you, sir?" Skylar asked, untying Willow while the man continued to look the mare over.

"I was driving my cart to the village. It's about half a day's journey from my farm. I was unlucky enough to meet two guards. They waved me down and told me they were taking my cart. 'Requisitioning it,' they called it."

"Can they do that?" Skylar asked.

"They were young, strong, and fully armed. They act as they please. I tried to explain that the cart and horses are my livelihood. Without them, I cannot sell my goods. They just laughed, and when I did not climb down fast enough, one of them pulled me from the cart and hit me about the head."

"That is disgraceful." Skylar was appalled. "I wish we had been here to help you."

"And then they would have cut you down. As well, you know," Calida pressed her fingers into Skylar's arm.

"It seems you are a brave fellow. But sometimes, there is nothing to be done," the farmer said sadly.

"And we have the children to think of," Calida added.

The farmer turned to the three little faces staring at him from the back of the cart. "Oh. You are blessed." He beamed at the children and then back at Skylar and Calida.

Skylar realized the farmer had taken them for husband and wife with their three children. Calida's eyes twinkled, but she did not correct him, and Skylar took the lead from her. "Can you ride without a saddle?" Skylar asked the farmer.

The farmer shook his head.

"And what direction is your farm?"

"A quarter day's north."

"Well then." Skylar turned to Calida. "Do you think we can all travel together? I can ride saddleless for that short time."

Calida looked at the sky. "I am more than happy to help this good fellow, but I am not sure we can travel together all the way.

We need to make camp for the night, and there is, perhaps, less than a quarter of the day before it will get dark with all this cloud overhead."

"You are right," Skylar said immediately. "The children are soaked from all the rain."

The farmer brightened. "But you can stay at my farm overnight. My wife would insist, if she were here, for your aid and for returning Willow to me. We have a room you can have to yourselves."

"A whole room to ourselves?" Raoul called out.

Skylar, Calida, and the farmer laughed.

"What do you think?" Skylar asked Calida quietly.

"It sounds warmer and dryer than anywhere we are likely to find," she said.

Moments later, the farmer had taken Skylar's place on the cart, and they had started along the track. Skylar softly asked Willow if she minded carrying Skylar and received a warm assent.

As Skylar and Willow set off behind the cart, the farmer began to teach the children a lively song. The rain finally let up. Could it be their luck had changed at last?

❖

The next day dawned warm and bright. Following an invitation from the farmers, Calida proposed they stay for at least a day. She felt they needed a break from traveling, especially the cart horses.

Skylar was up with the sun to help the farmer, Nathaniel, repair a section of his barn. Raoul and Petro tended to the horses. While Florian and Calida assisted Nathaniel's spouse, Mary, with the many kitchen tasks. Skylar would have been content to prepare meals, but binary etiquette dictated their tasks. Skylar was irked with the strict division of labor but did not mind the actual work. She relished the chance to keep her muscles strong while building something useful. Calida showed no interest in sawing, nailing, or heaving heavy logs.

At suppertime, they gathered at the kitchen table. Mary and Nathaniel were remarkably cheerful considering the loss of their cart and livestock and the five extra mouths to feed.

"We made fine progress today," Nathaniel said, passing a plate heaped with slices of dark bread to Calida. "Your young fellow is a good carpenter."

"We are indebted to you. To you all." Mary beamed at Calida. "It gladdens my heart to see the children running through the fields. It has been such a long time."

Skylar felt sadness within Mary, although she could not tell why.

Nathaniel smiled kindly at his spouse. He cut through the slab of pale yellow cheese in the center of a rough wooden board and handed a chunk to Skylar. "Are you fixed on continuing north?"

"Why do you ask, sir?"

"There is a rumor of trouble building in the region close to the wastelands." Nathaniel glanced at Mary.

Mary sliced a juicy, crimson tomato for each of the children. "Some unruliness, we have heard. The guards that stole—"

"Requisitioned," Nathaniel interjected mildly.

"The guards that *stole* our cart and horses were marching to the far north," Mary continued. Her voice was mild, but her eyes flashed anger.

"The two I met so unfortunately were catching up with a platoon that passed through the village a few days past," Nathaniel added.

"I dare say they needed the cart for all the goods and livestock they would be *requisitioning* from other poor citizens along the way," Calida said.

Mary and Nathaniel nodded wryly.

"It is dangerous on the road at the moment. You could stay here. At least for a time or until the trouble settles. With your help, we can work the land and provide for us all." The farmer looked at Skylar. "The life is meager at times, but you can get extra work on market day, I am sure, a strong fellow like you."

Skylar glanced at Calida. She looked as surprised as Skylar felt. She was sorry to quash the couple's excitement, but she had to, at least concerning herself. "I have no choice but to keep traveling, I'm afraid. My business lies in that direction." Skylar resolved to speak to Calida out of the farmers' hearing. Calida might wish to stay.

"You'll want to keep the family together, of course." Mary seemed disappointed.

Calida glanced at Raoul and Petro, beginning to fall asleep in their chairs. "The little boys are not ours. They lost their parents. But they are in our care now."

Skylar noted Calida's use of the word *ours*. It certainly implied Calida and Skylar were Florian's parents. Florian grinned at Skylar but said nothing.

"They are darlings." Mary smiled tenderly at the sleepy boys.

"And so helpful. So polite. Their skill with horses is astounding," Nathaniel said.

"Indeed." Calida looked amused at the farmers' enthusiasm.

Skylar finished the last of her bread and cheese, relishing the salty, creamy taste. "That was good fare. Thank you." She began to collect the empty plates.

Mary raised an eyebrow.

"I cannot sit while there is work to be done," Skylar said.

"You are an unusual fellow." Nathaniel rose and took the plates from Skylar. He carried them over to the sink, glancing over to Mary.

She got up as well. "I will see to the clearing up. You need to get the children to bed."

"*We* will see to the clearing up," Nathaniel said, rolling up his sleeves.

Mary nudged Calida. "See, you are bringing nothing but goodness into our home."

❖

The little boys were asleep before their heads dropped onto their bed rolls.

Skylar lay on one side of the simple wooden bed. The straw mattress was comfortable. Even though they had camped out several nights together and Calida had often lain near Skylar, it felt strangely intimate to share a bed. Florian lay between them. Skylar felt peace and joy radiating from him. The little boys were content, but she knew they were happy enough to be safe, warm, and fed. Florian, though, had taken to her. The feeling was mutual. The child had stolen her heart. It was both wonderful and terrible because she must return to Gaea. She did not know if she could leave him in this dangerous, cruel country. But leave him, she must.

And then there was Calida. Skylar heaved a sigh. She was increasingly drawn to her. It was not surprising. Calida was brave and powerful, devastatingly attractive, and capable of such tenderness with the children. There was another awkward thing. Skylar felt desire flowing from Calida in return. She dampened her awareness of it as best she could. Her telepathy was an intrusion, especially since Calida was unaware of Skylar's abilities.

"Skylar, are you awake?" Calida's voice was barely above a whisper.

Skylar turned toward her. Florian's breath rose, and fell, sweetly asleep. "Yes."

"Do you want to leave on the morrow? The horses are rested."

Skylar was surprised. Everyone seemed so content. "I think so. Weather permitting." She was ridiculously happy that Calida wanted to journey on. "Are you sure, Calida? I wondered if you and the children might want to stay."

Calida shifted toward her, raising herself onto her elbow. "Oh no. It would not be right. I could not be myself here."

She offered no further explanation, and Skylar did not ask. She shielded to preserve Calida's privacy.

If only she could be herself with Calida. There was the prospect of a different life in the little room. A home with a beautiful and powerful woman, a child she loved already, and good, solid work on the land. It was as far from Thale as anywhere could be.

But this was Alba. It could never be.

❖

Skylar walked from the kitchen to the barn. A quarter of the day had passed, and it was blisteringly hot.

Nathaniel had borrowed the cart to trade the last of his tomatoes and the first of his corn harvest in the village. He had taken all three children with him. Mary and Nathaniel were kind to the little boys and gave their attention to Florian, also. All around, they appeared to be decent folks. They were the first honorable people Skylar had met in Alba, save the pieman, Calida, and the children.

The break had been welcome. Skylar's burns were healed, and the little boys' wounds were almost mended.

Outside the barn, the farmers' field stretched to the foot of a hill. Forest lay to one side, and a trickling stream ran past the other. Skylar sensed someone by the linden trees at the edge of the forest. She peered through the heat haze and found a ruddy, furry face observing her. Kit had disappeared from the back of the cart when they had driven onto the farmer's track. Skylar sent him warm greetings. He came out of the forest and trotted lightly over the plowed earth. He stopped close enough for Skylar to read the amber in his eyes. He stared at her, unblinking, one foot still raised. A thought blew to her, carried on a welcome breeze.

Freedom.

It was another promise made. Skylar nodded solemnly. She walked on to the barn. She had embraced the rest gladly, but there was no getting away from it. Skylar must return to Gaea, however sad the prospect made her.

She turned back to the vultrix. There was just the earth and the trees and the sway of the yellow corn husks in the haze.

❖

Calida sat with Mary, spinning yarn. She knew the principle of the task. In Freymar, she had acquired clothes for herself and Florian by whatever means were at her disposal. Blistering her fingers with yarn and wool had not been one of them. She'd have sooner taken the jerkin from a rich man's washing line than sit of an evening spinning and knitting.

Mary's skills put hers to shame, and Calida found she did not mind the work so much in this comfortable kitchen with the back door open to the breeze and a cup of fresh mint tea on the table before her. In some ways, it would be a wrench to go, especially as Florian and the boys were happy and safe. They had seen too much danger, hardship, and cruelty in their short lives.

She had slept fitfully, thinking over her decision. Was it better for the children if she stayed? She had not seen her cousin, Anton, since Florian was small. She hoped he would welcome them, but she had no assurances. Was his homestead in Bareglen a place where she could be truly free? If she was discovered to be a lover of women, she could be put to death. She had kept to the shadows for Florian's sake. But it was a path that left her lonely and dishonest. Was there no quiet place she could truly be herself? They were both courting danger. Florian was old enough now to face prison or worse if he were discovered.

"I like your young husband," Mary said.

Calida smiled and kept silent. She did not want to lie further to someone who had treated them kindly. Assumptions had been made for safety's sake, and there was little point in correcting them now. Would Mary and Nathaniel be so welcoming if they knew Skylar was a woman? Calida had been as sure as she could be moments after Skylar appeared in the shack, all swagger and confidence. And her instincts had been proved right the night before. Waking before Skylar, Calida had to tear her eyes away from the soft breast exposed beneath the open buttons of Skylar's undershirt.

Calida understood why Skylar might pass to protect herself from prison or death. Skylar was not the first virago Calida had known, nor the first woman living as a man in Alba. How curious they had been thrown together, all three of them hiding their true selves.

"And Raoul and Petro are not yours, you said?"

Calida sighed. "They lost their mother last winter. She fell to grippe. The illness swept the..." Calida had nearly forgotten herself and said "settlement." "Swept our part of town. Many were taken."

Mary looked solemn. "We had the grippe here three winters ago. We all succumbed to it. There was a fever and a terrible croup. Nathan and I recovered, but our daughter did not."

"Oh." Calida let her spindle rest on her lap. "I am sorry, Mary."

Mary bit her lip and looked away. "I miss her terribly. I had her for just eight years, and she was bonny and kind, a truly sweet-natured child."

Calida took Mary's hand. Mary wiped her eyes and resumed teasing out her yarn.

Calida did the same. Some pain was best worked through, especially when there was nothing, nothing at all, to be done to ease it.

❖

Skylar paused mid-hammer at the fast clip of hooves on the dirt track by the barn. It sounded like the horses and cart, but it was not even time for the midday meal.

She reached for her sword and remembered her weapons lay inside the farmhouse.

She went outside cautiously, still bearing the hammer.

Nathaniel reined in the horses and jumped down. He looked worried.

"Boys, pray take the horses to the barn, rub them down, and give them water and feed. Florian, will you pack your things while I talk to your mama and papa?"

Florian nodded solemnly and ran inside the house.

"What is wrong?" Skylar asked.

Nathaniel raised his hand. "One moment, Skylar. Can we talk inside with Mary and Calida?"

Skylar followed Nathaniel into the kitchen. Mary and Calida rose in confusion as they entered.

"You are back early? Did you trade well?" Mary's brow creased with worry.

"Some, Mary, but I've returned with bad news. Let us sit so I can keep my voice low. I do not want the children to hear before you do." Nathaniel pulled out a chair.

"What is it?" Calida sat beside him.

"The bailiff came into the village with several of his men. They are searching for felons who killed two travelers in the woods, some leagues from here."

Skylar glanced at Calida. Her face betrayed no emotion.

"That is shocking. Why are you so troubled, Nathan? Do you expect them to come this way?" Mary asked.

Nathan shook his head. "I do not think these people are a danger to us, Mary. But one of the men killed was the bailiff's brother."

"I can not say I am saddened by that news," Mary said. "He was a violent thief. He did as he pleased with his brother in the post, and no one dared challenge him."

Nathan nodded. "Indeed. Searching for his brother, the bailiff met two of his friends, a bad pair. They gave a description of their attackers."

Skylar swallowed. "Who are they looking for?"

Nathaniel met her eyes. "A light-skinned man, a brown-skinned woman, and three children traveling in a cart."

"*They* attacked us while we were sleeping," Calida said grimly.

"They meant to kill us all and take everything we had," Skylar added.

"I do not doubt it." Nathaniel's eyes were kind but full of concern. "The bailiff is coming this way, and he will check every farm. He was fond of his brother. You are not safe here."

Calida rose. "We must go."

"Hold a moment, please. I have a proposal." Nathaniel patted Calida's arm. "Leave your cart and horses. Take my pack horses instead."

"That is a good idea. We can travel faster, but we cannot manage with two horses. We need the cart for the children." Skylar pushed her chair into the table.

Mary took a deep breath. "Leave Raoul and Petro with us," she said.

Skylar turned to Calida.

"I do not know…" Calida began.

Skylar searched Mary and Nathaniel for cruel intent and found only compassion and hope.

Calida took Skylar's arm, leading her outside. "They seem good people, but can we trust them?"

"How can I advise you? I am not their guardian," Skylar whispered.

"Neither am I. We both took them on in the chaos of the fire."

"My instincts tell me the farmers are kind and will treat the boys well. They have been honest and generous with us," Skylar said.

"They are mourning one of their own. Perhaps this arrangement is good for them all, but it must be the boys' decision. Let us ask them."

Within the whirlwind of departure, Skylar and Calida sat with Raoul and Petro. The children agreed immediately. With great excitement, they ran to Mary and wrapped themselves around her knees.

Skylar and Calida left Mary in the kitchen with the boys, holding them close and wiping her eyes on her apron.

Skylar sent a message to Kit as they prepared the horses. She took one steed with most of the supplies and Calida the other with Florian sitting behind her. Kit joined them halfway along the track, running beside them.

As they galloped away from the farm on the dusty track, Skylar was filled with trepidation. May the Goddess help them avoid the bailiff and his men.

Chapter Five

They rode hard and fast, skirting the village. The sun beat down relentlessly, but at least the breeze from riding cooled Skylar's skin. A short while after they passed the road to the village, clouds gathered over the sky, giving welcome relief. Skylar took it as a sign that they had made the right decision. She felt Calida brooding on the wisdom of leaving Petro and Raoul behind. Thundering along the road, there was no opportunity for discussion. Skylar missed Calida's steady presence beside her at the front of the cart.

Kit kept pace with them for a time. When he lagged, Skylar pulled up and opened the top of one of the packs. Kit jumped in, eyeing the horse's flank suspiciously, but settled in well enough.

It was the middle of the afternoon when Skylar sensed hoofbeats behind them, and then she felt Kit's mind link with hers. Skylar had connected with other telepaths in Gaea. The combination emphasized their abilities, and so it was with Kit. Skylar quickly sensed five power-hungry males. They were hunting for someone. Kit yearned to evade them.

Skylar reined in her horse. Kit jumped out of the pack and bounded into the forest at the side of the road.

"Calida," Skylar said urgently. "Riders are coming. Take Florian and your horse into the woods. I have a hunch it is the bailiff and his men."

Calida galloped back to Skylar. "Why do you think that? Nathaniel said they were going to his farm." She peered back along the road. "I do not see anyone."

"Trust me. If it is them, they are looking for five people on a cart, not one man on a packhorse."

Calida frowned at the deserted road while Florian stared at Skylar with frightened eyes. But then Calida turned her horse into the trees, and they quickly disappeared. Skylar pulled out a cloth, hurrying to wipe her horse down. She needed to appear leisurely and untroubled.

She remounted and rode forward at a slow trot.

Skylar had only gone a short distance when she heard the gallop of horses. She glanced behind and saw five riders. Their faces were buried behind the hoods of their cloaks. The energy of their spirits bore down on her, brooding and oppressive.

Within moments, she was surrounded. The riders drew their swords. Skylar did not. Instead, she projected the image of a common man with little status.

"Good day, sirs," she spoke hesitantly, her head bowed.

A light-skinned, light-haired fellow prodded her shoulder with a riding crop. "Dismount."

Skylar did so. The light-haired man and two others dismounted also. They formed a triangle around her with their swords pointed at her chest.

Skylar felt Kit's presence at the edge of the forest, watching. *No,* she sent. Skylar did not want to lead the men into the woods, not with Florian there.

"Lay down your weapon," one of the mounted men commanded. His cloak and breeches were hewn from fine cloth. Arrogance pulsed from him. He was a petty tyrant, used to pushing folk around. He pulled his hood back. Skylar was struck by his resemblance to the bearded, fiery-haired bandit. One of the men who had intended to leave them dead on the forest floor.

Skylar pulled her sword from its holster and put it on the ground. The man nearest her kicked it away.

"Sirs, I mean you no harm. There are some provisions in my packs. Take them if you have need," she said in a weak and timid voice.

"I am the bailiff of these parts." The haughty man's lip curled.

The blond man cuffed her on the head. "How dare you presume us thieves. Why would we want your miserable possessions?"

"I beg your pardon," Skylar tried not to snarl through teeth clenched with pain. The blow had not been soft.

"Why are you traveling on this road?" the bailiff asked.

Skylar glanced up at him. "I came in search of work, but now I am returning to my village. I have heard there is sickness there, and I worry for my parents."

She sensed the bailiff thought her a simpleton to return anywhere there might be sickness. That was good.

"Show your traveling papers," the light-haired man demanded.

But the bailiff dismissed him with a hand. "We are looking for a man, a woman, and three children traveling in a cart. Have they come this way?"

"I have not passed them."

The light-haired man took a step closer. "He could be the fellow." The tip of his sword was a hair's breadth from Skylar's chest.

If she ducked and rolled, could she pull the dagger from her boot before one of the swords cut her down? Her chances were poor. But she would take the blond brute with her at least. She shrunk her shoulders down as if cowed by the men. Surprise was the only advantage she had.

"He is olive-skinned," the second man, still mounted, said.

The blond man turned to him. "Olive, light. It's all the same. He is not brown or black-skinned."

The bailiff tossed his head impatiently. "This cowering laborer is not our man. Pay heed, sniveling wretch. I'll warrant you are traveling without leave. If I meet you on this road again, that will be the end of you. Am I plain?"

Skylar kept her head bowed. "Yes, sir."

Several of the men laughed. She felt their surge of power. The blond kicked her knees from under her, and they laughed harder.

She stayed on the ground while the men climbed back onto their mounts.

Still laughing, they rode away, coating her with dust and grit.

❖

Skylar uncurled herself and straightened. The bailiff and his men were small figures in the distance. She felt their intent, and it was to search onward.

She was dusting the muck from her cloak when she felt four life forces at the forest's edge. Two beasts and two humans.

Skylar walked her horse to the trees. She felt Calida and Florian, Kit and the horse, but could not for the life of her see a soul. The vultrix was a master of camouflage. Perhaps Calida and Florian were experts also. But hiding a horse? That was unusual.

Skylar whistled. "They have gone," she called softly.

Florian stepped from between two slender and tall silver birch trees. Their leaves fluttered as he moved through them. The branch of a broad oak shifted. Calida jumped lightly down from it, clutching a knife in each hand.

"I was worried for you." Florian ran to Skylar and threw his arms around her.

"Why did you do such a stupid thing?" Calida's eyes were fierce with rage. Her breath came in short bursts.

"She wanted to come to your aid," Florian explained. "It was horrible when that man hit you and kicked you onto the ground."

Calida's mouth twisted. She gripped her knives tightly enough to break the handles.

"You were supposed to disappear deep into the forest," Skylar told her.

Calida glared at her. "That is not my way."

"She is protective of those she loves," Florian said.

Skylar and Calida both turned to him in shock.

"Loves?" Calida croaked.

"Well, perhaps likes in your case, Skylar." Still hugging Skylar, Florian looked up at her thoughtfully. "But I do love you already. You have been kind to me when you had no duty to be."

Skylar swallowed and hugged Florian back. "You are an easy person to be kind to, Florian," she mumbled into the top of his head. She looked up to find Calida glaring at her.

"Let me make one thing plain. I do not need anyone's protection."

Skylar blanched. "I know that very well. But you have a child. That is why I put myself forward to distract them."

Calida narrowed her eyes. "I see. And if Florian were your child, you would have agreed to me putting myself in their path?"

Skylar considered Calida's words. After some moments, she nodded. "Yes."

"Hmm. Well then, good. We understand each other." Calida slipped her knives back inside her coat. "Come then, *sniveling wretch*, we have found a place to camp. There is water for the horses, and it is not far. I thought it best to stay the night quietly and move at dawn. Unless you have other ideas?"

Skylar caught a note of challenge in Calida's words. "I bow to your judgment," Skylar said softly, bending in an actual bow for emphasis.

Florian giggled, and Calida rolled her eyes, but her lips were Skylar's friend. They twitched with laughter in a most fetching manner.

❖

Summer breezed on as they continued north and entered grasslands. Calida walked through a sea of slender, tall green stems topped with ripening seed heads. Dense blue stalks wove between them. There were no bushes, no trees, just the endless arid waves.

The grasses stretched well above Calida's head. It was strange and disorientating, wandering in a world with no views save the sky. The stems swayed in the breeze with a sound like the ocean. Skylar was somewhere nearby, hunting birds. Calida searched for sorrel, groundnuts, or edible seeds. She hoped to trap a rabbit or two and carried a net within a rush frame she had woven.

Florian walked with her. He had not ventured far from her side since leaving the farm.

"Do you miss Raoul and Petro?" Calida asked. Florian had been quieter than usual for the last few days.

"Yes." Florian glanced at her. "It was nice. Like we were a big family. Did you like it?"

Calida smiled. "I did. I think the boys are safer there with Mary and Nathaniel. I hope they will be happy. They will be better fed than us, at least."

"I am glad for them." The statement was typical of Florian. He was always generous. "Are we a family with Skylar now?"

Calida was startled. "Well, no. We are traveling together, that's all."

"I wish we were. You like him, don't you?"

"Yes." Calida was always honest with Florian. It was their way.

"I think he likes you."

"Do you?" Excitement welled before she staunched it. "Florian, that is not for you to think about. Likely nothing will happen."

Florian paused. "Mama, I know Skylar is not a man."

"I see."

"Do you think that is why he helped me in Freymar?"

"Perhaps."

"Has he told you about himself?"

Calida shook her head. Skylar had not. And Calida wished she would trust her enough to do so.

"He must be very frightened."

Calida spied a bunch of fat-leafed plants growing low and bent down. They were indeed sorrel.

"Florian, pick a few leaves from each, will you? You know why we pick just a few, don't you?"

Florian had already rushed over to the plants. He looked up. "Yes. We leave plenty for the animals and insects who rely on them."

"Very good." Calida shook her head, smiling at Florian's imitation of her voice. He was growing up, perhaps even more swiftly, on this journey. He could be right about Skylar being too fearful to reveal her gender.

She heard Florian cooing and a telltale rustling in the grass near him.

Calida gathered her net. The rabbit was distracted by Florian's gentle murmurings. She crept up on it and swooped.

The net landed and tightened. Without pause, Calida killed it swiftly and cleanly.

"Mama!" Florian cried in horror.

"Florian, we need to eat." Calida tried to smooth her words into something that sounded kind. Florian was sensitive. He did not truly care for flesh because he loved animals. When food was plentiful, and there were enough nuts or beans, Calida was content for Florian to eat what he wished.

This was not one of those times.

"He was gentle and full of life." Florian's face was upset and angry as he gazed at the rabbit dangling limp from Calida's hand.

"I am sorry." Calida *was* sorry. She would not change Florian for all the riches in the world. She loved him for his tender heart.

"I will not eat it." Florian choked back tears. He looked at her, furious and distressed, and then he turned and ran.

"Florian!" Calida yelled. Running away was dangerous and foolhardy. Anyone or anything could be lurking in these grasses. She rushed after him. There was a trail of trampled stalks, but it was impossible to spot him through the dense maze.

"Florian," she called again. She could be alerting a predator to Florian or herself.

"It's okay, Florian is with me," Skylar's voice came sailing through the rustling of the grasses. She was nearer than Calida had realized.

Florian was safe. Calida allowed herself a moment of relief.

And then she turned back to camp. The rabbit must be skinned and prepped for cooking. Calida sighed. Florian's reaction had reminded her the rabbit had been content and alive moments before. But their bellies were empty, and there were no vegetable alternatives. They would not survive on a few sorrel leaves.

Calida did what she had to do. It was the way of the world. The way she had learned to be.

❖

Twelve years previously, Southern Alba

Mama had been behaving strangely for weeks. People arrived at the kitchen door after nightfall. Calida recognized some of the voices, but others were strangers. Each time someone knocked, Calida; her sister, Freya; and the baby were sent to the bedroom before Mama opened the door.

Freya did not mind. She was tired from giving birth five moons previously. Florian was a lovely baby, plump and content. Freya's milk was rich from Mama's vegetables and the eggs from their chickens. They were luckier than most. Living on the outskirts, the collectors did not always bother to trudge leagues through the woods for a couple of eggs and a cabbage.

The rest of the villagers were not so fortunate. The village lay on the road to the capital and was convenient for plunderers of all kinds, whether they were the King's collectors or his guards. The new king was callous and greedy. His father had been wiser. He had known not to lean too heavily on the backs of the common folk. Everyone had a breaking point.

The day they came for Mama, she was outside, weeding her vegetable bed. Calida heard the horses and rushed to the kitchen door. Mama looked through the trees, then jumped up and ran to the house.

"Get Freya and the baby and hide. You know where." Mama's voice shook. She pushed Calida roughly inside and pulled the door shut fast.

Calida wanted to scream, "Come with us," but there were already hoof clips on the path and cries to "Halt."

Freya cradled Florian. Calida shoved aside the stack of wood by the hearth and pushed Freya and the baby into the hidey-hole. Most homes in the area had one left over from when the old king took the throne, and overnight, people found themselves on the wrong side of justice.

Calida returned the stack, leaving just enough room to squeeze past it. Then she backed into the hide and pulled the door to.

It was dark, hot, and dry inside the tiny space. Freya's body shook as she suckled Florian. She mouthed the words of Mama's song without making a sound. Calida's heart raced as outside Mama started to cry.

A man's cold voice cut through the thin cottage walls to where they crouched, trembling.

"You are charged with the crime of organizing rebellion against the King. And you are charged with the crime of witchcraft."

"Sirs, you are mistaken," Mama cried. "I beg you—" The crack of a stick stopped her words. She yelled in pain.

Freya pushed the baby at Calida, but Calida would not take hold of him. "I will reason with them."

"There is no reasoning," Freya spat. "They will kill her where she stands. I will go. I am the better swordswoman and stronger."

Freya was good with a sword, but what could she accomplish against the King's guards? Calida saw in her sister's eyes she would not be deterred. She began to push at the door. "I'll come as well. We will have a better chance of succeeding."

Freya slipped past Calida and thrust the baby into her arms. "No. You must protect Florian. Promise me. Do not let my baby die."

Calida looked into her sister's eyes and gave her word. Freya shut the door, plunging Calida and Florian into darkness again. The stack of firewood groaned as it was pressed firmly against the door.

Calida crooned the baby, whispering.

The cottage door swung open with a bang.

Mama's voice rang out, "No, Freya. Let them take me."

"Drop your weapon and kneel," the soldier commanded.

"I will never kneel to you, motherless bastards." Freya was never one for diplomacy.

Steel rang on steel. Then, a duller, slicing blow, and a man screamed in pain. Freya must have taken one down. But then a horrible cry rang out, part agony, part anguish, part choking wetness. Calida closed her eyes. She knew the sound came from Freya.

Mama sobbed. Footsteps marched along their front path.

The kitchen door burst open. Boots crunched on the flagstone floor. Wood splintered. Pots crashed to the ground. Calida clasped Florian into her breast and tucked his head under her chin.

She breathed into his soft, milk-sweet head, willing him to stay silent. She waited for the firewood to be slung aside. For the hide to be found. For the little door to open. For a sword to thrust in.

A long time later, the crashing, banging, and tramping of boots faded. Horses rode away, and Mama's steady weeping grew fainter.

Calida crouched stone-still through it all, with the sleeping baby warm against her chest.

It was nighttime when Calida pushed against the door. She was so cramped it took several attempts to push the wood away. She crawled from the hiding place to a house that was deathly quiet.

Calida put Florian in his crib and tiptoed through the cold kitchen to the door. She inched it open, holding her breath.

It was pitch dark outside. The front garden was empty of horses and men. The only shapes were trees and bushes and something…a bundle on the path. Calida lit a lantern and took it outside.

Freya lay on her back, staring up at the moonless sky. Her stomach gaped where she had been run through. Blood pooled under her, returning to the earth. Her eyes were open. Calida bent and pressed her fingers against Freya's chest. It was still. Freya had gone. She was cold and beginning to stiffen.

Mama must have been taken away. Or the brutes would have left her body there beside Freya's.

Calida buried her sister. There should have been the proper rites, but there was no time. Calida mumbled any words she could remember over the heaped earth and scattered purple vervain petals on top.

Then she dried her eyes, packed what she could, and left with Florian as dawn broke. They could not stay. Someone would come and claim the cottage for the King or themselves, and she would be arrested as a conspirator.

The morning of that day was the last she had woken with peace in her heart.

It was also the day Calida vowed she would never hide, never ever wait in the darkness again.

❖

Florian and Skylar had beaten her back to camp.

Florian had built a fire. He or Skylar had somehow found logs and dry twigs. With the grasslands this dry, there was no shortage of kindling. Florian ran his knife over his flint. Smoke rose from a twisted knot of grass. Florian blew on it, and a flame crept across the kindling. Calida was glad to see that Florian had surrounded the firepit with stones. Nothing destroyed land like fire. Except perhaps the King's soldiers.

Several cleaned pale yellow roots waited patiently on one of the stones to be roasted. Knife in hand and sitting cross-legged, Skylar scraped the skin from another.

She looked so kind and handsome sitting there that Calida forgot, for a moment, her concern for Florian.

But then Florian turned, saw the rabbit in Calida's hand, and glowered at it. Calida glowered herself but curbed her irritation. It was not fair. Florian was thirteen. Nearly but not yet grown. He had a right to childish feelings. In truth, if only he could have them for many years still. She would do anything to stay the innocence in his eyes.

"Florian," she said as gently as her fear and exhaustion allowed. The words were not soft but less harsh, at least. "When we are settled, I will cook dried beans and fresh vegetables. We can eat eggs. But out here, with winter coming, you must eat meat to survive, Florian. I will not protect you from the hard truth of life." *No matter how much I wish I could.* "You are my child." And he was. Florian had stopped being her nephew a long time ago. "I am always honest with you. We travel in strange and dangerous lands. Please let me keep you strong and healthy and as safe as I am able until we can find a new home."

Florian shut his eyes and tipped his head up to the setting sun. The orange light painted his brown skin umber and his dark hair chestnut. His shoulders relaxed. Birds twittered somewhere close by, hidden amongst the grasses.

"Mama." Florian's voice was gentle. "He sniffed me. And his nose was so curious."

Calida sighed. It was easier to insist on the right thing when Florian was angry. Her heart rebelled against chiding him when he was soft and sweet.

Skylar put her hand out toward the rabbit. "I will clean it." It was clear she had sympathy for Florian, but she said nothing. Calida was glad. If Skylar had intervened on Florian's behalf, it would have been annoying. And unhelpful. Calida was his parent. She had no idea if Skylar knew anything of child-raising. There was a lot about Skylar she knew nothing of.

Skylar looked away and began to prepare the rabbit for cooking. The way she turned so fast was curious. At times, it was as if she had a sixth sense.

Calida took up the abandoned root, unsheathed one of her sharpest knives, and stripped a piece of peel away. She sniffed it, gratified to inhale the scent of carrots. "Who found these?" she asked casually.

"I did." Florian's voice was full of pride, and rightly so. Wild carrots were not easily harvested by the uninitiated and could be confused with hemlock—a mistake the forager would grimly make only once.

Calida smiled. "You have learned well."

Florian smiled back at her. "I recognized the leaf."

"And how did you know this was carrot, not hemlock?"

"I crushed the leaf, Mama."

"And what if the leaf had smelled sour and musty?"

"I would have found water and washed my hands until the skin reddened."

Calida chuckled. "Just washing them thoroughly would have been fine. But it is good you know the precautions."

Skylar had tied the rabbit meat to a stick and placed it above the fire. Florian glanced at it and quickly away.

"Florian." Calida had no trouble speaking gently now. "What if you eat the carrot root this evening?"

Florian wrapped his arms around her. The abandonment of it, the generosity of his embrace, was like he was four or five again.

She held him tightly. She had to reach up now to kiss the top of his head. He was not that small child now.

When they had eaten, Florian sat with Kit curled at his feet, feeding the vultrix the cooked meat.

"Kit does not worry about these things," he explained.

Kit most certainly did not. He gulped back chunks of meat as if it were the last meat he would see. Calida stroked Kit's soft fur. He gave a whine of pleasure. Calida smiled. To be so petted! Fed by one friend and caressed by another. Kit's life was better than her own.

Skylar sat on the other side of the fire, whittling away at a piece of wood.

Calida watched her for a while. "What are you doing?"

"Making a fox charm. For Florian."

"Now? When wood is so scarce?"

"Exactly now. When times are hard, we need something to hold on to. This will be something in Florian's pocket signifying luck and family."

Skylar passed the figure to Calida. She examined it. It was finely done. Florian would love it.

Calida returned the figure and gazed into the fire, musing about Skylar and her secrets.

Florian had curled up with Kit. They both breathed easily, relaxed in sleep. Calida held back for a moment, loath to break the easy silence. But reticence was not her way. The truth was both her weapon and armor.

"Who are you, Skylar?" she asked. "You are traveling without papers and with no provisions save for your precious block of resin."

Skylar patted the pack lying beside her. "My most important treasure." She grinned. And then grew serious. "My business in the north is somewhat secret."

Calida studied Skylar's face. It was a nice face. She should not trust her heart to such a face. At this moment, the face was earnest and grave. "Secret?" Calida repeated.

"Calida, I'm a woman."

Skylar spoke so urgently, so rapidly, that Calida was startled. She drew back.

"Oh. You are shocked." Skylar shifted on the verge of standing.

Calida touched Skylar's arm. "No. I am not shocked at all. I knew."

In a crouching position, Skylar blinked. She held onto the half-formed wooden fox and her knife and looked confused and uncomfortable.

"Why don't you sit back down?" It would be so easy to reach out and take Skylar's hand. Calida almost did.

But then Skylar flopped down with a thump. Her face twisted in pain. She had likely bruised more than her dignity.

"You are not the first woman living as a man I've encountered," Calida said.

"I am not?" Surprise flickered across Skylar's face, then a touch of fear. "It is dangerous, though."

"Of course." Calida felt Skylar pull away. It was to be expected when the revealing of secrets could mean a death sentence. "Do not worry. You know about Florian. I know about you. We will not put each other in danger. Of that, I am sure."

Skylar nodded. She smiled shyly. They sat awhile in a comfortable silence. Calida could have chosen to disclose the secret of her sexuality, but she did not. Living as a man did not mean that Skylar preferred women for her lovers. And Calida was convinced Skylar still kept something from her. Being forthcoming was not advisable. No matter how much the firelight flattered Skylar's complexion. No matter that Skylar's smile sent the most pleasing shivers all the way to her toes.

Until and unless Skylar was prepared to trust Calida completely, Calida's secret was best kept to herself.

CHAPTER SIX

The few meager provisions they had gathered traveling through the grasslands soon ran out when they crossed into the coastal plains. There were no forests, and the little common land was flat and dry. Hunting and trapping were allowed by permit only. Calida kept them from starvation with surreptitious plant foraging in the early hours of daylight. When Skylar got home, and she was determined that would happen, she would talk to Captain Noro about the importance of including plant lore in basic training. Even with Calida's skills to aid them, they were desperately hungry. The people they met were barely able to eke out a living. The few that would speak to them counseled they should head northeast to the seaside town, Farehaven, and seek work there.

Skylar stopped at the edge of a causeway, eyeing the boggy sandbar with suspicion. Farehaven was an island passable when the tide was out but cut off when it was high. Skylar did not relish the prospect of traveling into a town she could not easily escape from. But their bellies had been empty for days, and they could not journey on without food. "Will this carry our weight, do you think?" She turned back to Calida.

Calida shrugged, looking as doubtful as Skylar felt.

The strip of sand had been reinforced with stones and planks of wood. The water on each side of it was too deep for the horses, even at low tide. Skylar urged her horse forward. He went slowly, testing the ground beneath him. Skylar did not like how the sand oozed into the water at its edges, but after several steps onto it, the causeway held.

Florian jumped down before Calida brought her horse onto the sandy path and skipped ahead to Skylar. Kit refused to accompany them. He turned around, flicked his bushy tail at them, and disappeared. How Kit could do that in such a flat environment was a secret known only to foxes.

Skylar dismounted to walk beside Florian.

"Do you think we might find something to eat here?" Florian asked cautiously.

"I hope so. I think it is worth the detour from our route." Skylar looked out over the waters that lapped at each side of the causeway. "There should be fish here, at least."

Florian followed her gaze. "But what if food is scarce and people are always watching us, like on the plains?"

"Then we will have to notch in our belts again." Calida strode up behind them. She seemed as unafraid on the strip of sifting sand as on the streets, trails, and forest paths they had already traveled.

Florian nodded and walked ahead. Skylar felt his spirits rise, and hers rose with him. It was cooler by the sea. She took in a lungful of salt air. White gulls wheeled overhead. Their cries were bold enough to carry above the turn and crash of waves. One swooped down to the water and soared a moment later with a flash of silver between its beak. They were in the middle of nowhere, with the somewhere of Farehaven waiting for them a few leagues in the distance.

It was a joyous moment. If only they were safe in Gaea and still together. Skylar pushed that regret swiftly aside. It was best to live in the moment.

At the end of the causeway, beaches stretched away on either side. Skylar looked for boats. In Gaea, rowboats and small fishing craft were always hauled onto the sand. She would have felt happier knowing she could borrow a boat should they be trapped here at high tide. But there were none to be seen.

An elder sat at the quayside. He waved to them as they approached and called a welcome.

Skylar smiled at him. "Good day, good sir. Can you help me? I seek work. Are there fishermen in need of paid hands? Or, perchance, farmers who want help with the harvest?"

"The harvest is finished this late in the season, young man. And the fishermen, well, the protectorate is clamping down on itinerant workers. Even if they wanted to engage you…"

Skylar's hopes sank. It looked like a long walk for nothing. Florian's gaze dropped to the sand.

"However, you are in luck. The circus has come to town. There is great excitement. They need strong fellows." He lowered his voice. "I do not think they will ask for papers, should you have mislaid yours." Skylar sensed the elder had known hardship and was a kind person. "I thought you were the last of the circus people. I like to sit here and see who is crossing over. I traveled myself, in my day, all across Alba. I do not have the growing fear of strangers in these parts. Be warned, mistress." He turned his gaze on Calida. "Keep the maiden close and stay together with your husband. Most islanders wish you no harm, but there is growing unrest farther north. It serves the bailiff and the protectorate if the townsfolk are wary of visitors."

"Thank you, Uncle," Calida said.

The elder smiled. "Ah, a southerner. I have a fondness for the south. I might have settled there had I not loved my hometown so much. It is a pleasant custom you have of making kin of everyone."

Calida nodded. "Thank you for your assistance. We are indebted to you. Can you tell us where we can find the circus?"

"Setting up on the common in the center of town. Follow this road, and you will come straight to it, by and by."

From the size of dwellings and farmhouses they passed, it was clear that the islanders had more wealth than the plains folk. They crossed over a hill before they cantered down into Farehaven town. They dismounted and led the horses toward a large, green field where carts were parked and many people were gathered.

Skylar handed her horse to Calida and stepped toward the men unloading the carts.

Calida curled her fingers around Skylar's arm. "I do not think we should dally here."

Skylar followed Calida's gaze to a group of townsfolk. Children watched the activity with excitement, but suspicion and hostility lined the faces of the adults.

"I agree," Skylar said. She found herself relying on Calida's instincts more and more. They made a good team.

Skylar walked to a tall fellow who stood in front of the carts, shouting orders.

"Do you need more hands, sir?" Skylar asked him.

He assessed her before nodding. "Can you haul and lift?"

"Yes, sir."

"The pay is four pennies. You will work until the job is done."

"And the job, sir?"

"There are three large tents to put up, some fetching and carrying. Is there somewhere you need to be?"

Skylar's concern was leaving the island before high tide, but she pushed the worry aside. "No, sir."

"I am glad to hear it. Consider yourself engaged." The fellow stretched forward and clasped Skylar's hand, squeezing hard enough to hurt.

It felt like a test. Skylar ensured her face remained impassive and joined the men carrying poles, tools, and thick swathes of cloth from the carts.

When the cart was unloaded, Skylar partnered with a local teenager named Adam. Their task was to fit the outer poles to the biggest tent. Adam was adept and cheerful. Skylar steadied a thick, circular timber pole while Adam climbed wooden steps to hammer it into the ground.

A man's voice carried above the chatter and thud of hammers. His voice sent shivers along Skylar's spine. She turned her head to look.

In the nearby market square, a man was perched atop a stack of crates. He spoke to anyone gathered in the square like a preacher, but his words were not benevolent.

"The bailiffs in our region have been warned about a nest of deviants up north. We must take care they do not flee from that region to ours. Good folk of Farehaven, I implore you to be wary of strangers."

Skylar felt the gaze of the crowd gathering in front of the speaker.

"Why would they come here, and why should we fear them?" a brave townsperson called out.

"A fair question. I will tell you," the speaker responded. "Maybe it is the poisonous ground in the far north. Maybe it is treachery. Something has infected ordinary men and women and turned them deviant. They hide their sex beneath clothes of the opposite gender and perform acts I cannot speak of with children present. A man is a man, and a woman is a woman, but these defilers of our sacred truths would turn that all about. And they are bent on spreading their unnatural ways to all of Alba."

"Shame on them," cried an older woman at the crowd's edge. Skylar shuddered at the hate and fury in her voice.

Adam stopped hammering. He stared at the crowd, his cheer having evaporated.

"Who is the speaker?" Skylar asked him.

"The bailiff's deputy."

Skylar felt Adam's disquiet mirror her own. Without prying into his thoughts, she realized Adam was a lover of men, and she sighed. It was surely not an easy life in Alba without evil people stirring up hatred. She looked for Calida and Florian and found them sitting by one of the carts. Florian stitched a torn pocket on a bright yellow dress. Skylar guessed that it was a costume of some sort. Calida had a coil of half-braided rope on her lap, but now she was turned toward the square. She caught Skylar's eye and gave her a grim nod.

Adam went back to hammering. Skylar glanced around and found the circus man watching her. His expression was smug and devious. They moved on to the next pole, and Skylar took over hammering. After she drove the stout timber firmly into the ground, the circus man walked away.

Some hours later, when the tents were complete, the men lined up to receive their pay.

Adam shared a little bread and cheese from his pack. Skylar took it gratefully.

"You are not local, and you are not with the circus?" Adam asked quietly.

There was no malice in Adam's question, just curiosity.

Skylar kept her voice low in return. "I came to the island in search of work. I had no idea there was such unrest in the region." She took a bite of the bread and an even smaller bite of cheese.

"You are welcome here for me." Adam tapped her arm lightly. The line had moved forward, and it was his turn. He stepped forward.

Skylar pocketed the rest of the bread and cheese, conserving it for Florian and Calida. The circus man grinned at her as she approached. She tried to read him, but his motives were obscure. When she held out her hand for her pay, he put two pennies into it. Skylar frowned.

"I thought you said—"

"Four pence for *men*." The fellow cut off her words. "If you are not satisfied, there is always the bailiff."

Skylar closed her fingers around the coins before any observer could count them.

She stepped away, simmering with rage. There was nothing to be done with such hostility all around.

As she turned to find Calida and Florian to leave the accursed town, an official cantered briskly to the group of workers.

"Step aside, circus folk. The rest of you men with no gainful employment gather on the main road," he called atop his horse. "There is work for you at the mayor's house."

Tension swept through the fellows around Skylar. She saw a flicker of movement beside the big tent, where a man was trying to slip away. Unfortunately, the official saw him too. He galloped over, raised the short staff in his hand, and savagely beat the man.

There was no further resistance. Skylar followed Adam to the street that flanked the market square. As she passed Calida and Florian, she flicked her eyes to them. Both looked grimly back at her.

Well, there was nothing for it. She would have to complete whatever tasks the mayor required.

Perhaps they could still escape the island before high tide washed over the causeway.

The mood of the group of men as they trudged behind the official's horse did not feel hopeful. But Skylar's resolve was deep. She had earned two pennies. It would feed them going forward.

Now, she just needed to slip away from this team of forced labor at the mayor's house.

❖

The mayor's residence was an elegant, well-appointed house at the top of a hill outside the town. The midday sun had burnt away the morning cloud, and it was a hot, steep climb on foot with no water and no rest stops.

Skylar walked next to Adam near the back of the group. "Will we be paid for this work?" she whispered.

Adam glanced at the mayor's officer ahead. "No. And you must take heed. The mayor is a cruel man, and so is he." Adam tipped his head toward the official's back. "Do whatever he asks without question. And do not tell him you are not from the island. He is newly drafted here and does not know everyone. He will throw you in jail if he knows you are from outside. After he has worked you until you drop, of course."

Adam fell silent, and Skylar asked no more questions. Adam knew she was not a local, and probably many of the other men pressed into service did, too. She hoped they would not betray her to the official.

The group halted on lavish grounds before an elegant two-story, pale stone house. There were many windows, indicating lots of rooms. Skylar had heard of leaders and officials being gifted houses far larger than their needs, but this was the first time she had seen such a residence. Officials in Gaea lived in spacious buildings, but they accommodated all the people who worked for the officials, as well as their families. Private quarters were pleasant and modest.

It was a glorious view from the top of the hill over sweeping fields abundant with row after row of crops. This was a fertile island. Skylar could see all the way to the ocean. At the moment, the tidal causeway was clear, but the waves lapping along its course reminded Skylar that it would not remain that way. To the west was the beginning of the wastelands. A hard day's ride away.

Adam pulled at her arm. The mayor's officer glared at her. She quickly joined the line of workers filing around the grand building to the back of the house.

❖

Skylar stood inside the great hall near the doors with a tray of clay cups and a jug of wine. Guests took a cup as they entered. No one thanked her. Skylar had offered one of the guests a cup when she was first stationed. The mayor's officer had cuffed her on the back of the head. After that, she spoke to no one and met no one's eye.

The island bailiff spoke with his deputy a few steps away. Their presence agitated Skylar. She searched their minds, but all she could glean was that they did not trust her. Then the bailiff muttered, "Circus man."

Hopefully, that meant they thought her to be part of the circus.

"The mayor has sent word to the King asking for more guards," the bailiff said.

"To hunt down the deviant rebels?" the deputy asked, throwing back his third cup of wine. He nodded his head at Skylar to refill his cup.

Skylar went over, careful to keep her eyes low and head bent while not walking into an obstruction. All the servants and forced workers did so.

"They are clearing out the rebel nests. We must ensure they do not creep into our territory."

Skylar returned to her position. The furnishings and decoration were splendid. The guests' clothing was finer than any Skylar had seen in Alba. They laughed and talked and gorged themselves on food, wine, and ale served by the strained, unhappy fellows who had been pressed into service. Should one of the workers drop a morsel of food or not tend the guests fast enough, they were beaten by the official or one of his lackeys. The guests either did not notice or did not care. They blithely laughed, ate, and toasted each other's health as if oblivious to the brutality.

A large, ruddy fellow took the jug from Skylar's tray and walked away. She waited for him to return it. He did not. The mayor's officer glanced over and curled his lip. He expected Skylar to resolve the situation.

She decided to go and get another jug.

Skylar was glad to escape to the kitchen, although it was stiflingly hot. The cook and her helpers sweated over several large pots strung over the fire.

Skylar went into the wine pantry and picked up a jug. She was poised to fill it when she heard a muffled cry and a series of dull thumps. The noises came from outside.

She crept to the back door and cracked it open.

In the shadow of the woodshed, Adam lay on the ground, rolled into a ball. Two of the officer's lackeys were beating him with sticks. Both had their backs to the door. They exerted themselves until they ran with sweat. Skylar longed for her sword or staff, but they had been taken on arrival. Adam's knees were drawn up, and his hands pulled over his head as he tried to protect himself. He cried into his arms as the blows landed.

Skylar pushed the door quietly open. She stepped behind the nearest fellow and smashed the jug over his head. He dropped before he knew who had attacked him.

The second brute advanced, swinging his staff. Skylar turned her shoulder into the blow and reached for the man's wrist. The staff whacked against her shoulder. She ignored the pain and gripped and twisted the fellow's wrist. It cracked. The man paled. Skylar swept up the staff as it fell. The man sank to his knees, cradling his arm.

Skylar pulled Adam to his feet.

"You must go," she told him. "I will make sure they do not follow."

Adam was bloody and trembling. "The mayor will kill you for this," he whispered.

Skylar glanced at the lackeys. One was unconscious, the other shaking. She disarmed them and darted back into the kitchen. As quietly as she could, Skylar dropped the weapons onto the pile that sat next to the wine pantry. She snatched up her staff, sword, and some rope.

Outside, she tied their hands, dragged the unconscious man into the woodshed, and forced the other to follow at the end of her sword. Finally, she locked the woodshed door on them.

Adam watched her, trembling. "They know me. What will I do?"

Skylar could feel Calida and Florian hidden in the village below, waiting for her. They needed to get away before high tide. Time was running out, and now she was in worse danger than before.

But one look at Adam, and she knew he could not get down the hillside without her help.

She put his arm around her good shoulder, gritting her teeth against the dull pain in the other. Together, they hastened from the mayor's house along the darkening path.

❖

Halfway down the hill, they met Calida and Florian. Calida came instantly to support Adam's other side.

Adam sagged between them, murmuring directions to his house. Skylar explained what had happened on the way. Calida's concern multiplied at the tale.

Florian gripped Skylar's jacket in the manner of a much younger child. "I was worried about you," he whispered.

"What about your shoulder? I can see you are in pain," Calida said.

"It will have to wait until we are off the island." It was the least of their worries at that moment.

A slightly older version of Adam opened the door to their abrupt knock.

"This is Skylar. He is a good man," Adam managed before collapsing into his brother's arms.

When Skylar explained Adam's injuries, the brother's face paled beneath his dark coloring. "My family is indebted to you. I heard the mayor's officer had gone to fetch workers from the town. This mayor is a brutal and dangerous man. You must leave the island at once."

"But the causeway is covered," Calida said. "Is there not some place we can hide?"

Adam's brother's face was grim. "There is nowhere. The island is ruthlessly policed. All this trouble up north has whipped the islanders into a frenzy of prejudice. No one will shelter you. We cannot risk it."

"But we are headed north," Florian said.

The brother looked aghast.

"What will Adam do?" Skylar asked quickly.

The brother frowned. "We will spirit him away. You should tend to your troubles. If the officer's men have been found, they will call out the bailiff and his folk. The ferryman is the only way off the island at high tide. Go down to the beach as if heading for the causeway, but instead, keep going for three leagues. The area will become rocky, and you will come to a cove. That is where the ferryman will be found."

As they turned to go, Adam's brother waved Skylar back. "I have heard there is a rebel stronghold at Greendale," he whispered.

Skylar was unsure why he had mentioned the fact, but she thanked him anyway. If there was as much unrest as the islanders feared, they might need to seek out these rebels.

But that problem was some distance hence. First, they had to find the ferryman before the bailiff found them.

❖

Mist rolled in from the sea, and clouds obscured a pale moon. Skylar held fast to Florian's hand as they slipped and scraped their way down a treacherous cliff path.

This must be the cove. As they descended, the crashing of waves grew louder. The tidal wash was high indeed, and the sea was rough. If they tried to swim, it would be the last thing they did.

They had not dared risk returning to the town for the horses. Skylar and Calida had been loath to leave the steeds and saddlebags but had agreed escape must be their priority.

On the beach, shingle crunched underfoot. There was no boat waiting on the water, just rocks. Skylar searched the shoreline desperately.

Then, the clouds rolled away from the moon for an instant, and Skylar spied a shape out of place. There was a boat a short distance to their right, camouflaged into the craggy shore, and a hunched, hooded figure in it.

They hurried across pebbles slick with water and seaweed. Calida's foot twisted, and Florian slid. He would have fallen, but Calida grabbed his arm in time to keep him upright. Florian was fearful and tense, but there was no time to comfort him.

As they neared the boat, the figure reared up. Through the gloom, Skylar made out a weather-worn, whiskered, and unfriendly elder. Her heart sank. His spirit reeked of greed. He was a mercenary type. He would row them if they could afford his price. If not, he would sell them to the bailiff as happily.

"The price is tripled," he called out. "Ten pennies per rider. The wind is as high as the tide. And it will be two trips. Trip one, I'll take the woman and the child. Hand over the coin first."

"I only have two pennies in coin. What else will you take?" Skylar flinched from the bitter wind. By the open water, it struck her face with a vengeance.

"Gold."

Skylar shook her head. The ferryman laughed unpleasantly. "Then there will be no trip across the wash for you." His eyes narrowed as he watched Florian shiver. The child's body shook from the cold, but Florian's eyes betrayed his fear.

Calida studied the boat. "Your boat is large enough. Why can you not take us in one trip?"

The ferryman grunted. "She took a bash to the hull, And there's no way to fix it, not with the bailiff and the mayor commandeering materials the way they do nowadays." He laughed. "Now, if you had some block…"

Skylar's hand was already emerging from her pack. "Resin?"

The ferryman gaped. "How did you…where did you…my God, man. Resin is rarer than gold in these parts." He eyed the block hungrily.

"It is worth twice your price," Calida said.

"Perhaps so. Costs have risen beyond sense with the mayor's greed," the ferryman grumbled.

"You can have the block if you take us in one trip," Calida pressed him.

The ferryman pursed his lips. "Get in then and be quick about it. You, sir, will have to bail as we go. Help me push her into the wash."

Skylar heaved beside the ferryman, striding knee-deep into the foaming waves. At the ferryman's nod, Calida lifted Florian into the boat and jumped in after him.

"Gently, woman. You'll turn her over."

Calida tossed him a look but held her peace.

The seats were damp. Water lapped in the bottom of the boat, soaking their feet. The wind whipped about them and seeped under Skylar's hood. Florian shivered, pressed next to her.

"Bail, man. There's a bucket at your foot." The ferryman turned the oars with great power, forcing them through the strong current.

Skylar felt around and found a wooden pail. She pulled it through the growing pool under them and dumped the icy water overboard. As they neared the middle of the estuary, the wind picked up further. It roared in Skylar's ears, cold and furious. The waves rose, too, slapping against the boat and rocking it. Skylar was impressed with the ferryman's strength and skill. He kept them afloat and somehow pushed them through waves that seemed hell-bent on forcing them back to the island.

She sensed several men riding fast along the cliff top.

The mainland shore glimmered a furlong or so ahead. Skylar could not tell how close the riders were, just that they were traveling at great speed and searching for them.

As the shore neared, the waves relented, and the boat sailed faster. At last, the bow hit sand.

Calida jumped into the water and straight away pulled Florian out. Skylar peered across the estuary. There were riders on the beach of the rocky cove. Skylar knew it was the bailiff and his troop.

The ferryman eyed them with distaste.

"Will you bring them across?" Skylar asked.

She sensed his calculations. How much could he make if he sold them out?

He shook his head. "Help me pull the boat behind those rocks. Quickly. A few moments more, and they will be able to see us."

Florian ran ahead while Calida, Skylar, and the ferryman dragged the boat across the beach.

They were obscured behind the sea stack just as the clouds pulled free from the moon overhead, and the beach lightened.

The ferryman sat back in his boat and draped his cloak around him. "Your wife was right. The resin is worth twice my price. And now we are even."

Everyone had their code of honor. This was the ferryman's.

Keeping to the shelter of the sea stack, Calida, Florian, and Skylar made their way up the beach. Skylar turned to Calida. "I know it is dark, but should we walk awhile, farther inland at least?"

Calida nodded. "I'm sure we are all tired, wet, and hungry, but I agree. We should put some distance between ourselves and the island bailiff. One moment before we leave." She reached down to grasp a thick strand of bulbous, brown seaweed. "That shoulder will no doubt bruise. This will be your best friend in the next few days."

Skylar smiled, moved by how Calida thought of others, even at such a time. "Thank you, Calida."

They left the beach and started on the road that ran north. "I have something to cheer you up. It's not much." Skylar pulled the small packet of bread and cheese from her pack.

Florian brightened instantly. He took his share and began to chew happily.

A short distance later, Kit ran to them from a grove of trees. Before Calida could stop him, Florian shared his cheese with Kit. Skylar was not concerned. Foxes did not eat cheese, surely? But Kit snapped up the chunks and nuzzled his thanks into Florian's hands. Even Calida laughed.

They had lost their horses, bedding, cooking pots, and bow and arrows, but they were safe. And now they were all together again.

❖

To Calida's displeasure, the weather turned noticeably cooler as they entered the far north. She tolerated heat in abundance. It ran in the blood of her southern ancestors. The cold was not her friend.

The going was slow without horses. Days passed, and they covered little distance. Hunting was difficult, too, with no bow or arrows. Calida foraged and thanked her mama for schooling her in plant lore. Without it, they would have been half-starved.

After a long day's hike, as the sun dropped low, they stopped at a meadow with a small spring gurgling over stones. Kit ran straight away to the water and lapped there delicately. Calida had grown fond of the witch fox. He was an efficient predator, strong in limb and mind, yet graceful in his movements. He was loyal as a hound with a cat's independence. He had protected Florian twice. Indeed, Calida liked Kit very much.

Now that they had no horses to attend to, Florian's new job was to replenish water for all. He knelt at Kit's side to wash his face. He had cupped his hands to drink when Kit shook himself vigorously. Florian shrieked. Then he laughed and wrestled Kit until they were both soaked.

Kit pushed Florian away with his head and ran off into the long grass. His eyes twinkled, and his lips were pulled back, very much as if he were laughing.

Calida would not have been surprised to discover Kit had splashed Florian deliberately.

Well, it was no good standing idle. The sun would set soon. Skylar stepped into her path.

"How about Florian and I find supper tonight? Foraging seems always on your shoulders. Florian has seen wild carrots behind the stream."

Calida followed Skylar's pointed finger to Florian digging in the grass.

"If you are sure." Calida turned instead to collecting firewood.

There was a flat spot near the spring, near a large oak tree where someone had made a firepit sometime before. Calida began to build a fire. It would need to be a long-burning one. Their bedrolls and blankets were with their tent and horses back in Farehaven. She missed their barrier against the cold, hard ground.

She put knife to flint, and the kindling caught with a whoosh. Calida sat for a moment, warmed by the flame and the last rays of the sun and comforted by the scent of woodsmoke and the gentle trickle of water. She could close her eyes and be completely at peace here. They had little money and scant supplies, but life was abundant with Florian, Skylar, and Kit.

Hell's teeth, those were dangerous thoughts. Her eyes flew open. Pointless thoughts.

Florian flopped down by the fire. He dropped their three canteens and a small pile of cleaned wild carrots. "We found berries and pears. Skylar will be along soon. Kit has gone hunting." Florian carefully placed the carrots on stones near but not in the flames.

"Well done. Florian, I am very proud of you. You have adapted well to our changed circumstances."

Florian smiled. "I am happy, Mama. Especially when it is quiet and safe, like this."

Calida hugged him tight as Skylar arrived with a kerchief brimming with fruit. The pears were good. They ate them while the carrots roasted. The berries were overripe and past their best. Calida tried one and tasted fermentation on her tongue.

"I am not sure…" *we should eat these*, she began to say. But Skylar and Florian had already scooped up great handfuls. Calida shrugged and joined them, laughing as her fingers turned purple with the juice.

"What do you think about going to Greendale?" Skylar asked. "On the map, it is near Bareglen, the home of your cousin."

Calida frowned. Leaving Skylar at Bareglen was not something she wished to think about. "Is it on the way?"

"The shortest way is to go through Greendale, in fact."

"It makes sense, then." Calida was distracted by movement on the branch above them. It was a squirrel. She reached for a knife. It was paltry, but meat, at least.

Florian stayed her hand. "It is preparing for winter, Mama. Maybe it has a family that relies on it?"

His expression was so sweet, his question so poignant that Calida relented. It was almost dark anyway. She could miss and lose a knife. And there would be barely a few mouthfuls of meat for the cost of killing a creature and upsetting Florian.

Kit returned and curled up with his snout on his bushy tail, staring passively across the darkening meadow.

Skylar winced, shifting on the ground. She patted her breeches pocket and drew out something she examined in the firelight. "I had forgotten about you," she told a lump of resin about the size of an egg.

"Is that the extent of your riches now?" Calida teased her. "What can be done with such a piece?"

Skylar smiled shyly. "Perhaps not a lot. I was cheated when I bought the block, but it saved our lives. It may be silly, but I feel it is lucky."

"You were prepared," Florian said. "Like the squirrel."

"Ah," Skylar murmured. She pulled her short dagger from her belt and began to whittle at the piece.

Calida watched a bushy tail take shape. "I have never met anyone quite like you," she said with tenderness.

"That is a good thing, I hope."

It was. It truly was.

Florian's mood turned giddy. He sang a boisterous and ridiculous song, made up a jig that he performed to a most bemused Kit, and promptly fell asleep.

His mood was contagious. Calida felt light and silly, as if she had drunk too much wine. The night air was sweet with the scent of grass and crushed berries, and Skylar was inconceivably handsome in the firelight. Warmed by the flames, Calida watched Skylar magically create an animal from the resin. She was strong, skilled at combat, kind, gentle. Calida yearned to be honest with Skylar. She wanted a better hand than the one life had dealt her. She was so deeply tired of hiding who she was.

"I love women," she announced.

Skylar looked up from her carving, and cold shock roused Calida from her stupor. By the seven realms of hell, what had possessed her to blurt that out? Calida did not dare look at Skylar. How could she be so witless? There was danger at every turn, and they needed each other. If Skylar were horrified and left, it would be a disaster.

The flames crackled on. Crickets continued to chirp. Skylar did not leap to her feet and walk away into the night.

"You love women," Skylar repeated.

Well, it would be pointless to deny it now. "Yes. All of my lovers have been women."

"All of your lovers?" Skylar seemed only capable of repeating Calida's words. Calida studied her. Skylar's eyes were big and wide and somewhat dazed. Why would that be?

Then Calida remembered the fermented berries. Good heavens, they were intoxicated.

Maybe Skylar had not understood. If so, it was undoubtedly for the best.

Calida sighed and leaned back, strangely disappointed. Her secret felt heavier, more taxing.

"That is wonderful." Skylar gushed.

Calida blinked. "I beg your pardon?"

Skylar took both of Calida's hands. "That is wonderful, Calida." Skylar's palms were rough and calloused. Of course, they were. She worked so hard. Yet the skin on the back of her hands was surprisingly soft.

Before sense could deter Calida, she bent forward and kissed her.

Skylar kissed Calida back. She tasted of berries and salt and summer days. Days that led to hot summer nights.

"I like women, too. I like you," she murmured.

"That's good. That's very good." Calida gave in to all the parts of her that saw no sense and heeded no reason. They kissed for a long time.

They might have gotten entirely carried away had Kit not yawned the most delightful yawn, full of contentment. They broke apart and laughed.

Florian was asleep right there. It would not have been right to go further. But, by all that was holy in the heavens, it was devilishly hard to stop.

Chapter Seven

Skylar walked the road to Greendale with a light step. The length of the journey ahead no longer mattered. If anything, Skylar wished the leagues to mount before them so she could stay at Calida's side. She had kissed her. Calida had kissed her. And it had been everything a kiss should be. Granted, Skylar had been fuzzy-headed from fermented berries. That elation was nothing to the joy of Calida.

The air was pleasantly cooler as they traveled steadily north. Clouds drifted across the sky. The trail led through farmland. Kit trotted at Florian's heels. They had quite the bond now. Kit would miss Florian, she realized with a jolt. They would all miss each other.

Dread at their parting served no purpose. She pushed it away.

They had been walking for more than a day without passing a soul. Even the farms were quiet.

"I am very hungry, Mama. Do you think they would miss a cob or two?" Florian gazed wistfully at a field of tall golden corn.

Calida and Skylar looked at each other. Skylar shrugged. In Gaea, food would be gladly given.

"If you see cobs that would spoil, especially something nibbled by mice, something the farmer may not want. I don't suppose that would matter." Calida grabbed Florian's sleeve as he ran past. "But be very careful. Do not be seen."

"Is it safe?" Skylar asked as Florian disappeared amongst the corn rows.

"No. Neither is starvation." Calida sighed and then reached across to link fingers with Skylar.

Her touch ignited a trail of desire. It was best to keep distracted. "Do you think it is strange we have passed no one so close to Greendale?" Skylar asked.

"Well, I do not know this area. We are, what, about three leagues away now?" Calida looked thoughtful. "Indeed. Yes, it does seem odd."

They continued on the road, and soon Florian joined them. He peeked open his pack to show three plump and partially nibbled cobs.

Skylar smiled at Florian's easy happiness. But as they walked on, despite the pleasure of Calida's fingers laced through hers, she could not shake off a feeling that snaked uneasily through her gut.

❖

Two leagues outside Greendale, she understood why.

Scaffolds rose from the verge ahead. Three of them, each bearing a poor soul on its crossbeam. Skylar pulled Florian to her, tearing his eyes from the terrible spectacle.

"Do you think they are rebels?" Calida's voice was hushed. They had all halted in shock.

Skylar started walking, holding fast to Florian's hand. She felt him twist to look back. "Let us keep going. There is nothing we can do for them now."

Calida took Florian's other hand. They walked close together, even Kit. There was a strange solemnity about the place. No birds sang, and even the tree branches moved silently in the wind.

As they traveled on, Skylar tried to shake the faces from her mind. They were people murdered by their government for what? For being different? She had heard no mention of the rebels wanting to overthrow their king. But perhaps that was their intention.

The scaffolds were far behind them when they passed a signpost that said Greendale was a league hence.

Then, Skylar noticed a dust cloud in the distance, and she felt faint vibrations on the road beneath their feet.

Calida stopped dead. She squinted against the sun. "Guards ahead!" she cried. "Quick, quick. We should not be found on the road. We must find somewhere to hide."

❖

Calida saw no friendly trees or rocks to hide behind. Only a ramshackle barn a short distance from an equally run-down farmhouse.

"Over there," she said. She was loath to risk running into a local farmer, but surely, a farmer would be more sympathetic than the King's guards.

They ran around the side of the barn. The roof was barely in place, and the walls were crumbling. Florian started to go inside.

"No, no," Calida called. "We need to be out of sight, but we do not want to be trapped in a building."

"Are they soldiers, Mama, the King's men?" Florian was trembling.

Calida hated seeing his terror. She nodded. "Keep going, Florian, where they cannot see us from the road."

Florian crept behind the barn, Kit at his heels. Calida followed the little fox, looking cautiously for any sign of the farmer or his kin. She had not had much to do with northerners. They had the reputation of keeping to themselves.

Skylar passed Calida, moving to the far side of Florian to sandwich Florian and Kit between them. It was strange being able to rely on another adult. Calida passed two knives to Florian. He gripped them hard and nodded bravely. Calida drew another two from inside her coat. Skylar had unsheathed her sword and staff.

The thud of boots on the packed dirt road drew closer. Waiting had never been Calida's great skill. Skylar appeared calm. She had the training of a warrior, so she said. And she certainly had the combat skills. But she did not have the disposition of any guard Calida had met. It was a puzzle. The marching feet were louder now.

Calida checked quickly on Florian. He was no longer trembling. His breath was slow and even. Pride surged through her. He was growing before his time. How strong his mind was.

The boots were almost upon the road in front of the farm. They were many and rhythmic as the soldiers marched in time. The clatter of swords and shields mixed with the crunch of their footsteps. The smell of their sweat assailed her nostrils. The flicker of fear she felt was for what might befall Florian. She was not concerned for herself. She would die to protect him.

The marching feet did not falter. The sound grew excruciatingly loud until the dilapidated barn seemed to shake.

When the noise began to fade, Calida let out a breath. Skylar shrunk inward, away from the far edge. Calida took a step back and saw a bend in the road where the dusty backs of uniforms could be seen. She stepped in again.

At last, the marching of the guards quietened. Calida hugged Florian with relief. She bent down to stroke Kit, saving the pleasure of embracing Skylar until last. She rose, but before she could turn to Skylar, a noise at her elbow pulled her sharply around.

A tall fellow stood at the corner of the barn in dirty farm clothes. His expression was hostile. He raised the scythe in his hand.

❖

Skylar ran forward. "Good fellow." She hastily tucked away her sword and staff and raised both palms peacefully. "Forgive us for trespassing upon your land."

The farmer looked Skylar up and down, a cold and nasty glean to his eye.

"We seek food. There is little upon the road." Skylar flooded the man with as much good feeling as she could muster.

"Nor in my fields, thanks to the rebels and the King's guards." The farmer spat the words out. He seemed equally disgusted with both parties. "What is your business in these parts?"

He was suspicious.

"We visit kinfolk." Calida had secreted her knives and affected a placating smile. It was far more alarming than her regular expression.

"We are a small hamlet. Everyone is known here. What is the name of your kin?"

Calida's smile faded. "They live some distance hence."

"Toward Greendale?" the farmer persisted.

Silence stretched until Calida reluctantly nodded.

The farmer noticed Kit and grimaced. "What in God's name is that?"

"He is my dog," Florian said sweetly.

"You think that animal is a dog?" The farmer's hand tightened on the scythe.

"He *is* our dog. Admittedly, he has the look of a fox." Skylar bent down to Kit. She stroked him while projecting the appearance of a red dog around him.

The farmer continued to frown but looked away. Skylar rose. "Do you have any food we can buy?" It was the best course of action. Pay the fellow something, and hopefully, they could be safely on their way.

"Come with me." The farmer led them toward the farmhouse. Inside a falling-down store in the yard was a pile of dry, husky corn cobs. He picked four from the top of the pile. The corn was shriveled. Parts were more nibbled than those Florian had found. "One penny."

Calida tutted, but she dug into her pocket and paid the man.

"We will take our leave now. Thank you, sir." Skylar nodded at the farmer and turned.

He watched them as they returned to the road, and then he disappeared into his house.

"I know why you did it, but I resent paying that swindler, that extortionist," Calida grumbled.

"Indeed." Skylar did not trust the man. She kept an eye on the farm as they walked on.

"It was a clever move to buy food. I would not be surprised if there is a reward for informing on rebels." Calida glared at the cobs. "Did you see the condition of this corn?"

"I will eat one, Mama. I'm still hungry," Florian piped up hopefully.

Calida passed him one. He bit into it with relish.

The farm was behind them now, and there was a signpost at a fork in the road. Greendale was in one direction. The other simply said, North.

Skylar could still make out the farm. A young girl ran out from the farmhouse. Skylar nudged Calida.

They watched as the girl sped past the barn to the road and kept going in the opposite direction.

"She's running after those soldiers," Calida said. "Damn! I did not want to mention Greendale. The farmer forced it out of me."

"And now we know why. We will take the north road then." Skylar started to walk. "Perhaps we can double back or travel across country to your cousin's place later."

"Agreed. We better move fast," Calida said, stuffing the cobs into her pack.

And they did, all running at full pelt along the north road.

❖

It was some time before they found a path that wound east toward the hamlet of Bareglen. Calida had never visited her cousin there, but Anton had told her the way long ago. She hoped her memory served her well.

After consulting Skylar's map, they took a bridle path stretching across open fields and meadowland. The land should still be plump with wild and farmed crops ready for harvest, like the fields they had passed south of Greendale. But the crops had either been taken too early or trampled beneath boots. Calida's mind protested the outrage, but her belly protested it more.

More than injustice plagued Calida. Before long, they must say good-bye to Skylar.

Skylar had been clear her destination was Alba's northernmost territory.

Florian would miss her terribly. And Calida, well, in truth, her heart ached at the thought of their parting.

It was ridiculous. When had she become sentimental and romantic? As if Calida could ever have a relationship. Not in the whole of Alba, and most certainly not in the north where apparently they were blighted with prejudice against those whose only crime was love.

They had shared a kiss, that was all. And Skylar, who in so many ways promised openness and equality, had not been entirely honest. What was it, in the far north, that claimed Skylar's attention? Above Calida. Above Florian. She could not feel the way Calida did. It was the only explanation.

In which case, their parting was for the best. She could not entrust her heart to one who kept secrets. Not when Florian's and Calida's had been revealed and lay open.

She was both glad and further confused when Skylar insisted on accompanying them to Bareglen. The practical thing would have been for Skylar to remain on the north road.

Florian was not plagued with such ill thoughts. He talked excitedly with Skylar about all manner of things. What if Calida followed suit? What if she turned to Skylar, kissed her, took her hand, and demanded answers?

But this was not a daydream. Calida yearned to speak to her, and she was sure there was an answering pull from Skylar. But they dutifully or stupidly repressed their feelings, walking closer and closer to their parting.

It was not just leaving Skylar that haunted Calida. What if Anton was not there? What if he turned them away?

After Freya died, the only place Calida had thought to go was to her aunt and uncle, ten leagues west of Freymar. They had taken them in and were settled as a family until Florian was three and announced he did not want to wear masculine clothes. Calida argued with her uncle over Florian's choices. Anton had supported Florian, but even with him on their side, it became impossible to stay.

Calida took Florian to a humble rented room in Freymar, where they eked out a living. Before long, they moved to the shanty settlement.

They did not see Anton again for many seasons. It was a chance meeting in the central market when Anton, now a young man himself, called out to Calida. She invited him back for a meal. He was gracious, funny, and kind. If he was horrified at how they lived, he did not show it. That was when he told them he had moved north, gave his address, and issued an invitation to visit at any time.

On top of a low hill, Calida saw a cluster of buildings below. "There, that must be Bareglen," she cried.

Skylar joined her, cupping her hand to her forehead to shield her eyes from the sun. She frowned. "Is that smoke?"

Calida saw then that the shape she had taken for gray cloud was too low, too dense, too dark. It changed and spiraled in a way clouds never did.

They started down the hill. Her anxiety mounted as they neared the hamlet. The air reeked of smoke. Calida looked for the river Anton had spoken of as the waypoint. She found it running along the west side of the settlement. It had dried to a brook. Listening intently for any signs of unrest, they stopped to drink and fill their canteens.

Nothing stirred except the water.

Calida led them west along a dirt path following Anton's directions. She stopped when she saw the papery bark of silver birch trees, remembering his homestead was beside a birch grove.

The smoke was thickest here. Calida could not force her feet forward. A great charcoal plume rose into the sky. Little remained of what had been a small house but gutted panels of walls, black and crumbling. Charred and sticky clumps were scattered across the ground where things had dropped or burnt where they lay. The lumps glowed white and amber. The fire could not have been burning very long. There was tilled earth behind the house where crops had been planted. The fire had spread, or the crops had been deliberately set aflame. The ground there was scorched and smoldered still.

"I see no trace of people," Skylar said gravely.

Calida turned to Skylar, struck silent with horror. Skylar put her arms around her. Calida let herself be held as her mind turned over.

What had happened to Anton? And what would they do now? This smoking ruin was to have been their refuge. The might of their plight threatened to overwhelm her. The long journey had been perilous, and Calida was so very tired. She leaned against Skylar. It was too much. Would there ever be a place in the whole of Alba for herself and Florian?

Kit walked gingerly across the darkened soil, sniffing. He looked at Calida with a sorrowful expression. He came and nuzzled against her legs. She bent to stroke him. He rested his face against her hand.

"Mama." Florian tugged sharply on her arm.

He was right. This was no time for despair. She straightened and surveyed the burning canvas. "There is nothing here for us. We must go."

"But, what was planted there, Mama, do you think?"

Calida looked at the blackened patch of land. It was a good observation. "Let us see."

They dug carefully using rock slabs and an old tin plate Florian discovered in the debris. Calida unearthed potatoes. The earth was warm to her fingers as she pulled them out.

Florian bent at the furthest edge. "Look, Mama." He waved a carrot like a flag.

"My clever child," Calida said softly.

They filled their backpacks with vegetables. It was the first uplifting thing that had happened in many days.

"We have food now, at least." Skylar wandered over. "And the carrots we can eat…" Her head turned to the right.

Calida followed Skylar's gaze. Something moved in the grove of trees. Calida stared until she made out a figure behind one of the tree trunks.

A man shuffled forward, old and bent-backed. He came toward them with a wary expression.

"Who are you? I do not know you. You should not be here," he cried when he was but a few steps away. "This is not a safe place."

Calida drew herself up. "Where is Anton? I am his cousin."

"Oh." He stopped mid-step, a look of deep sadness upon his face. "Anton spoke of you." He cast an eye over Florian. "And your child. I am sorry to say I do not know where he is. The King's guards came. This is the result."

Calida wanted to scream with rage and anguish. Why was it the same everywhere, up and down the land? Yes, there were rebels in the north, but this very thing happened years ago in the south when Mama was taken and Freya killed. It happened all the time for little excuse.

"They will not bother me," the old man continued. "I have lived here all my life. There are many who can vouch for me." He looked down at the vegetable patch. "I come to take up the harvest. It will serve no one to let it rot in the ground. And we are all so hungry."

Calida nodded. It made sense.

"Soldiers arrive without warning. They keep some of whom they take alive." The old man cast a look at Florian and lowered his voice. "And *question* them to discover who else is involved. Strangers are arrested on sight. Many poor travelers just passing through are sitting in gaols. For your sake and the child's, do not tarry here. Do not head toward Greendale, either. My nephew said it is worse there."

Skylar turned to Anton's neighbor. "Thank you, good fellow. May fortune keep you well."

"And you, sir." The old man took up the spade he carried with him.

"Why? Why did they do this?" Calida swept her hand across the smoking devastation.

The old man took a ragged breath. "They burn out the homesteads of rebels. Maybe Anton was. Maybe he was not. I do not think the guards care much either way." He turned to dig.

Risk punctuated each instant they dallied. The guards could sweep back at any moment.

When Skylar walked forward, Calida followed.

❖

They returned the way they had come. Calida walked as if asleep with Florian close beside her.

Calida's thoughts were of Anton. Was he alive? She had no way of knowing or discovering. Anton was a good man, sensitive and kind. A man not obsessed with masculinity. Did he join the rebels because of that disposition? God! Why could people not just be allowed to be?

Calida had been looking forward to seeing him. She'd wanted to ask about her aunt and uncle. She had no idea what had become of them after their cold parting. She had hoped that Anton knew stories of her uncle's childhood, stories about Mama.

Those possibilities had vanished in an instant.

"Calida." Skylar stood on the north road. They had arrived back to where they had started.

It was the moment of parting.

Calida halted. She wanted to keep traveling with Skylar, but Skylar was heading to the tip of the land. It was wild country, close to the poisoned wastelands, and it was madness to think about taking Florian there.

They would have to turn south. And she knew there was no safe place in that direction, not for days and days.

Well, they had faced tough choices before, and here they were still, alive and together.

But Skylar. She must say good-bye to Skylar. Skylar, who gazed at her so sadly.

Calida walked right up to her and kissed her.

"Oh, Mama!" Florian muttered. Calida ignored his embarrassment. He could turn away.

She kissed Skylar like it was the first and only kiss of her life. As if it would be the only one. Skylar kissed back as fiercely. For a perfect moment, it was just the two of them in a future devoid of choices.

And then Skylar stepped back. "Calida." She took Calida's hands in hers.

Calida went to shrug her away. She wanted to stay the moment. But the urgency on Skylar's face stopped her.

"Calida, what if I know somewhere you can go with Florian and be safe?"

Calida's pulse quickened. She searched Skylar's eyes for a reason to believe her. Safety, truly? And a chance to remain with Skylar? Her heart lifted foolishly.

"Where is this place?" she asked.

"In the far north."

"The far north is barren and wild. Little grows so close to the wastelands. Close to poison, Skylar. You wish me to take my child to a noxious place?"

Skylar squeezed her hands gently. "I cannot explain everything now. You must make your choice, Calida." Skylar's face was bare and hopeful.

Against all sense, Calida trusted somehow that Skylar's impossible words were true. Her mind screamed that she should turn around and walk away. But her reckless, wanton heart kept her standing there facing north.

Florian coughed to clear his throat. "Skylar, do you lie?"

Skylar shook her head.

"Is it safe to go with you?" Florian asked in the way of a child, trusting the answer given would not betray them.

"I suspect there will be similar dangers to those we have already faced. It seems there is unrest throughout the region," Skylar said. "But I do not lie when I tell you, there is a place not far from here where you both can be free."

Florian turned to her, his eyes bright. "Mama, we should go then. During all of our travels, we have not found any such place. Freymar was not safe, nor any place between there and here."

Calida was afraid to put her faith in Skylar's word alone. She was not in the habit of heeding her heart's desires. Her first duty was to protect Florian. She had half a plan to return to Mary and Nathaniel. "What about the farm?"

"The farm in the area governed by the corrupt bailiff?" Skylar raised her eyebrows in a ridiculously fetching way. And then waited with such vulnerability on her face.

Calida wanted more than anything to believe her. She grappled to make sense of this new information. How did Skylar know of this place? Unless she was a rebel.

It would explain much.

"We cannot stand here all day. I want to go with Skylar, Mama." Florian shifted from foot to foot impatiently.

When had he grown up so?

Kit rubbed against her legs.

It was against Calida's better judgment. It could prove to be the most foolhardy choice she would ever make.

"All right then, Skylar. But if you break my trust…"

Skylar grinned. "I would not dare. I would rather face fifty warriors than the one of you."

"Indeed." Calida smiled wryly, and they started forward.

Florian skipped along. Skylar brought out a carrot and began scraping it with her knife. Kit walked next to her, and she could have sworn he grinned up at her. There was a lightness of spirit among them all.

But Calida was not so foolish she relaxed her guard entirely. They faced peril still, and the place of safety Skylar had spoken of, well, she prayed it existed. But until she stood before it, all she had was a promise.

❖

They trekked on in silence. Skylar was glad, for her thoughts raced. She had acted impulsively. Recklessly.

The day was ending. A lot had happened since sunrise, and they had covered many leagues. They needed rest and sustenance. Skylar began to search for a place to bed down for the night. They would have soup. It was something to look forward to after so many hungry days.

Dry, barren meadowland lay on either side of the trail. She saw a pile of sacking ahead and wondered if there was something usable within it. If the sacking were dry, it could be a soft layer on the ground or a blanket for Florian. Skylar sped up.

She was a few steps from the road when the sack moved. She stopped. Kit trotted up with his ears raised and shoulders flattened. He sniffed at the pile, wary, too. A brown wool sleeve poked out from under old, tattered sackcloth. Skylar reached out with her mind and sensed a slow heartbeat.

Sword in one hand, Skylar carefully pulled back an edge of the cloth, and the breath caught in her throat. A waif of a child was curled up, asleep. No, not sleeping, unconscious and weak. Skylar lifted more of the sacking away and saw blood stains on the child's tunic and trousers. She swallowed. Kit looked at her and whined.

Kit was right to be concerned. This small child was near death.

"Skylar, scout the area, will you?" Calida had approached behind. "We need to be sure there are no soldiers in the vicinity. Or farms. I will tend to this child."

Skylar reached out and sensed no one. But then, she had not felt the life force of this small being. She set off across the field in the fading light with Kit at her side.

❖

Skylar found nothing except a small pond. The sky was overcast, and the twilight was fading. Soon, the birds stopped chattering, and it was so quiet that even Skylar's careful footsteps sounded loud. She had walked a wide perimeter around where they had discovered the child. She was satisfied they were alone. Kit yipped a short cry and disappeared to hunt.

Calida and Florian had made a rough camp. "He has not awoken," Calida said at her approach.

"We guess he is he by his clothing," Florian said from the campfire. A small pot sat atop a stone set into the flames. Whatever was inside smelled good.

"Where did you find that pot?" Skylar asked.

Florian stirred the contents with a stick. "My cousin's house. It's a bit sooty. I have made potato soup. Mama's spices are in there."

"That's why it smells so good!" Skylar grinned. "And because of your cooking skills, of course, Florian."

Florian smiled proudly back.

"I have dressed the child's wounds," Calida said.

Skylar knelt at her side. "Are they grave?"

"Yes. Skylar, they are stab wounds." Calida looked distressed. "I got him to take a sip of water, but he is febrile and weak."

Skylar sighed. "What happened to him, I wonder?"

Calida shrugged. "I cannot leave him, Skylar. He is all alone."

Skylar nodded. "I agree. I am as certain as I can be that we are safe for now. We should take turns keeping watch tonight, though—you and I. Florian should sleep."

Calida nodded. "That is a sound plan. I will take the first watch." She glanced down at the sleeping child. "Let us enjoy a good, proper meal at last." She smiled at Florian and took a cup of soup.

They sat comfortably by the fire, enjoying its warmth and the excellent soup. Whatever was in Calida's spice mix transformed even the simplest ingredients.

Afterward, Florian settled down to sleep, and Skylar cleaned their dishes with a rag. Calida bent over the injured child, holding a cup to his lips.

"This would bring his fever down if I could only get him to take it."

Skylar felt Calida's concern. "You are worried?"

Calida glanced at Florian and lowered her voice. "This child is very ill. He may not last the night, but it is not just that. I do not trust this area. Where there is unrest, people behave lawlessly. I fear I will not sleep well."

Skylar lay down and gathered her cloak around her. "I understand, Calida. It has been an awful day. All the same, you should try. Florian needs you fit and rested tomorrow."

We all do. Assured Calida would protect them while they slept, Skylar closed her eyes.

❖

The wind picked up, rousing Skylar from a state somewhere between reflection and the edge of sleep. It was her watch. She sat beside a fire that had reduced to glowing embers.

Something had changed. She peered through the darkness and listened. There was the sound of the others' breath in sleep, the wind rustling the dry grass, and nothing else. Still, the atmosphere had been disturbed.

Calida was asleep with Florian cuddled into her. Skylar went to the wounded child. His forehead felt cooler. Skylar picked up the cup that Calida had left on the ground and lifted it to the child's mouth, cradling his head in her other hand. He murmured and took a long drink.

Heartened by the child's progress, Skylar sent her mind out to their surroundings. A ways off, something moved.

There was also the light padding of familiar paws running through the grasses in their field. The sky was heavily overcast, making it impossible to see much of anything. At least a quarter of the night remained before dawn.

Kit bounded into their clearing. His eyes glowed amber in the dim firelight. He was anxious. He had broken off his hunt to connect with her.

"Do you feel it, too, Kit?" Their minds linked. Her reach surged and extended beyond hers alone.

There were humans in the vicinity. They were on the road some distance away, approaching.

Skylar heaped earth onto the embers. Neither firelight nor smoke must betray their presence. She shook Calida's arm. Calida leaped up, knife in hand.

Skylar jumped away from the blade, suppressing a chuckle at Calida's speed. "I think I heard something nearby. Stay here with the children. Kit and I will investigate."

Calida nodded.

Kit slinked across the field several steps in front. Skylar did not attempt to overtake him. He was an accomplished hunter.

There were low shrubs at the roadside. Skylar positioned herself in their shadow. Kit crouched next to her, one front paw raised, back paws poised to spring. His ears were pressed back as he waited.

Skylar sensed the travelers coming from the left, moving south. A moment later, a steady clop of hooves and rumble of cartwheels confirmed her intuition.

She eased out a breath, hoping they were a cartload of ordinary folk. But a wave of misery blew in with their approach.

The front of the cart appeared with lanterns strung from poles on either side of the driver's seat. Skylar pressed herself farther into the bush. The lights swung with the movement of the cart, casting an eerie, flickering glow before them.

A bearded, stern-faced guard drove the cart. Three more rode behind. Skylar carefully shifted a branch so she could see.

Three people sat on the wagon floor, their hands tied behind their backs and their cloak hoods pulled over their faces. She could not tell their age or anything about them, but she felt their wretchedness. It hung heavy in the air, mixed with a strong smell of smoke.

The smell worried and perplexed Skylar. How could the smoke from their small fire create such a pungent scent? If the guards noticed and went in search of the fire, it would be their undoing.

It was so strong. Too strong, she realized with relief. The smell had arrived with the group. Skylar wanted to help the prisoners, but she had to think of Florian and the other child. She was one warrior. They were four.

And if she succeeded, it would be four more deaths on her conscience, for she would have to kill them. She bore the weight of the one man she had killed. She saw his face, sometimes on the edge of sleep, and her stomach roiled with guilt.

While she deliberated, the cart lumbered on and disappeared into the night.

With a heavy heart, Skylar turned back toward camp, Kit at her heels.

❖

At dawn, the child opened his eyes and cried out. "Who are you? Let me go."

Calida was at his side immediately. "Shh, young fellow. Do not be alarmed. We will not hurt you." She tried to test his forehead, but he flinched from her touch.

"Indeed. Calida has tended to your wounds and brought down your fever." Skylar looked over from the fireside.

"Why would you help me? Oh!" The child noticed Kit curled up by the fire with his tongue indelicately poking out. "Is that a dog or a fox?"

"He is a fox." Skylar rubbed Kit behind the ears. Kit groaned and purred. He opened one eye to look at the boy, decided he was no threat, and closed it again.

Florian bounded across the field, carrying their recharged canteens. Skylar delighted in Florian's exuberance, even in their present circumstances. He stopped, mouth agape when he saw the young boy sitting up.

"Oh good," Florian cried. "Are you thirsty? Here, this is fresh." Florian held a canteen out.

The boy eyed Florian carefully. But then he reached out, took the canteen, and drank from it heartily. "Thank you. You are a kind girl."

"I am Florian. Who are you, and do you want some soup? It's potato."

The boy's eyes widened. He looked toward the fire and sniffed. "I am hungry," he said quietly.

Florian dipped out a cup of soup and passed it to him with a spoon. The boy tested the temperature of the contents and then began to heap spoonfuls into his mouth as if he had not eaten for weeks. Perhaps he had not.

Some moments later, he noticed they were all watching him. He swallowed. "My name is Deakin." He began to eat again, more slowly this time.

Skylar dished out soup for Florian and Calida. Deakin was eating from her cup, so she waited patiently, stroking Kit absent-mindedly as she considered their situation. This soup was the last of their potatoes. They must continue north. They had risked discovery already. It would not do to test their luck further. "Deakin, is there someplace we can take you? Reunite you with kin, perhaps?"

Deakin looked down into his soup. "I have no family," he mumbled.

"We are traveling, too. We are running away," Florian blurted out.

Deakin sat up straight. "From who?"

"The guards."

"Florian," Calida said.

"Do not worry, mistress," Deakin said. "I will not turn you in. I am a rebel."

"A rebel, are you? You can be all of seven? Eight?" Skylar said incredulously.

"I am a rebel," Deakin insisted. "I am going to join them in the far north."

"How do you know the way?" Skylar asked.

Deakin looked sad again. "My parents told me when the soldiers came. I tried to get away through the back fields, but one of them caught me. He cut me. I fell and pretended to be dead. He was too busy setting fire to our farm to check on me."

Calida broke a twig between her fingers. "Damned cowards." She threw both ends onto the fire.

Florian put his hand on Deakin's. Deakin smiled. "I can take you if you like. Because you have been kind to me."

"The far north?" Skylar asked.

Deakin nodded.

Skylar caught Calida's eye. "We are traveling that way. I would see you safely with people who will care for you. What say you, Calida?"

Calida stood and dusted herself off. "I agree. There is safety in numbers, especially for this young one."

"Is he well enough for travel?" Skylar asked.

"I think so. Deakin, you must say if you feel weak on the road."

Deakin nodded solemnly up at Calida.

As they gathered their few possessions together and earthed the fire, Skylar took another look at the map. It looked like they were a day, two at most, from the wastelands. And from there, it should be a day on foot to the border. She sighed. She was more impatient than ever to cross the magical line. But she chided her impatience. She could no more desert a child in need than Calida could. They were well-matched in that regard.

May it please the Goddess to prevent further delays.

❖

Deakin would not reveal the directions to the rebel hideout, but as long as they were traveling north, Skylar had no argument with him.

Calida stole a look at Skylar from time to time but said nothing. They trudged on, their fatigue and hunger growing. Skylar swung between her impatience to be done with Alba and her concern at returning to Gaea with Calida and Florian.

She could not stay. Alba was not suitable land for a butch lesbian, and if it were ever known that she was Gaean, she would be triply executed, should such a thing be possible. Impressive to be such a threat to humanity.

And yet, she could not cross the border and leave Calida at the mercy of these lesbian-hating zealots.

Neither could she leave Florian. He was a beautiful and gentle child. He would thrive in Gaea, where his gender would be welcomed and applauded.

What a naive and daring heart she found beating within her chest. This new heart imagined possibilities that were forbidden. It knew the right thing, the only thing to do, was to take Calida and Florian across the border.

She had already broken the law to help Kit. To return with Alban citizens was a hundred times more serious.

If only she could contact Gaean officials to harness their consent.

But it was not possible. Skylar was a warrior, trained to decide the right course of action in the moment. That was what she had done. Therefore, the decision had been made. All she could do now, for safety's sake, was not to reveal Gaea's existence until the very last moment.

They had been climbing uphill for a time with the sun high in the sky above them. Skylar wiped the sweat from her brow. Deakin stopped suddenly. He looked to the left, scrutinizing the terrain. Then, he set off on a small track with renewed vitality, limping on the side of his sword wound. It was astounding how fast children mended. But then, Skylar had carried him for a good part of their journey.

"Where are you going, Deakin?" Florian ran after him.

Calida looked at Skylar. "Is that the right way?"

Skylar frowned. "I do not know." Why did Calida think she would?

Deakin disappeared around the side of the hill.

"Wait, Florian," Calida called. But Florian vanished as well.

When they cornered the bend, a rocky hillside awaited them. At first glance, there was nothing but dirt, boulders, clumps of dry grass, and a lonesome, scraggly tree. Then Skylar saw a cavity. She took a few steps forward and realized a tunnel led deeper into the hill.

The children were nowhere to be seen. Skylar rushed after them inside the cavity.

She had taken but a few steps when she was grabbed from behind. Before she could draw a weapon, she faced a group of six or more brandishing swords and bows.

One of them stepped forward. Skylar heard Calida grunt sharply behind her, but she could not turn because the rebel had a knife at her throat.

Chapter Eight

The rebels were an angry, suspicious band. After their dramatic appearance, Calida waited for them to recognize Skylar and for the location of the wondrous, safe place to be revealed. But the rebels remained closed-faced and tight-lipped.

Calida and Skylar were forced forward, swords at their backs, into a large cavern. Florian ran to her and was allowed to embrace her.

One rebel took Deakin away while another ushered Skylar, Calida, and Florian to a damp nook secluded between jutting rocks. Two of the rebels stayed nearby as guards.

"Do they not know you?" Calida whispered to Skylar.

"No," Skylar replied in a guarded voice that made Calida wish she had not listened to her foolish heart but rather heeded the advice screamed by her head.

Florian nestled close to her. "What do you think has happened to Deakin?"

"They are questioning him, I suspect." Skylar sounded annoyed.

It confused her, but Calida did not blame Skylar for her ire. She was equally frustrated at the poor welcome. The air was dank. The ground was cold and dirty, and there was nothing to sit upon. Water dripped somewhere, though they had not been offered so much as a sip. The rebel guards conducted a hushed and grunted conversation in the semi-darkness.

Calida did not understand Skylar's part in this. "Are they not your people?" she whispered, trying to keep the irritation out of her voice and failing.

Skylar glared at her with an expression that was confused and angry in equal measure.

Before Calida could demand an explanation, one of the rebels approached.

A wiry, young, masculine woman, taut with muscle, waved a sword at Calida. Calida was not impressed. A simple "Come with me" would have sufficed.

She led Calida through the cavern to a tunnel. Calida took advantage of the darkness to reach for her smallest knife, one she could secret within her sleeve. She slipped it into a lip she had sewn for that purpose. Ahead was an alcove lit by fluttering torchlight.

A woman of later years sat on a stool next to a crude table. She rose as they entered and stared at Calida for several long moments. Calida was not intimidated. They had taken Skylar's sword and staff but neglected to search Calida or Florian. Her smallest knife was as deadly as an axe in Calida's hands.

"How did you find us?" The woman sounded angry and tired.

"The boy, Deakin, brought us here. We found him near death on the road."

"What district are you from?"

"The south, originally. Most recently, we came from Freymar, where we lived until zealots burned our settlement in the night."

"That is convenient," the virago said. "Freymar is too far to corroborate her story."

The woman nodded at her companion. "Say I chose to believe you. Why did they burn you out?"

"Because we were poor and different. Because they were full of hate. Because the sun shines in the morning and the moon at night. Is there a reason for their prejudice? They had been tormenting my son for some time."

The woman frowned. "But you just said you met the boy on the road."

"He already told us you are not his parents." The virago watched her sharply.

Calida was beyond annoyed at the pair of them. She had been pursued and plagued by the King's men, bailiffs, and ignorant townsfolk. Now these rebels had the nerve to test her? "Not that boy. My child, Florian."

"I see. Florian is a boy?" The woman appraised Calida with one eyebrow raised.

Calida nodded.

"And the man you travel with. He is Florian's father?"

Calida paused. Her ire turned to disdain. During their conversation, she had gleaned the older woman was a feminine person like Florian, and the other was a masculine woman. The two seemed remarkably inept at recognizing their kind.

Calida sighed. She was weary of games and deception. So she told them how she had met Skylar and the events of their journey to her cousin's home. She did not mention any romantic feelings. They were none of their business. Besides, she was deeply confused and annoyed with Skylar at the present moment.

"She is Anton's cousin?" the woman asked the virago.

The virago nodded. Calida did not understand the exchange, but it seemed they knew Anton. "Do you know where my cousin is? Is he alive?"

"No news has come out of Bareglen except for yours," the woman said gently, her manner entirely changed. "The King's guard leaves no one alive to carry a warning to other rebels."

"Damn them all to the coldest pit in all of the seven hells," Calida said. "And the King."

The virago laughed. "She is one of us, even if she does not know it yet."

"You are welcome here." The older woman turned an exhausted smile on Calida. "We must speak with your traveling companion. A comrade will come for you and Florian and show you where you can bathe and eat."

Calida nodded cautiously. Being fed and clean was appealing, but this was not the safe place Skylar had alluded to. She did not want to be caught with a band of rebels if the King's guards came knocking.

There was nothing to be done until Skylar had been questioned.

❖

Skylar stood weaponless before the fae woman and the young butch. Two more of the rebels stood guard outside the small alcove.

"What district are you from, and why are you here?" The fae woman spoke like an interrogator.

Skylar opened her mouth to answer and felt the familiar touch of an empath at the edges of her mind. She barriered automatically. That was interesting. But, on reflection, not surprising. Why should empaths and telepaths be restricted to Gaea?

The butch was the empath.

"My family were circus folk," Skylar lied. "We traveled a lot."

"You have a strange accent." The butch spoke and reached out again.

Skylar projected honesty as she invented her answer. "Circus folk keep to themselves. We do not mix with outsiders."

"I would not know." The fae woman watched Skylar closely. "No circus comes this far north. Why are you not still with them?"

"When their girl turned out to be a butch, my parents disowned me. I was forced to leave."

"A butch? What is that?" the fae woman asked.

"A virago," the young butch said. "It is an old word. I have only heard it used as an insult."

"I hoped to find others of my kind. I did not. I was lost until I met Calida." Skylar did not want to deceive them, but she could not reveal the truth. They might be trustworthy people, but that was no matter. She could not break the cardinal law of Gaea over and over.

The butch nodded to her compadre. The fae woman returned the nod. So, this was how they questioned outsiders—using empathy. A practical method, no doubt.

The butch had relaxed. "Did you ever hear a tale of a group of deviants and rebels who fled the country to create a free land?"

"I did," the fae woman replied. "It is the reason there is no land outside of Alba. The king before ours deployed a terrible weapon against them. It is how the poisoned wastelands came to be. It is a shame they were all destroyed. A free land composed of our kin, how grand that would be." The fae woman spoke like a leader. "You may stay for the time being." She sank onto a small stool with a weary expression.

Skylar was sorry for her and for their situation. She wished with all her heart that they were not subjected to such atrocities because of their country's ignorance.

"Follow me." The young butch led Skylar out of the alcove.

Skylar wanted to help the rebels—they were gender warriors, after all. But her primary and only mission now was to get her group of four across the border to Gaea. And that mission was urgent. They must go at first light.

❖

Calida had had no chance to question Skylar, and now she walked toward the market in Kirkdale with a nervousness she resented. Not since she had hidden behind the fireplace in their southern homestead had Calida wasted energy on fear.

But this town was alive with gossip, hate, and something feral that crept through the marketplace. It was reckless to ignore it.

Calida had barely finished bathing when the young virago had come running to fetch her. The hideout was taut with news of guards gathering in the town. Calida had been deemed the only person capable of scouting for information.

Lucky her. She understood it was because her gender would be deemed acceptable by the townsfolk. Florian had been told to remain behind. That, Calida knew, was to ensure her return. Another could have gone. Calida was sure of that. But it would have been more dangerous for them. And the rebels gave her little choice.

She found a suitable spot beside an old woman selling vegetables from a handcart. Calida set down the rebel leader's stool and sat on it with her basket of eggs on her knee. She nodded at the woman, who smiled cautiously in return.

She had arrived later than most. The marketplace was bustling with traders, customers, and livestock. There were no cookshops, but the baker's shop was doing a brisk trade, and the tavern was lively.

The mood was not jovial. Calida thought back to Galamoor on market day with fondness. Skylar had been remarkably unworldly that day, falling victim to a cutpurse. *Hmm.* Calida tucked that thought away to ponder upon anon. It was one puzzling inconsistency among the many surrounding Skylar.

Kirkdale marketplace was not festive. A large number of guards wandered the square and spilled from the tavern. Where they went, unease followed.

Calida had sold most of her eggs and had not acquired any information when four soldiers approached the vegetable cart. Without so much as a greeting, they began to load carrots, potatoes, and parsnips into a sack.

The woman watched them with eyes of burning coal. When over half her stock had been taken, she threw a blanket over the cart.

"The rest is spoken for." The snap of her teeth at the end of her sentence defied them to challenge her.

The guard holding the sack was the oldest and meanest looking. "By rights, we could commission the lot." A nasty sneer and an untidy beard blighted his face.

Calida's fingers itched to shave it and use the cut hair to wipe the sneer away.

"You want us to do your dirty work and rid you of these heretics, but you balk at feeding us?" The guard stared at the woman until she looked down. Her hands trembled on the cloth, but she kept them stubbornly atop her wares.

Just when Calida was sure there would be violence, the guard huffed dramatically and walked away. The others followed. Calida was angry on the woman's behalf, but nothing could be done. This was the way of the King's guards. They were bandits legitimized by royal decree.

"Glorified thieves," she muttered too quietly for the guards to hear but loud enough for the trader's ears.

The woman let out a grunt of agreement.

When the guards were out of sight, townsfolk surrounded the cart to grumble and complain. After a time, just a few townswomen remained, and the talk turned to gossip.

Calida surveyed the market as if looking for customers whilst listening for snippets of news. She could tell by the tone they discussed something salacious, but the conversation was held in whispers.

Until a middle-aged woman cried excitedly, "Deviant hunt!"

Calida stopped herself from turning sharply. They were bound to talk low if they were directly observed. Feeling sick to her stomach, she strained to hear more.

"Women who take women as *lovers*," said one.

"In truth? But how? How do they…manage?" The vegetable stall woman sounded perplexed.

"Well, I am not about to explain in the middle of the marketplace, Milicent," the first replied. "They do not look how they should either. Some of them look like men. And some of the men look like women."

"Goodness. But I do not see why the King's guards should get involved. Or why people should be arrested."

Calida was beginning to like Milicent. She had bravely stood up to the guards, too. Unfortunately, the other women were vicious in their remarks. Calida tried to tune out their ignorance and prejudice while continuing to listen. There would be an attack on the rebels, but when and where? If everyone stayed holed up in the cavern, could they wait it out?

"I wonder at you, Milicent, I really do."

"I do not see the harm in it, that is all. We did not have a problem before the guards arrived, and if these people are far northerners, they are our extended kin."

"It is their fault the King's ruffians are here stealing your vegetables. We do not want them in our town. In any case, it is out of our hands." The woman lowered her voice. "They are hiding in Bride's basin, and the guards know. I heard them talking. There they are now, gathering in front of the guildhall. We will get some peace from them, at least."

With horror, Calida looked toward a tall, stone building at the south end of the market square. It was teeming with soldiers. Some were preparing horses. Others sharpening weapons. Calida rose as unobtrusively as she could. Milicent glanced over and gave a small smile.

Calida nodded in reply. She did not want to attract attention, but all her concentration was on returning to Bride's basin with utmost speed. She must warn them. She must get Florian and Skylar out of there.

She had to get there before the soldiers. And she would ride like the hounds of hell to do it.

❖

Skylar sat with Florian in an area of the cavern set aside for dining and recreation. They had not been assigned sleeping quarters, and Skylar hoped they would not need them. The area was volatile, and the rebels felt it, too. The atmosphere in the cave, called Bride's basin, was tense.

No one had spoken to them since Calida had left for the town. They were kind enough to Florian but disinterested. Presumably, they were occupied with their concerns. Some cast furtive looks at Skylar, and she sensed she was not trusted. It did not matter to her. She itched to be on their way.

Come back soon, Calida.

Florian sat next to her on a rough wooden bench, picking at a crust of bread.

"You should eat what you can while you can," Skylar said.

Florian glanced at her. He seemed disappointed, tired, and scared.

"What is wrong?" Skylar asked.

Anguish washed over him. "Skylar, will we ever, ever be safe?"

Skylar held him. He gripped her tightly, tears dropping silently onto her neck. It was a bad sign when a child cried without making a sound. "I will keep you safe." She should not make a promise she could not keep, but Skylar made it anyway.

When Florian spoke, his voice was dull. "Mama said not to expect a future with you in it. She said we might not be able to trust you."

"Florian." Skylar lifted his chin and spoke in a whisper. It was important that no one but Florian heard. "What if there was a place, a different place from Alba? A place we could all be together."

Florian took a breath, his eyes full of hope, and she wanted to cry. She wanted to sing. She did not know what to do with herself. She held fast to a dream of herself with Calida, Florian, and Kit all home in Gaea.

Then fear swelled in Florian again. "I cannot stop thinking something terrible is about to happen."

Intuition pulsed through Florian's words. Skylar sat up. "Since when have you felt this?"

"Not very long. The feeling was not there when we arrived or even when Mama left for the town. It has been growing, though, and Skylar, I am so afraid. Am I being foolish?"

Skylar clasped Florian's hand. "Is your mother in danger?"

Florian thought for a moment. "No. Skylar, we are."

"Is a threat coming here? Is it the soldiers?"

"Yes. Yes, that's it," Florian said quickly.

Skylar jumped to her feet. "Come with me."

Skylar hurried to the rebel leader's alcove. She was seated with the young empath, sharpening weapons. They started when Skylar burst through.

"Florian has a prediction that the guards are coming here." Skylar felt their alarm but was not prepared to dally. She meant to take Florian and go, even if it meant finding Calida in the town. "We are leaving. You should do the same."

"Wait." The young butch gripped Skylar's arm. "We cannot move everyone on a child's whim."

"Do what you must. Florian's prediction may be right or wrong, but Florian feels it. This much I know."

"How?" The young butch was skeptical.

"The same way you do. Search Florian's feelings."

Shock flared in the empath. And then Skylar felt zir mind reach out.

"I wish you all the luck in the world." Skylar locked eyes with both rebels before grasping Florian's hand and hurrying to retrieve their packs.

They ran along the entrance tunnel, Skylar already calling with her mind to Kit.

❖

The two rebel sentries at the entrance turned with shock when Skylar and Florian ran along the tunnel toward them, Skylar with sword and staff in hand.

Skylar had barely opened her mouth to explain when Kit burst into the tunnel with a growl. The rebels, caught off guard, had only a moment to stare at the vultrix before the sound of galloping hoofbeats drew them all out onto the hillside.

Skylar scrutinized the goat track below, bracing herself for a regiment.

A single rider came around a bend in the track, riding fast. Dust obscured the rider, but Skylar knew in a heartbeat it was Calida.

Calida ignored the treachery of the loose, stony path and the hard breath of the horse beneath her. She bent over the horse's neck, holding tight to the reins and urging the horse faster.

A furlong away, she yelled, "Guards are coming. Warn the camp."

The rebels disappeared. Calida galloped up to the tunnel and dismounted. "We must leave immediately. I stole a horse. He is no further use to us, I think?"

Skylar studied the stallion. He was damp with sweat but still with stamina. "Thank you, friend," she whispered to him. "He will serve us until we reach the marshes. They are not far. You two ride. Take my pack. Kit and I will run beside you."

Calida gripped Skylar's sleeve. "Where are we going?"

Skylar faced her. "To the safe place I told you about."

Calida frowned, but she mounted the horse with Florian and galloped forward to the north road.

❖

Ahead was a burnt-honey sea of reeds and grasses. It stretched on and on to a horizon that was darkening fast. A line of something rose beyond the vast stretch of marshland, but whatever it was was too far and shadowy to identify.

Underneath the whispering of grasses was the lazy drift of water, its gentle lap creating a soothing rhythm. Insects chirruped, their chorus blending with the wind. The air was heavy with the distinct odor of silt. It was the smell of the bottom of a pond brought to the surface and thrust into the air. And it was a pungent reminder of the treacherous swamp soil beneath.

"This is where we say good-bye to our stallion." Skylar stood at the edge of the marshland, reaching with all her senses toward Gaea. Her country was there, beyond this great wetland. They were almost home.

Kit sat on his haunches at Skylar's side, looking out like she. Skylar heard Calida and Florian dismount. Then footsteps and Calida appeared next to Skylar.

"You expect us to cross that?" She eyed the marsh as if it were her personal enemy.

Skylar kissed her gently on the cheek. "We must."

"These are the beginning of the poisoned wastelands, Skylar." Calida looked incredulously at Skylar. "The water must be tainted, apart from the fact it will likely drag us down as soon as we set foot in it."

"Look." Skylar went to point at a clump of reeds to the right. Before her finger had marked the place, Florian gasped. The child had a strong affinity with creatures. When they were home and safe, he could explore his skills.

"An otter, Mama," Florian murmured.

A dark brown head peeked out from the hollow reed stems.

"She's caught a fish," Florian said in awe.

"Oh good," Calida said wryly. "We will have something to eat as we sink to our watery deaths."

"Mama!" Florian sounded horrified.

"Not the otter, Florian, the fish." Calida chuckled.

Skylar felt hope bubbling within Calida. But she was scared, too, and for good reason. "Right, we are close, but we must not delay. Florian, turn our strong stallion loose. Persuade him to trot far away so no one is drawn to our position."

Florian threw his arms around the horse's neck and whispered into his ear. The steed nuzzled Florian's face. When Florian released him, the stallion set off at a gallop.

Skylar stepped into the marsh with Kit. Florian came behind them, and Calida brought up the rear.

The sun was low in the sky. There was a chill in the air this far north, and the water was cold. It was shallow at first and sound underfoot. Skylar relaxed a fraction when they stepped into the reed banks. Calida and Skylar could be seen by anyone approaching the marshes, but Florian and Kit were hidden at least.

Skylar was torn between pushing them on and keeping a pace that ensured nobody became entangled in the grasses. They had no choice but to travel through the night. She could only hope that they crossed the wetlands before darkness fell completely.

And that the guards were occupied elsewhere. Though she could not bear to think of the nature of that occupation.

❖

The sky had darkened to purple, and they were still wading through sludge. The marshes mocked them by standing in the way of the safe place Skylar promised was ahead. Calida grunted. It better be there. She detested the slimy water up to her waist and the shifting silt under her boots. Something brushed against her, and she shuddered. God knows what was in this water, swimming along with them. It was too dark to see, and whatever it was was already two steps behind. She fought to stop her teeth from chattering.

Calida pressed on. Florian was her main concern, as always, and now, well, now, maybe there was Skylar, too. Her heart danced a jig at Skylar's name. A ridiculous jig, but it was a good distraction from the sludge.

However uncomfortable the marshes were, ahead lay the poisoned wastelands. By all the bells in seven hells, how would they cross that? Calida pushed the worry from her mind. One unpleasant and potentially deadly situation at a time.

Skylar carried Kit. Calida had tied a rope between herself and Florian. He waded quietly beside her, being exceptionally brave. That child truly deserved something good in his life.

She swiped a mosquito away from her cheek, already feeling the sting. The watery plain was thick with the tiny devils. The air stank of pond weed. Calida could think of no other way to describe the dank, mushed green plant smell. There was no sound save the slosh of six legs wading.

Except there *was* something else. Calida stopped. She tugged on the line to halt Florian.

Something large crashed through the water a distance behind them. Actually, a few large somethings.

Calida turned. She peered through reed banks under the moonless sky and could make out human-sized shapes. They came fast and noisily through the water.

Skylar must have heard them, too. "There are rebels in the marsh. They are trying to flee." Skylar went quiet, staring intently at the bank from whence they had come. She snatched in a breath. "Guards are nearing the bank on horseback with torches. We must move forward quickly."

Calida was astounded. Did Skylar have the eyesight of an owl? Calida could not even see the far bank, let alone riders. But she did not doubt Skylar's words or warning.

They waded on swiftly. Calida kept the line taut, ready to catch Florian should he slip. Kit growled softly. It was a chilling noise, coupled with the splashing that grew closer and louder. Silt underfoot sucked at Calida's boots as if the damned marsh wanted to consume them. Well, it could go unsatisfied, like most of Alba's population.

She then heard galloping horses. There were shouts, male voices, from the bank. Still moving forward, turning, praying not to trip, Calida looked back. Torchlight threw flickering light on grim, bearded faces massed at the far edge of the marsh.

"Deviants in the water, escaping." The cry went up, and the riders turned their horses into the water.

The marsh slowed them, thank the heavens, but they had the advantage still.

The splashing grew louder. Several desperate rebels were half across.

Calida stopped worrying about poisoned land. She took Florian's hand, rope be damned, and pulled him along.

"This way." Instead of taking the direct path, Skylar turned sharply left, heading back into the marsh.

"What?"

"We will not make it to shore," Skylar grunted, her words breathless and laced with tension. "Quick. Kit knows the way."

But how do you know what Kit knows? Did Skylar speak Fox now? It did not matter. Calida's only choice was to trust or not. She chose to trust Skylar.

A horse whinnied a distance off. Something thwacked through the air, and a man cried out.

"Got one." The deep voice carried. The tone was smug and cruel.

They had reached a dense forest of reeds. They were pressed so tightly together it was hard to get through them. Calida pushed harder.

"Protect your eyes," she whispered to Florian. *Out of my way, damned plants.* At last, the stems bent aside.

It was quieter inside the reed bed. The ground was more solid. Reeds and grasses entwined together and stretched high enough to cover them all.

Calida spoke into Florian's ear in barely a whisper. "We must be absolutely silent."

He clung to her. Skylar held Kit to her chest and gripped Calida's arm. Skylar's fingers were strong and warm and sure.

Splashes continued beyond. The guards taunted those they chased. They mocked. They insulted. They laughed. There was a horrible scream.

Calida forced herself to remain crouching, to keep holding on to Florian, to concentrate on Skylar's warmth, to the steady breath of the little witch fox. Those poor souls were desperate. She wanted to help them. Tears sprung to her eyes. She wanted to take up all her knives and thrust them into the King's guards.

She could not aid the rebels and save herself. Florian needed her.

They must not be discovered. Words of a song sprung to her mind. Half-forgotten, they were words her mother used when she wanted their homestead to be left alone. They were the words Freya mouthed in the hidey-hole behind the fireplace.

Dampen sight and smother sound, so thee and me cannot be found.

Light as air, not even there. Peril pass us, unaware.

❖

There was powerful magic in the air. It flowed in a circle around the reed bed. Skylar's skin tingled with it. She sensed Calida's lips moving. Skylar had already sent out a circle of protection, but her witchcraft was rudimentary. This new spell floated into Skylar's weak circle and snapped a wall around them.

Skylar sent out a message suggesting the reed bed was impenetrable and completely silent. She focused on the scent of each of them and submerged it beneath the pungency of marsh water.

Kit was pressed against her. Calida's arm was warm under her hand. Florian's breath was slow and even.

But beyond their haven, horses thrashed in the water. Hounds, determined to do their masters' bidding, tore across the shallows and swam through the deeps. Skylar turned their minds away from the reed bed. She tried to turn them from the others. Their terror ripped through her heart, assaulted her mind. But she could not protect both them and her new family. She did not have the skills for it. It was unbearable. Skylar damned her lack of foresight. Why had she not studied witchcraft? She had put all her faith in the ways of a warrior. She could not help them. Yet she must endure their cries.

The purple night faded to the gray before dawn. Riders moved more slowly as if searching the marshland inch by inch. A hound scouted in the water just beyond the reed bed. Skylar had not hurt an animal in her life, nor did she wish to now. But she was bitter. She had felt this dog's teeth bite down on a man. She sent him a message, perhaps too sharply, and the hound turned away.

Neither horse nor hound were to blame. The guards were the monsters here.

Kit trembled. Skylar was soaked through, and it was cold. Why did the riders not return to the far bank? There was no one left now but them.

She had a horrible thought. What if one of their number was a telepath? Skylar shielded hard. She linked with Kit, and together, they reinforced the sense of nothingness around them. Kit's energy was strong and comforting. Camouflage was his primary skill. His power increased Skylar's threefold.

And yet a horse came steadily toward them. Calida was aware. Her arm moved away from Skylar's hand as she reached for a knife. Skylar did not want to let go of Kit. She could not risk the splash of him dropping. She maneuvered inelegantly to unsheathe her sword. The angle was wrong. She could not unhook it, and stronger movement would create noise.

The horse was steps away. Skylar gave up on her weapon and concentrated on reinforcing their nothingness. She tasted fear. Not for herself. For Florian, for Kit. And for Calida. Calida, who had stolen her heart.

The horse stopped. She could see it, a chestnut bay near the edge of the reeds. A guard in a hooded cloak sat on top of the horse, staring solidly at the reed bed.

Skylar hardly dared breathe. *Nothing but grasses. Tall, swaying grasses.* She took hold of his mind. It was forbidden in Gaea, this thing she was doing. It was nothing to her need to keep them alive.

There was faint resistance to her touch. She slipped past it, becoming fog that seeped into the guard's thoughts. *It is finished. All is done. There is no one here.*

He had gone so very still that doubt began to creep along Skylar's spine. She quenched it. Her telepathy turned from mist to wave. *There is no one here.*

The guard drew up with a start. He turned the chestnut bay around. "We are done here," he called into the true mist that rose now with the coming of the dawn light.

The guards and hounds retreated. Skylar held Kit tighter. He shook in her arms. Poor, sensitive vultrix. They were truly bonded. He had absorbed her fear. Calida's back was curled into her, her arms around Florian, the knife still gripped tight in Calida's hand.

The four of them had survived a terrible night. Skylar drew a ragged breath. She must hold fast. It was not long now, and they would need her guidance. For the last steps might test them the most.

❖

When there was nothing but soft bird calls and the regular gentle lap of marsh water, Skylar stood. Calida felt her gaze.

"We should move on."

Kit gave a low whine. He looked alert and ready for anything.

Florian's fingers tightened around Calida's arm the way they used to when he was a small child. She embraced him and kissed the top of his head. "We cannot stay here. It is freezing cold, for one thing. Do you not want to be out of this icy slush?"

"I do not mind it." Florian's voice was barely above a whisper. He stared fearfully toward the barren landscape on the nearby bank.

Calida shared his trepidation. What was Skylar leading them into?

But Skylar had already left their reedy protection and was skirting the left edge of the bed. Kit looked back over Skylar's shoulders with a *what are you waiting for* expression.

A rush of warmth pushed back the soaked-through chill that suffused Calida's body. She had a pack now, a little family. At least, she thought and hoped she did.

"Come, darling." Calida set off after Skylar, gently pulling Florian in her wake.

Her cramped body was glad of the movement. She could not help but scan the marshes as she moved, wanting to be sure the guards had truly left. She pushed the horrible sounds of the night to some quarter of her mind where she might never have to hear them again. God help those poor souls.

The water had receded to the height of her knees as the bank of the wasteland loomed. It took all of Calida's courage to keep wading forward.

Mist as thick as smoke drifted across skeletal trees and clumped twigs that had been bushes. The ground was dark, as if it had been burnt. No grass grew, no trailing plant. There was nothing green save pools of slime.

Calida stopped a footstep from the wasteland. The air was acrid. Her throat began to sting. Her eyes watered. She turned to Florian. "Take out your head covering." All Albans carried them, especially females, in case they needed to pass through a religious area. She fixed the scarf across her nose and mouth. Florian copied her. The barrier helped, but still, Calida could not understand how any safe place could exist here in these poisoned lands.

Kit looked up at Skylar with an expression that said *this is not what you promised me.* Calida was in agreement with the little fox.

But Skylar did not seem perturbed. She was already standing on the charcoal earth, breathing without protection. She bent down and whispered something in Kit's ear, and when Skylar walked forward, Kit padded behind.

Calida did not trust as easily. "Skylar," she called. There was already a rasp in her voice. They could not last here long. A few days at most. What in the seven frozen leagues of hellish hell was Skylar thinking of?

Skylar turned back. Her eyes glittered with excitement, and her smile was broad. "Do not be afraid, Calida. Florian, all is well. Follow me. We are so very close now."

Calida's mouth fell open. She looked from Skylar to the desolate landscape. There was nothing but tree after broken tree. Yellowish clouds swept down from the sky. Calida imagined those clouds full of poison and shuddered.

"Calida, please. You cannot stay there. You cannot turn back now."

Against all reason, Calida stepped onto the wasteland. Slime had congealed upon the bare tree branches. A drip fell to the dark earth with a hiss.

"This place will kill us, Skylar."

Skylar turned back and took Calida's hand. "Do not trust your eyes, your ears, your nose, any of your senses. Trust only me."

Trust. Now, there's a thing. A precious commodity with so much at risk.

But Florian surged forward, taking Calida with him.

They trudged on. There was nothing living. Not plant, nor animal. No bird sang. No insect fluttered or chirruped. Calida was sure her boots were burning away beneath her.

They came to a line of trees, beyond which was nothing. It was a strange sight. The land behind the trees, if there was any, fell away.

Calida turned to Skylar. She had put her faith in a madwoman. There was nothing here but poison. And nothing at their back but persecution.

Skylar stepped close to a broad and broken oak, carrying Kit. "Stand on either side of me and link your arms with mine. Be ready to move when I do."

Calida did as she was bade. There was hope in Florian's eyes. Calida said nothing. Let the child dream. Calida hardened her heart as she should have done a moon or so ago. She did not berate herself. There would be time enough for that later.

Skylar stared into the scorched tree bark, mouthing words with Kit pressed to her chest. A high-pitched droning sound resonated in her ears. Perhaps it was one last stray insect. But then Skylar surged forward and kept walking as if the tree was about to magically disappear.

Calida braced for the crash. For the scrape of bark on her skin. For poison to burn and sting her face.

And the tree vanished.

Chapter Nine

A fresh breeze caressed Calida's face, and the mist cleared away. Calida was in a cool, quiet forest, enveloped in the glorious, velvety green of holly and hawthorn. Ivy trailed over branches, and moss sprung underfoot. Beech, oak, and birch trees in full leaf stretched languidly upward. The forest was healthy and vibrant. A little ways off came the sound of water falling and splashing. The invigorating scent of it filled her lungs.

"We're here. We're here!" Skylar's voice startled her. Skylar was on her knees kissing the earth. "I told you. Did I not tell you?" Skylar spoke to Kit. She swept him into her arms, and he nuzzled under her chin. If an animal could beam, the vultrix was indeed beaming.

Florian skipped from one foot to the other, half jumping, half dancing. "Is this the safe place? Is it? Oh." He hushed suddenly, glancing into the trees. "Should I be quiet?"

Skylar jumped up, took hold of Florian, and swung him around. Calida was amazed at Skylar's strength. Florian did not weigh much, but he was no longer a small child. Their laughter rang through the forest. The sight was comical and wonderful.

Skylar set Florian down, and they both staggered. "Florian, my dear, you never have to be silent again," Skylar proclaimed.

Calida took a long and cautious breath. The air felt clean. She removed her scarf. Her skin did not sting. Her throat was already healed. "Where are we?"

"In the southwestern forests of Gaea." The lines of worry had vanished from Skylar's face. "These are wetlands, too, but clean ones."

"I can see. I can smell." And Calida could hear the life in the forest. Bird song, the buzz of insects, the flap of wings. A squirrel scampered along the horizontal branch of a great oak.

Florian stood very still, taking in every inch of the chestnut-colored, furry creature.

The squirrel jumped from branch to lower branch until it dropped to the ground, a footstep away from Florian. It sniffed, poised as if to spring away at any moment.

A slow smile spread over Florian's lips. He was the picture of gentleness and innocence. Calida swallowed hard. It had been such a very, very long time since Florian had looked like that.

Florian and the squirrel shared a look, and then the squirrel noticed Kit. It darted off immediately.

"Animals are more tuned to humans here," Skylar said.

"Gaea?" Calida found her voice. "I have never heard of such a place."

"This is my country, my land. I could not tell you before." Skylar came to Calida and took her hand. "Calida, I hardly dared hope I could bring you both back here. But, well, here you are." She kissed Calida lightly on the lips. "You are both free. You can be yourselves here."

Calida let her forehead rest against Skylar's. She understood the words, but they were impossible. As impossible as a vanishing tree.

Skylar pulled away. "Come. Let us wash the marsh water from our clothes." She ran ahead through the forest. Skylar seemed to have reverted to a teenager since their arrival.

Florian raced beside Skylar. Kit bounded at their heels.

Calida followed more cautiously.

The sound of falling water grew louder. The trees opened into a clearing filled with a large, green pool. Calida shook her head in wonder at the great stream falling from above. A river had forged a cleft between trees, splitting the forest in two. It had created a pool deep enough to swim in. And Skylar, Florian, and Kit had already plunged into it. Skylar and Florian splashed each other, shrieking with laughter. Kit was caught in their deluge and did not seem to mind.

Calida watched them laughing. She shrugged off her pack, pulled her boots off, and sat on the ground, soaking her feet in the cool water. She began to wash the grime of the marshland away. She bent her face, and suddenly, two arms pulled her into the pool.

The coldness was fierce and shocking. Calida rose to the surface, soaking wet, somewhat annoyed at being taken by surprise, but the laughter bubbling up inside did not care at all. Skylar tread water beside her, delighted at her daring.

Calida met Skylar's eyes and was aflame. She longed to kiss her, to hold her. But Florian was there. She contented herself with dipping her eyes at Skylar before swimming back to the bank.

Skylar grinned wickedly. Calida shot the cocky butch a look. Skylar need not think everything would go her way so easily.

❖

Skylar saw Florian's head droop forward as he leaned into the horse's neck. The child was shattered. They'd had the good fortune to run across an ostler. He'd recognized Skylar's uniform, dirty and ragged as it was, and lent them horses.

And now, at last, they had reached a traveler's rest. A steady drizzle was starting to seep through Skylar's cloak. She pulled on the reins of her mottled brown stallion. The horse was fresh. He could trot until sundown, but the humans could not. The terrible events of the past few days had exhausted them.

"Let us stop here for the night." Skylar swung down from her horse and strode to the door of a log cabin beside the main forest road. They needed warmth, food, and sleep. They would be safe here. Even bandits, scarce as they were in Gaea, would not defile the sanctity of a travelers' rest.

Calida frowned. "We have no coin, Skylar."

"And we need none. This is a resting stop for any traveler passing through this area. Where there are no inns, or if folk cannot afford one, we provide a place to eat and sleep. It is open to all."

Calida's eyes widened in surprise. She dismounted, walked to the cabin door, and carefully thrust it open.

The interior was as Skylar expected: a cooking area for bad weather with provisions neatly stowed, a place to wash, and an ample open space with bedrolls. The cabin had been built near a stream. An animal shelter with hitch posts, three sides, and a roof was situated next to the cabin.

There is no meat here. Skylar sent a message to Kit, who immediately disappeared into the forest. Florian took charge of the horses.

Before long, Calida had a fire crackling merrily in the grate. Florian had brushed down and fed the horses from the animal supply bins, and Skylar had pulled dried lentils and crushed grains from the food stocks to create a quick and hearty stew.

Florian placed three bowls on the rough wooden table. "What is a free season? The ostler said we could have the horses because they had finished their free season."

Skylar turned from the stew pot hooked over the cooking fire. "Nearly all the horses in Gaea come from wild stock." She was about to explain the skill of empathy, but she hesitated. She must then broach the subject of her skills. "They have a free season, where they roam and do as they please, and then we persuade them to work for us for a season."

Florian smiled. "And they agree?"

"Usually. We treat them well. Give them food they love and would not otherwise have. Horses make it clear if they do not want to assist us."

"And you do not make them?"

"We do not." Skylar noticed how thin Florian's undershirt was. It was suited to Alba's warmer climate. "Go look in those wooden crates by the door, Florian. You will find spare clothing there. It is for anyone to use."

Calida narrowed her eyes. She had draped their cloaks and outer garments within drying range of the main fire. Now, she crouched beside it like a cat about to spring. "I cannot believe we are permitted to stay here," she said in a rush.

Skylar understood. Calida could not know that Gaea cared about its citizens, especially the ones without resources.

She sat next to Calida. "I am a warrior, a member of the butch regiment. I am respected here. Even if you cannot believe there is no charge for these accommodations, you are safe traveling with me."

Calida swallowed. "I trust your word, Skylar. But this puts me on guard. Theft in Alba is treated more harshly than you know. For Florian's sake, I will eat the meal you prepare and sleep here. I will ride upon the horse your ostler friend gave us. But I will not take anything from those crates." She tossed her head toward the box Florian stood by. "If guards come after us, I can turn the horse loose, but I will not run naked through the forest for you or anyone."

Skylar bit her lip to stop laughing aloud. The statement, delivered with heat, conjured an astounding image. "I cannot imagine you without your coat. Where would you put your knives?" It was a falsehood. Skylar had that very moment, imagined Calida without a stitch of clothing. It was Calida's own fault. She had put the image there. Thank the Goddess she was no telepath.

Calida met Skylar's eyes boldly. Then her lips twitched to a smile before she returned to tending the fire.

Skylar pulled a shift and tunic out of the box and held them toward Florian. He shook his head.

Skylar sighed. It would take some time for Calida and Florian to shake off the ways of Alba. She would support them until they did.

❖

By noon the following day, a promising start turned dark and damp with the onset of rain. This was not unusual for the southwest of Gaea, where rain was all too common. A chill wind blew from the north, adding to their discomfort.

Florian rode on his steed behind Skylar with Kit tucked into a sling under his cloak. Calida rode at Skylar's side. She stared truculently into the rain as if the Goddess had sent it to test her. Her hands gripped tight to the reins. Skylar sensed how cold she was.

Calida turned her head to Skylar. "What?"

Skylar resisted mentioning the rejected cloak and the thick chemise and tunic lying back in the traveler's rest. "This is unpleasant riding. Perhaps we should stop to build a fire and feed ourselves?"

Calida shot a defiant look at the heavens. "The rain has settled in for the day. The horses are fresh for a while yet. And where would we find dry firewood amongst this bog?"

Either side of the trail was lined with fir and spruce, silver birch, and hazel trees. Rivulets crisscrossed the trail. The forest they traversed was a patchwork of greens and browns. The road was springy with the moss that covered everything. The misty rainfall dampened the splash of the horses' hooves. Skylar linked minds with Kit, snuggled into his sling, and found him asleep despite the damp weather. Skylar sighed. Calida and Florian deserved a better welcome. They reached a stretch of road Skylar knew, and an idea came to her.

"A half day's journey from here is a shelter much bigger than the rough dwelling we rested in last night. This one has comfortable lodgings and hot food, much like an Alban inn."

Calida brightened. "But still, we have no coin from your employers."

"The double axe on my forearm denotes me as a warrior. I can also show my ragged uniform." She patted the saddle bag where her uniform lay. "And we are travelers in need. We would not be turned away. Besides, I know the woman who runs the place. She is kind and will welcome us. And there is another reason I would have us stop there. I wish very much for Florian to meet the steward's child."

Calida sat up in her saddle. "Is the road wide enough ahead to gallop?"

"For some leagues. As far as the shelter, at least."

"Then ready yourself, Florian," she called behind before turning to Skylar with a challenging look. "And you, my butch warrior friend, tighten those strong calves of yours and spring up. We should quicken our pace. This sky is preparing to throw a deluge upon our heads. If we hurry, we may escape the worst of it."

Skylar knew not how Calida read the weather, but she did not question her abilities. The conversation about unseen skills could be had soon enough. Preferably somewhere warm and dry.

❖

Calida was delighted to pull up before a medium-sized stone dwelling on the edge of a small grove of silver birch. A stream ran close by. It was undoubtedly convenient, and it would be pretty on a sunny day. But in the midst of pounding rain, the swollen, churning water provoked a shiver that bit deep.

Heavy rain had come, as Calida knew it would, and she was soaked to the skin. It was all she could do to stop her teeth from violently chattering. She kept her discomfort to herself. It would be churlish to complain of what would likely seem to Skylar to be a minor matter. In truth, she was still shocked to discover a whole land lay over the border from Alba. And they were here in it, here and free. Meeting Skylar had changed their lives. Calida knew she was reacting to things in what must be to Skylar, a strange way. But she could not throw off the habits of a lifetime in just a day or two. She could not truly believe they were safe. Not yet.

She wanted to. Her emotions veered wildly between joy and concern. She could put up with the cold as long as they were safe. Calida was prepared to make the best of any situation, though she secretly hoped Gaea had nice, warm, dry regions to settle in.

Skylar dismounted, strode to the front door, and knocked.

A round-faced, bright and friendly woman in a simple, cornflower blue, long-sleeved robe opened the door. She looked about thirty years old and wore her long, blond hair tied back with a sapphire-blue ribbon that matched her eyes. She was pale-skinned and feminine, with a curvy physique. She stared at Skylar in surprise and then smiled broadly.

"Skylar! Come in," she cried, backing away from the door. "Come in, everyone. Tie your horses off to the rail and come out of that downpour."

"This is Calida and Florian," Skylar said as she stood back and waved them inside before her.

Calida stepped gratefully into a dry, airy entrance room with a small hearth where logs glowed red under a layer of white ash. She gravitated immediately to its warmth.

"I need to see to the horses, Ramona." Skylar's words were muffled by the house owner's enthusiastic embrace.

"They can graze there for a while, sheltered by the overhang," Ramona said. She pulled slightly away while keeping Skylar enveloped in her arms. "I had no idea you were in the region, Skylar. The village council received word that you were missing. I am overjoyed to see you."

Skylar smiled back. The two were clearly close. "Well, yes. I have been missing. Ramona, I have been to Alba."

Ramona drew back, looking at them all with startled eyes. She shut the entrance door against the rain. "To Alba?" she repeated in a hushed voice. "But?"

Skylar shrugged off her dripping cloak and hung it on a rack near the door. "It is a long tale, Ramona. Perhaps one we should not broadcast. Do you have other guests?"

"One or two." Ramona noticed Florian was struggling to untie his cloak with cold, wet fingers. She went to help him. "Let me show you to—Ah!" Ramona jumped about a foot in the air.

Kit's head peeked out of the top of the bundle Florian had fashioned to carry him. He yawned, revealing his teeth.

"You have a dog? No, no dog is that color. Surely not?" Ramona stepped gently close to Kit. "Are you a fox?"

Kit sniffed Ramona's outstretched hand and whined.

"He is a vultrix," Skylar said.

Ramona's eyes widened again. "No!" she breathed. "Oh, my goodness. You are so beautiful. May I stroke you?" she asked Kit.

Kit blinked slowly and relaxed when Ramona gently stroked his head. "I was about to show you to rooms where you can wash, change clothing, and rest if you wish."

"Can you spare any garments?" Skylar added. "All we have are the packs on our backs."

"Of course." Ramona set off through the doorway ahead. "I will send Linden to tend to your horses."

It all sounded wonderful, but Skylar had not spoken of payment. Calida could not accept anything without discussing the terms. She hurried after Ramona. "I must explain that we had to leave in a great hurry, and I do not have the means to pay you for our accommodations."

Ramona turned, looking as startled as when Skylar had mentioned Alba. "That is not a problem, Calida. It is my pleasure to aid you."

Calida was still not entirely comfortable, but things were different here, and, oh, it was good to be out of the rain. Dry, fresh clothing would be so very welcome.

"We are not entirely dissimilar in size, Calida," Ramona threw over her shoulder as they ascended a staircase. "I should have some traveling clothes to suit you. There is a spare clothing store you may riffle through, Skylar. And my son will have something to fit Florian."

Florian gave a small sigh. Calida waited for him to catch up and squeezed his hand. He looked downcast. Of course, he was. In Alba, despite the dangers, Florian wore the clothing of his chosen gender. Calida opened her mouth to tactfully explain when a light-skinned, green-eyed, blond-haired feminine child of similar age to Florian descended the staircase toward them.

"Ah, Linden," Ramona said. "Meet new friends of Skylar's, Calida and Florian. Can you help Florian with a change of clothes?"

Florian brightened instantly. "Are you sure you do not mind lending me some of your clothing?"

Linden broke into a beautiful smile. "Of course not. Come, shall we see what you might like?"

The two children ran up the stairs ahead. It was the first time Calida had met another child like Florian. She was taken aback at Ramona's openness and casual manner.

On the next floor, Ramona showed Calida to a charming bedroom. The small window facing the garden at the back of the house had real glass. Rain trickled down it, all but obscuring a misty view of the stream and grove of trees. There was a large bed, a cupboard for clothes, and an unlit fire in the hearth. The heavy oak furniture was old but polished and cared for.

Ramona turned down the thick, woolen blanket atop the bed to air it. "Calida, Skylar, will you share this room, or have you need of another?"

Calida drew a breath, glancing at Skylar and immediately away. Heat rushed to her face, and she blessed her brown complexion, trusting it to hide her blushes. "I will share with Florian. We will be amply comfortable here. Thank you." It was too complicated to consider sharing a bed with Skylar. Their first time should be…well, not so public. And when she caught Skylar's eyes for a moment, Calida was absolutely sure their time would come.

Skylar said nothing, but the look on her face promised Ramona further explanation. There was an intimacy between them that spoke of a deep friendship or a passionate relationship.

"Light the fire, Skylar. Can you not tell Calida is chilled to the bone?" Ramona said. "The privy is along this passage, next to the bathing room. Will you have a hot bath, Calida? Or shall I bring hot water here for your wash basin?"

Calida did not want to trouble her host with the work of fetching water up the stairs for a bath.

Skylar knelt by the hearth. She struck a flint to her knife, lighting the tinder. "Calida has earned a bath. I will bring the water." She rose, kissed Calida tenderly on the cheek, and disappeared through the doorway with Ramona.

The fire had taken hold nicely. Calida warmed herself in front of it, letting her worries fade away. She felt a surge of affection for Skylar. She could never repay her for what she'd done for them. And it was no light thing, the way she felt about her.

There had been lovers before. Most were brief affairs. One had lasted almost three seasons before word had gotten around that her lover was not a man. Skylar, though. Calida bit her lip as her body reacted to the name flowing through her mind. Skylar was different. Perhaps it was because of all they'd been through. Skylar was tender, and kind, brave, and exceedingly handsome. Too handsome for Calida's good, in truth. Her feelings for Skylar could run very deep in time. For the first time since Freya's death, there was someone in her life that Calida could rely on. If she could let herself rely on anyone, it would, perhaps, be Skylar.

A knock at the door disturbed Calida's musings. Ramona walked through with a bundle of clothes. She held out a shift and a robe. "You can wear these while waiting for your bath. And here are traveling breeches, a shirt, and a tunic. I am beside myself with curiosity about your journey. But please take as long as you wish to refresh yourself. Linden is tending to your horses. I will go down and prepare a good, hot meal for us all."

Calida was overwhelmed suddenly. She was in a strange land with no means to support herself, and Ramona was nothing but kind. She clasped Ramona's hands in hers. She wanted to say much. "Thank you," was all she managed.

It was enough. Ramona squeezed Calida's hands with a smile and left again.

❖

Calida stepped into the kitchen, warm, clean, blissfully refreshed, and ravenously hungry.

Ramona was busy at the hearth, stirring a pot of something that smelled wonderful.

"What can I do to help?" Calida said.

Ramona turned and smiled. "You look good in that blue tunic. It complements the color of your hair."

"Thank you. It must have been very expensive."

Ramona shook her head. "No. It is quite old now, but it was reasonable."

"Really? In Alba, such a deep color would cost a lot of money. And the cloth is thick and warm. I appreciate that!"

Ramona laughed. "I could tell that you are finding our climate uncomfortable. Skylar told me about your extraordinary journey while you were bathing. I cannot tell you how welcome you are. We are taught the basics about life in Alba. I do not believe any Gaean has been there for decades."

"We are taught you do not exist! We are told there is nothing but poisoned land beyond Alba's northern edge."

"I am glad to hear it." Ramona looked grave. "Not because I want your people to suffer, but because I fear Gaea would be in mortal danger from your king." She transferred the contents of the pot to a terracotta dish, which Ramona took through to a large room adjoining the kitchen. In it was a rectangular oak table, large enough to seat twenty or more. She was reminded of home, long ago, when Mama and Papa were alive, and their mealtimes were rich with family, friends, and neighbors.

Tonight, it was just five of them. Six, with Kit under the table. He ate roasted fowl from a bowl at the foot of Florian's chair. Ramona had prepared a feast of roasted meat, a lightly spiced vegetable stew, steamed grains, and fresh bread. Calida had not eaten so well since Nathaniel and Mary's farmstead. She spared a thought for Raoul and Petro and prayed they were happy.

Skylar sat beside her, looking fine in an orange shirt that complemented her skin tone and dark hair. It was the first time Calida had seen her in any color but tan. "Are all butch uniforms tan?" it occurred to her to ask.

Skylar broke off from tearing into a thick slice of bread with her teeth. "Yes," she said through a mouthful of crumbs. She reached for Calida's hand, her eyes dancing with amusement. "Had we been in Gaea, you would have known me for a warrior from the start."

"Oh, I saw the warrior in you," Calida teased her. Warrior was a word she could say with warmth. It was a different article from soldier or guard.

Florian wore a deep red dress delicately embroidered with beads that glittered in the lamplight.

"You look beautiful," Calida said.

Florian swelled with delight. "I could not resist such a wondrous robe. But, do not fear, Mama, I will wear it for this meal only."

"Why?" Ramona asked immediately.

"Too many people will notice me if I wear this." Florian was surprised at the question.

"That does not matter in Gaea," Skylar said. "You can be noticed here."

"No one minds, truly?" Florian was wide-eyed with wonder.

"Oh, Florian," Linden said. "I am sorry you had to hide and be afraid. I wish it had been different for you."

Calida leaned in and kissed Florian's cheek.

"We let our children decide how to dress and choose their toys. We do not have such a thing as boys' clothes or girls' toys like I believe you do in Alba," Ramona said.

"We do indeed," Calida said wryly. "Excuse me, Linden, do you like to be called he or she? We use she in public, do we not, Florian?"

"For safety," Florian added.

"We use he at home, though," Calida said.

"Neither," Linden replied. "I am ze."

"Some people use ze and zir as pronouns," Ramona explained.

"People like me, who do not feel either she or he. I am both and neither," Linden said in a gentle way.

"But that is how I feel, as well." Florian turned solemnly to Calida. "I would like to be called ze and zir. If I may."

"Of course. If that is what you wish." Calida smiled.

"Much is different here. For the better, I hope." Skylar sneaked a roasted fowl leg to Kit, who delicately separated the meat from the bone and wolfed it in a couple of bites.

"Skylar, will you visit Hera while you're here?" Ramona asked.

Skylar glanced at Calida and Florian. "I know we are close to my mother's homestead here," she sighed. "And it has been some time since I visited. All the same, I am unsettled until we have seen the leader and gained citizenship for Calida and Florian."

Ramona laid down her spoon. "That is important, I am sure, for all of you. However, you should know, Skylar, I had heard Hera is…" Ramona hesitated. "Ailing. She is not working much. Sometimes, she is not seen in the village for days, even weeks at a time."

Skylar's face twisted. Calida knew not if it was with pain or guilt. Skylar had not spoken of any family or friends during their acquaintance.

"Ramona, I am sure my mother will manage without me for a few weeks. She has lived this far without anything I say or do influencing her behavior. She needs her quieting potions more than she has ever needed me."

Calida slipped her hand over Skylar's. It appeared that Skylar's mother was addicted to sleeping plants. How was that possible in a free land? It was undoubtedly commonplace in Alba, where strife and pain were everywhere.

"I understand your motives, Ramona," Skylar said more gently. "But it is vital that Calida and Florian are settled in Gaea. That is all I can think of for the present."

Ramona nodded. "Well, Calida," she said, deftly changing the subject. "Are you also telepathic? Or empathic, perhaps?"

Calida laughed quizzically. "I do not understand these words." She winced. Skylar's tense grip on her hand bordered on causing pain.

"A telepath can read thoughts. An empath reads feelings. You do not have these skills in Alba?" Linden said.

"I am sure they do, but let us hear more about what you have been doing, Linden. How are you faring at school?" Skylar interrupted quickly.

Calida glanced at her before turning to Ramona. "Why do you ask?"

"Because Skylar is a telempath, of course," Linden said cheerfully.

Skylar went rigid.

Calida dropped her hand. She struggled to understand. Were they saying that Skylar could read her thoughts? Truly? Was she able to pry inside a person's head to know their private thoughts? Had she been doing it all this time? Had she done that to Florian?

Suddenly, she could not breathe. Calida pushed her chair back. She barely heard the scrape of the chair across the floor beneath the blood pounding in her ears.

She had to get away. She could not look at anyone.

She rushed from the room and through the front door, not caring if it rained or snowed or if she met a hurricane.

She did not care where she went as long as it was away from Skylar.

❖

Skylar ran after Calida, her stomach in knots.

Calida was not at the front of the house or at the side.

Skylar rounded the stable and saw her at the bottom of the garden where the woodlands began. She gripped the top rail of Ramona's low fence, her back to the house.

Skylar's boots crunched on the gravel path.

"I do not want company," Calida said to the dark outlines of the trees.

Skylar stopped mid-step. Not fire but ice flowed from Calida. Skylar's small spark of hope spluttered out.

"At first, there was no need," she told the back of Calida's head. "It was so dangerous in Alba, and I was sure we would part. I always had to return to Gaea." Calida's hair was loose. It fell, almost solidly black in the dark of night, across her shoulders and down her back. Animated by the breeze, strands of hair rose and fell as if encouraging Skylar's explanation. "And then I came to care for you, but you were Alban. You did not know of these skills, and prejudice is high in your country. Even here in Gaea, not everyone understands or welcomes my abilities. So I kept quiet. I believed we would have to separate, and I could not risk alienating my only friend..." Skylar's throat tightened. "...my only two friends in your land."

Calida's shoulders snapped upright with anger. The change was both welcome and filled Skylar with dread.

"I am sick when I think you have been slipping in and out of my mind with no knowledge or consent from me."

"I have not. There are rules. I realized you did not know how to shield, and I did not, would never pry."

"How can I believe that is true?" Calida spoke so softly, and sadly, tears welled in Skylar.

By the Goddess, why had she not been honest with Calida when she'd had the chance? "I do not know how or if you can trust me…" she began.

Calida raised her head, straightening her spine. Even her flowing hair lay flat and silent now. "I cannot," she sighed.

"Then what will we do?" Skylar asked.

Calida seemed to consider Skylar's question. There was no kindness flowing from her, nothing for Skylar to lean into. She had grown so very used to leaning into Calida. "I will come with you to your leader. I would have citizenship for Florian's sake. He is too good, too pure, too sensitive to return to Alba." She turned and faced Skylar then.

Skylar ached to reach out a hand, to pull Calida into her arms, even just to see Calida's expression soften.

"I know not what to do." Calida shook her head. "It is huge. That you did not tell me, Skylar. I do not know where we can go from here."

The words cut sharper than any knife, and Skylar knew she had made a terrible error of judgment. "I would change everything if I could."

Calida smiled sadly. "We went through so much. We have only known each other for a short time. I let things move too fast, Skylar." Calida was not angry anymore, and she was right there, so close. Skylar could reach out and hold her.

Except Calida had moved beyond her touch.

❖

Skylar stared at the surface of the table, unseeing. Calida had gone straight to bed.

Kit came into the dining room and padded over. Skylar rubbed his head. He snuggled down against her legs. "Thank you, my friend. I am glad of your gentle warmth."

"Oh dear, Skylar. Did it not go well with Calida?" Ramona stood in the doorway bearing two cups. She sat in the chair next to Skylar. "Chamomile tea?" Ramona held out one of the cups.

Skylar took it. "Thank you. And no, it did not go well."

"I am so sorry, Skylar. I thought Calida knew."

Skylar looked into the concerned eyes of her old friend. Ramona was not telepathic or empathic. She was lovely and cared for everybody, from the animals and birds who wandered into her garden to the guests and travelers who passed through. They knew each other from Elderwell. After her sister Cora's death, Hera had medicated her grief to the point that she rarely woke. Skylar had grown thin and unkempt and, after a few months, quite wild. Ramona had been the one to draw Skylar back into village life. They grew close. Years later, they became lovers for a time. When Skylar left for the butch compound, their relationship turned to the close friendship it was still.

"Why did you not tell her?" Ramona asked.

"There was so much to explain, so much I had to hide. Ramona, you have no idea what Alba is like. It's a terrible place—far worse than the tales describe. It was terrifying, even for a warrior."

"I believe it." Ramona reached across to hold Skylar's hand. "I am sure Calida will forgive you. It is not that big a thing, is it?"

"But it is. They do not believe in telepaths or empaths in Alba."

"They must exist, though, surely?"

Skylar shrugged. "I think they do. I met one. But nobody shields. I had to curb my powers. It was exhausting."

Ramona sipped her tea. "The children are sharing Linden's room. I asked Calida. Florian is a lovely child."

"Ze is." It was painful to imagine being without Florian. Skylar swallowed. She must try to repair this damage between herself and Calida.

"You are heading directly to Civitas, then?"

"Yes. I want to attend to Calida's and Florian's citizenship as soon as possible," she told Ramona. "There is also the matter of my crossing the border. I may be disciplined."

Ramona looked horrified. "Surely not? You were going to the aid of this beautiful fellow." She reached down to stroke Kit's back. He groaned happily in his sleep.

"I need to face my superiors. I can do that at the leader building at the same time that we gain an audience for Calida and Florian."

Ramona smiled gently. "You are in love with her, aren't you?"

"Very much." Skylar rested her head on Ramona's shoulder.

"Then you must fight for her, brave warrior. In time, she will see your patience and kindness the way I do. I am sure of it."

Skylar wished for that with everything she possessed. If only the Goddess would smile on her and soften Calida's heart.

Chapter Ten

Calida walked along the wide pavement of a great road in the astonishing capital. Civitas was packed with buildings and teeming with people, horses, carts, donkeys, dogs, and cats. The occasional green space or fountain relieved the noise, smells, dust, and constant traffic.

Shops and houses were plentiful but similar in size and decoration. Calida was impressed with the lack of beggars or shanty settlements. At least she saw none in the vast streets leading to the ruler's building. The sun shone from a cloudless sky. It was warm enough for Calida to unbuckle her long coat as they walked. Underneath, she wore a splendid auburn riding dress bequeathed by Ramona. It had flowing sleeves, and the lower half split to form breeches. It was embroidered with veins to resemble a leaf. She had tried to refuse it, but Ramona had pressed it upon her. Now, she was glad for it as she passed city folk, and she received more than one appreciative look.

The city dwellers were not as friendly as those in the small towns and villages, but they were not unwelcoming. Many smiled at Skylar in her freshly mended, washed, and pressed uniform.

Florian walked beside her, wearing zir red dress and carrying Kit in a traveling sling. Kit's fur and Florian's long dark hair shone with grooming. Kit was pressed against Florian, observing his surroundings with caution. Calida mirrored his trepidation. Skylar had said their citizenship application would be granted without issue. However, word had reached them on the road that they were called before the leader herself.

Calida could not relax until the permission to stay was granted. She had yet to make any decision about Skylar despite mulling things over for the last four days. They had rested for two days at Ramona's house. Calida and Skylar had been civil to each other if awkward. Skylar had looked unhappy but had not once urged Calida to talk about their situation. It was a point in her favor.

Calida's anger had cooled. Part of her wanted to forgive and move forward, but her head urged discretion, and she listened to it now. Maybe it was prejudice, but she shuddered when she thought of Skylar sensing her feelings and knowing her thoughts. The only things Calida owned were the knives in her coat and her mind.

They passed water troughs and drinking fountains. No one stood with their hand held out for payment. A man sat behind a small table. On it was a pot of soup and a large basket of bread.

"Is he a merchant?" Calida asked.

Skylar craned her neck to see where Calida had gestured to.

"No. That's a traveler stop. They offer simple food free of charge to any in need."

Calida was impressed. "Like the supply caches. Who pays for all of this?"

Skylar smiled. "The citizens of Gaea. All workers give part of their wages for the common good."

"Part of our wages are taken also," Calida said sardonically. "To line the King's pockets." She smiled brightly at the man running the traveler stop. He smiled back.

Calida swelled with a sudden burst of hopefulness. She felt like a young girl again. It had been a long, long time since she had dared to dream of better things. Here, she was in a grand city where the poor were cared for. She was safe. Florian was safe. By nightfall, perhaps they would have a real future in this country.

Calida glanced at Skylar and caught her breath despite her misgivings. She sighed. Their relationship could be discussed and decided later. This was not the time for differences. Let them walk into the leader building united.

❖

The leader's chamber was a large room built from pale stone slabs fixed together with sand-colored mortar. There were many weeks of work in the construction and as many again in the decoration. The walls curved to form an arched ceiling, giving the impression of standing within an airy cavern. Long, glassed windows were set into the walls and dressed with finely embroidered curtains. The curtains were open, allowing sunlight to shine through. Sconces on the walls brought fiery amber torchlight to the room.

Calida was struck by a large painting on the wall opposite a dais where the leader sat. The painting depicted a group of thirteen people in clothes similar to the everyday outfits worn in Alba. Three were seated. Ten others stood. Some presented as women or men, while many others seemed to be masculine females and feminine males. Their complexions ranged from dark to pale, with most being brown or black. An owl sat on the shoulder of one woman whose eyes were closed. Many were young, although there were also people of middle years and elders in the solemn group. Many had injuries. Some had weapons. Others the crystals and wands of witchcraft. The air around the painting shimmered with something that reached inside Calida and pulsed.

"The founders," Skylar murmured.

Calida pulled back from the painted scene. Florian was gazing at it, too, and looked as fixed as Calida had been moments before. She took Florian's hand and followed Skylar forward to the dais.

The leader was seated on a gilded chair, flanked by others. Calida did not know if they were servants or members of her government. Calida's footsteps on the stone floor echoed in the silence, and she felt suddenly self-conscious.

When the leader turned to face them, Calida was filled with such intense dislike she caught her breath.

The leader rose with a broad smile and opened her arms. A gentle grace danced in her eyes. She was simply and elegantly dressed. The cloth of her long robe was fine but was not ornately embroidered. She wore a ring and a pair of small studs in her ears but no other jewelry. Her long, brown hair, streaked with gray, was held within a plain black band. She was paler than Calida with a golden olive complexion. She had few signs of maturity on her face, but she was not a young woman.

Calida's reaction to her was puzzling. Perhaps it was because she was a governor. Calida had never interacted well with bailiffs, protectorates, justices, and their like. Calida had met none who treated commoners with fairness or respect.

"Skylar," the leader's voice was confident and pleasant. "We are delighted to receive you home."

Skylar swelled with pride. Calida was happy for her, but she looked at the leader and could not shake away the doubts that swarmed in her stomach.

Calida looked at the Gaeans, who had risen with their leader. They smiled. They seemed warm. They disquieted her, these people who were so secure and safe, especially the leader with her radiant glow and careful, calm words.

Can I trust no one who is not brittle and bitter? People forged strong from being made weak. Is trust so precious a commodity that I must eke it out?

"You are a treasured warrior. Brave and generous," the leader said.

Calida smiled at Skylar then. She *was* a hero. She deserved her country's praise.

The leader's smile faded. Looking into her pale eyes was like diving into spring meltwater. Early in the season, when the temperature has risen only enough to soften ice from the block.

"Before we get to the matter of your actions, you requested an audience on behalf of two others. Is that correct?"

"Yes, leader." Skylar's voice rang out loud and true.

"They are the woman and child who stand before us?"

"Yes, leader."

The leader tensed, and Calida's stomach twisted with the familiarity of fear. Instinctively, she reached for Florian's hand beside her.

The leader looked Calida in the face for the first time. "You have crossed our boundary without our consent." Her voice was so perfectly quiet, so perfectly cold, her animosity was palpable. "We have no way of knowing if you are genuine refugees or spies. The security of Gaea is my responsibility, and I will not risk the sanctity of our border. I am loath to imprison you for the entirety of your lives, and therefore, you will be returned to Alba."

Calida wished the words shocked her less. She wished she had lived a different life, and she certainly wished Florian had. Rage growled in her belly as she stared back at the leader, and she did not hide her contempt.

"Leader, you cannot," Skylar cried. Her voice was not confident now. She *was* shocked. "They will not be safe. They are not spies. Calida did not know of the border or Gaea."

"So you claim, Skylar."

"I *know*. I am a telepath."

The look the leader gave Skylar was unpleasant. "And you have violated your position if you have monitored minds without consent."

"But that is not what I did. Let me explain."

The leader beckoned to the guards standing behind the dais. "Lieutenant Larkrye, we will deal with you later. Guards, take the Albans to the detention cells." She met Calida's eyes again. Calida noted the leader had not looked at Florian once. "I regret this lack of hospitality, but I will not endanger my beloved country." Her eyes showed no regret. And Calida knew precisely what her initial dislike had forewarned. The leader's heart was built of stone. The chamber was a fitting environment.

Two guards, swords unsheathed, came toward Calida and Florian.

Skylar stepped in front of Calida. She raised a hand to the guards but spoke to the leader. "By the Goddess, punish me, but do not punish them."

"Do not disgrace yourself further, Skylar. Must I arrest you, also? If you do not end this behavior right now, you will be discharged from the butch regiment. A promising career will be entirely halted, and you will face prison charges."

Skylar stepped aside. She threw Calida a look of utter bewilderment.

"Escort the Albans." The leader waved a hand at the guards.

Calida squeezed Florian's hand. She could not bear to think what zir feelings must be. With the Gaean guard's fingers tight around the top of Calida's arm, she left the grand chamber.

It was a bitter acknowledgment that her misgivings had been right.

❖

The room where Skylar stood was not grand. Skylar was surprised the stark room existed in the leader building. It was barely big enough for the people crammed into it.

She had forced herself not to protest further when Calida and Florian had been taken away. The leader's mind was fixed for some reason Skylar could not determine.

Skylar had then been escorted to the broom cupboard or whatever it was by a second pair of civic guards. They flanked her now, swords in hand. A third guard was positioned at the door. A butch warrior of the rank of captain stood crisply to attention in front of the shabby wall opposite Skylar. The leader sat beside the captain on a chair grander than the room merited, and next to her was a second lieutenant from the fae regiment, the platoons composed of feminine male warriors.

Skylar swallowed. She reeled from what had just happened and struggled to focus on her situation. With the assembled personnel, it could only be a disciplinary.

"Lieutenant Larkrye."

Skylar snapped to attention. Neither officer had introduced zirself. Skylar supposed they belonged to local Civitarian platoons.

The captain was stern. "Larkrye, you have admitted breaking the law on two counts. One: you crossed the border without permission. Two: you illegally brought Albans into Gaea. As you have admitted the charges, we will proceed to sentencing."

What? "But I want to explain, Captain. Also, I am entitled to a representative, am I not?"

The captain was angry, embarrassed, and shielding firmly from Skylar. "You do not need a representative unless you are changing your statement. Did you not cross into Alba? Did you not bring two foreign citizens into Gaea?"

Skylar had thought warriors facing charges were entitled to representation, whether they admitted charges or not.

"Do you wish to change your statement, Lieutenant? Did you encounter the woman and child in Gaea?"

"No. No. Calida and Florian crossed with me. I brought them here." Was this why there was such resentment and fear in the room? Skylar was unsure from whom it emanated, just that it was powerful.

"Are you worried that the border is compromised?" she asked, blurting out a sudden thought.

The second lieutenant appraised her coolly. The lieutenant was older than Skylar and younger than the founders, but not by much. "Is it?"

"I do not believe so, Second Lieutenant. The Albans do not know Gaea exists, at least not any I encountered."

"You told them we exist?" the captain asked sharply.

"No. Only Calida and Florian. And that was immediately before we crossed. I have nothing to hide. Bring a telepath here to verify what I say. My mind is open."

"Lieutenant! That is not how Gaeans proceed." The leader spoke for the first time. "Your mother was a child founder. You were expected to have a distinguished career. We are shocked and disappointed at your conduct. Full information will be collected from you anon. First, we must deal with sentencing."

Skylar was thoroughly confused, and now she was worried. "If you will just let me explain—"

"Silence, Larkrye." The captain's eyes drilled into Skylar's.

"These are two of the most serious crimes in Gaean law," the leader said. "You have compromised our border security. There is no allowable justification. The punishment for breaking this law is life imprisonment."

Skylar stared stupidly at the leader, unable to believe she had heard correctly.

"However," the leader continued, "your record is clean, and we are indebted to your mother. Further, I believe you acted compassionately. Skylar, I will commute the sentence if you agree to tell no one what has occurred. You must never speak of Alba or of having crossed the border."

The captain gave a slight cough. "The leader has generously allowed you to remain in the regiment. But you will be stripped of your rank. Do you accept these terms, warrior?"

Skylar stared ahead, grasping at words that slipped away from meaning.

"We need your answer, warrior." The second lieutenant sounded impatient.

Skylar felt a connection between the leader and the two officers. What it was, she could not say, and she dared not reach out with her senses.

They wanted an answer from her. Skylar felt an insane desire to laugh. Did they really want her to say if she preferred to go to prison?

"I accept," she said numbly.

The atmosphere in the room eased by the faintest degree.

"With one condition." Skylar hardly believed her gall. The captain's eyebrows shot up so far and so fast Skylar feared they might fly from the captain's head entirely.

"You are in no position—" the captain spluttered. Skylar had some sympathy. The captain must be excruciatingly embarrassed that Skylar was butch.

The leader held up a hand. "I will hear it."

"Do not return them at the western side of the border. It is safer for them if they cross at the east."

After long moments, the leader nodded. And then she rose.

"I will leave you to question Larkrye, Captain, Second Lieutenant. Send me the full transcription when you are done with her."

The leader walked from the room, leaving Skylar in the stuffy room with two coldly furious officers and many questions of her own. She barely registered the shame of being demoted. She was so perplexed at what had just taken place.

"Start at the beginning," said the captain. "Explain exactly why you crossed the enchanted border."

❖

In the basement of the leader building, in a gaol cell, Florian lay slumped on a small wooden cot pushed against the wall. Calida perched on the end of the bed, staring at the metal struts that barred the doorway. The room was cold and bleakly lit, but it was a far cry from Alba's sodden, bug-infested cells. It looked too clean for roaches. Calida doubted bed bugs lurked in the folds of the thyme-scented gray wool blanket. Beds and blankets? Alban prisoners would be pleased to find a dirty rush mat on the floor.

Calida was acquainted with Alban gaol cells from visiting her mother. It had been a futile, hopeless visit. Five years after Mama's arrest, word had come through a cousin that Mama had not been executed but taken far south. Calida had left Florian and traveled to the prison with the little wealth she'd accrued. It was just enough to bribe the guards. She had been permitted to see her mother for a few precious moments. And then she'd had to leave her there in squalor.

In Gaea, even the chamber pot smelled clean. The cell was a metaphor for the country: sanitized, civil, and repressive.

Calida stiffened at movement beyond the cell.

"You do not have long. I will complete my rounds, and then you must leave. I already regret agreeing to this."

Calida recognized the guard's voice. And then another's, one she knew intimately.

"Thank you. I will not forget it," Skylar murmured.

"You should. You must," the guard's voice was low and tense. "Now, be quick. There are not many prisoners tonight. It will not take long to look in on them."

Skylar appeared at the cell door. She took a deep breath and smiled hesitantly.

Hope surged at the sight of her, but Calida checked herself. Perhaps Skylar had a plan. Maybe she did not.

"Florian is managing to sleep, then." Skylar took Florian in, reaching out her hand toward him.

"Why are you here?" Calida asked. Fear that Skylar would let them down roughened her voice.

Skylar looked upset, tired, and harried. The silver star was gone from her tunic, leaving a circle that was brighter and less worn than the cloth around it. "I can never repay your help in Alba."

Florian stirred. Ze sat up with a cry. "Skylar. Have you come to get us out? Can we stay after all?"

Skylar bit down on her bottom lip. "No. I have come to say good-bye."

Ze stared at her, zir eyes wide and zir body as stiff as the hard cot.

"I'm sorry, I should never have brought you here. I am ashamed I did so." Skylar turned her gaze on Calida.

Hope vanished, and fury swept through Calida in its stead. Skylar had given up on them entirely.

"Forgive me." Skylar dropped her head.

Florian started to cry. Calida took zir into the strong folds of her arms. She wanted Skylar to leave. She never wanted to see her again.

"Take this, please." Skylar pushed a fist through the bars and opened her hand. The resin squirrel sat on her palm. "I want you to have it."

There was an urgency in Skylar's eyes. Calida did not understand it, and she did not care. How could Calida have felt anything for this butch? She turned her face away.

Skylar tossed the squirrel toward the bed, where it fell onto the blanket. Calida let it sit there. Florian continued to cry.

And Skylar walked away.

Somewhere beyond their cell, a door closed softly.

❖

They were still in a cell, this time a carriage with bars at the window and a reinforced door. Calida shifted for the umpteenth time. One arm was cuffed to an iron ring set into the frame, and her feet were bound together. The position did not make for comfortable sleeping. She doubted the guards cared. She could see the flicker of their campfire through a crack in the carriage wall. She pulled against the cuff, wanting her coat and knives more than anything, but they had taken it from her. With a knife, she could release the cuff in seconds. The ring did not budge, and Calida was sure one of the guards was on watch at the front of the carriage. She had heard the creak of the woman's boots on the driver's footrest moments before.

Florian's hands were tied together, and ze leaned against her for comfort. She glanced at her child, and the breath caught in her throat. Florian's expression was relaxed, and zir eyelashes fluttered gently. Rage simmered as Calida reflected on Florian's deep and bitter disappointment. An owl shrieked nearby, compounding their captivity in the cold quiet of the night.

Florian's eyes opened. "Mama, I was thinking. Even though we must return to Alba, I am glad we came here."

"You are?"

Ze nodded. "If we had not, I would never have known it was possible to be free."

Calida bit her lip. It was true. But it made the pain of leaving all the sharper.

"Maybe there are other places like this. Lands that would accept us."

"What do you mean?"

"The King and his guards and bailiffs told us Alba was the end of the world. They said beyond the northern border was a wasteland. That was a lie." Florian sat up or tried to. Zir tied hands brought zir up short. Calida fumed again. Could any parent bear to see her child roped so? But Florian's spirit was not impeded. Zir eyes shone. "Mama, what if there are other lands beyond the Alban southern sea? They tell us there is nothing but Alba. But we know that's not true."

Calida was astounded. This child, this gentle soul, was full of hope. Ze was not thinking about the danger they would be plunged into in a matter of days. Florian rested back against her, and she let zir dream. She had not the heart to do otherwise.

She clenched her fist in frustration, and it hurt. It really hurt because she had forgotten the carving in her hand. Against her better judgment, she had kept the thing. She wanted to toss it far away. She did not want to think of Skylar and her broken promises. Florian did not need to dream of lands that did not exist. There was a safe land right here that would not accept them.

They helped their own poor. But they turned away from the tyrannized across their border.

Calida should never have let herself believe in the possibility of a better life.

Damn Skylar, and to hell with her carving. What was she trying to say anyway, to be prepared? As if Calida needed reminding. She had been prepared from the age of two. Mama had seen to that.

Damn her insolence. Did Skylar learn nothing about her in their time together? She dropped the carving onto the seat in disgust.

She had not taken Skylar for a fool.

Calida shifted to lessen the ache in her shoulder. She must conceive of a plan. Outsiders were not welcomed in the border regions, and they would return with nothing. She did not think the resin figure would aid them, and she was angry enough to smash it. But the lump in her throat when she looked at it stopped her. She kept thinking of the night Skylar had whittled away at it.

Calida sat up, stick straight. Skylar was many things. She was annoying, secretive, and rash, but she *was not* a fool.

Be prepared.

Calida slipped the figure into her pocket and nudged Florian awake.

Ze sat up, confused and sleepy. "What, Mama?"

Skylar's face in the cell flashed through Calida's mind. She knew that look. Skylar had been trying to send her a message.

The owl shrieked again. The guards murmured to each other, and then their voices retreated. It sounded as if they were walking away into the woods. Calida pressed her face to the crack in the carriage wall and saw the guards had indeed disappeared. This was new. But why had the guards deserted them?

Had they been in Alba, the King would not have gone to the trouble of returning them to a border that was not supposed to exist. He would simply have killed them.

Of course, in civilized Gaea, that would be unthinkable.

But Calida did not trust a leader who would so readily return a woman and a child to danger and persecution. What if the leader did not want word of Gaea spreading amongst the Albans?

Calida pulled at the iron ring. If she were right, it would not be the guards that came to kill them. They would send mercenaries.

"What is it, Mama?" Florian asked as Calida began to frantically now tug at the ring.

The iron cut into her wrist, but the iron fixings gave a little. She gave it a wrench and gritted her teeth against the pain in her shoulder.

Footsteps padded lightly on the ground outside. Hell's teeth, that would be the cutthroat sent to dispatch them.

With an almighty wrench, Calida broke the ring from its fixings. Pain shot along her arm from wrist to shoulder. Ignoring it, she bent to Florian's ropes.

The carriage door swung open with a crash.

Calida thrust herself in front of Florian, arms raised to defend zir.

A cloaked figure stood in the carriage doorway.

Before Calida could strike, they threw back their hood.

To reveal Skylar bearing a knife.

Calida's mind raced. She knew Skylar could not possibly have been sent to kill them. And if she had been, she would not be smiling so ludicrously.

She reached behind Calida and cut through the ropes that bound Florian.

Ze pushed past Calida into Skylar's arms. "I knew you would come."

Calida did not have Florian's faith or easy forgiveness.

Skylar put out her hand. Calida hesitated to take it.

"Seriously?" Skylar said, cutting through the rope at Calida's feet. "The guards will return at any moment."

Calida stepped out of the carriage. Kit bounded up to Florian and allowed himself to be enveloped in a hug. "What happened to them?"

Skylar tossed Calida her long coat. "I paid a child to come to them with coin and ask for aid in the village. They obviously did not feel you were capable of escape. We have mounts waiting. They will return and find you gone, and we need a head start if we hope to outride them." Skylar turned, running through the clearing into the darkness of the trees beyond. Kit trotted after her. Florian looked expectantly at Calida.

She took a moment to unsheathe a knife from her coat and force open the iron ring. After tossing it to the ground, she took Florian's hand, and they broke into a run, following Skylar and Kit into the dark depths of the forest.

❖

Dawn was breaking when Skylar dared pull up beside a meadow with a trickle of running water. She had taken the quiet roads, even though there was no chance of word having traveled faster than they had. Not yet.

Messenger birds would be sent by noon, and by the evening they must be cautious in the surrounding towns and garrisons.

She jumped down from her mount. "The horses must drink. Florian, there is feed in my saddlebag. Will you brush them down and tend to them?"

"Of course." Florian dismounted and flung zir arms around Skylar. "I am so pleased to see you again."

Skylar embraced Florian tightly. "And I you."

Calida stepped gracefully from her horse as Florian untied Kit's sling. Kit padded toward the meadow's long grass.

Do not stray far, Skylar sent to him. *We travel on shortly.*

Kit dipped his head and slipped away, his back arched and his senses focused on the hunt for his breakfast.

"Do we have time to cook and camp?" Calida handed the reins of her horse to Florian but directed her question to Skylar. Florian led all three mounts to the stream.

Skylar shook her head regretfully. "If you can ride on, I suggest we do so until noon. We should travel at the quieter times of day, in the late afternoon and evening. We must avoid officials."

Calida eased out her shoulders and loosened the braid around her hair.

Skylar glanced at her. "Calida, whatever may or may not be between us, there was no moment I considered deserting you. I would not leave either of you to your miserable fate."

Calida raised her eyebrows. Her mouth twitched. "I think we have managed to be jovial once or twice in the entirety of our *miserable* Alban lives."

Skylar smiled. She knew Calida mocked her, and she did not care. She was high on the thrill of adventure. The leader had made a rebel of her. Leader be damned! Calida and Florian were worth ten of her.

Calida leaned against the trunk of an aged oak. "Here we find ourselves again, Skylar. Thrust together and in peril. Where should we go, my great butch warrior?"

Skylar grinned at the warmth in Calida's voice. "East and then northwest. There is a powerful crone I would speak to named Osheana. I hope that she will aid us, but I know not where she is. If you agree, I would have us ride to Thale."

Calida's eyebrows lifted at that. "The compound where all the butch warriors live?"

Skylar frowned mockingly. "Not all. I am standing before you."

"Indeed you are." Calida took two steps. "Right before me." She tentatively wound her fingers around Skylar's. "I guess we must learn to live with each other's ways." She blinked up at Skylar, and then she kissed her.

Fire laced through her. They had been so nearly parted forever. And now Calida was pressed up warm against her with the scent of grass underfoot and wild rose somewhere near and the prickle of morning dew in the air.

After a while, Calida pulled away. "I do not trust easily, Skylar. For me, that is everything. You came back for us, and I love you for that. I do not know what to do about my feelings for you."

"You said you loved me for rescuing you. I will have to do that often." Skylar dared to tease her.

Calida looked distinctly unimpressed. "I need no one to rescue me."

Skylar smiled. She tossed words over her shoulder as she walked toward Florian and the horses at the stream. "We all need someone to help us every once in a while, Calida. Even you. Life is too hard and too lonely without the gift of support."

CHAPTER ELEVEN

B reathing in the familiar sweet scent of the dry plains grasses, Skylar crept along Thale's fencing. All regimental compounds were built with walls high enough to withstand attack, even though there had been none since Gaea was founded.

A quarter moon hung lazily in the velvet sky, throwing scant light. This was to Skylar's advantage. As would be the relaxed attitude of the sentries above. In all the years and seasons Skylar had lived at Thale, there had been no incidents for the watch tower to report.

She did not wish to provide them with one. She sent her mind soaring and sensed two humans. That was unusual. The night watch had been reduced to one warrior many years ago.

Skylar dampened her spirit. It was the telepathic equivalent of treading softly. She knew the compound intimately. She followed the sturdy, circular fence until she stood on the perimeter of the enlisted personnel's sleeping quarters. Efren had no interest in leadership. Bhaltair, by contrast, was four years their junior but had already risen to the rank of lieutenant.

That did not matter now. She was here to wake Efren and find out where her grandmother was.

Skylar sensed the block of slumbering humans that was the general warrior billet. She felt for Efren within the mass. And found her room on the other side of the wood fencing.

Skylar put two fingers to her lips and blew, emulating the cry of a night jay.

It had been years since Skylar had signaled this way. She prayed Efren would hear and remember, for she had no other plan. The crone, Osheana, though cantankerous, would help them for Hera's sake. Skylar's mother had crossed the border with the founders as a small orphaned child under Osheana's care. Skylar had known Osheana briefly before Osheana took the hermit's robes.

The call pierced the steady drone of crickets. For a moment, all was still. Then the crickets trilled again, and Skylar was left to wait and hope.

A faint noise startled her. It could have been the creak of a door. Skylar slowed her breathing to enhance her mind and aural senses.

Footsteps came now, and the muffled clop of hooves. Efren appeared, leading a brown mare.

"Whatever is going on with you, bredren, I will aid you," Efren said in a rush. She usually never worried about anything, but her body was stiff with concern. "Word has been sent from Civitas that you are a deserter."

Skylar slipped her arms around Efren. "I am no deserter."

"I knew you would not be." Efren held Skylar's gaze and sighed.

"I want to go to Osheana. I think she will help us."

"I see. Skylar, is it true you crossed the border?"

Skylar nodded. "I crossed to save a vultrix caught in a trap."

"In a trap?" Efren was horrified.

"I became lost. Journeying home, I met Calida and Florian. Efren, they are kind and clever, and both are at great risk in Alba. I thought the leader would grant them citizenship once she knew their circumstances. Instead, she ordered they be returned."

Efren listened intently. "I will come with you. You will never find my grandmother without me to guide you. I brought supplies."

A heavy boot scraped the dirt road. Skylar drew her sword, praying she would not have to battle another butch warrior to gain her escape.

Efren unsheathed her sword also.

"What is this?" Bhaltair rounded the perimeter bend. "It is early for combat practice, is it not?" He was fully dressed and armed for battle. He carried a pack and led the black stallion Midnight, clad with similarly muffled shoes. His eyes gleamed with the thirst for adventure. "They say you crossed the border, endangering us all."

Skylar met the accusation in his eyes. "Yes. To save a vultrix, and I returned with a fae and a femme."

Bhaltair gave a firm nod. "Good enough for me, bredren."

Skylar grinned. This was the Bhaltair who earned the love of comrades and stole the hearts of many a warrior.

Bhaltair grinned back. "Let us ride then before the snoring sentries realize there is something amiss for once."

Skylar did not attempt to deter either of her comrades. Captain Noro had trained them to act quickly and decisively.

They mounted up. Skylar's heart swelled with a butch on each side of her. Although she rode away from Thale, she was home.

They slipped into the long grasses to be swallowed by the quickening night.

❖

Skylar waited with Calida and Florian, out of sight of the road, for Efren and Bhaltair's return.

The two butch warriors had ridden into Hazelmere. The town forded the great river Shuimu. The Shuimu was deep and wide and ran tumultuously across the northern tip of the central plains. Hazelmere Bridge was the only bridge for leagues. Skylar hoped Efren and Bhaltair would return with the news that Hazelmere was quiet, and they could pass through it quickly and unnoticed.

Three riders came toward them. Two of them were Efren and Bhaltair. The other was a stranger. Skylar observed the stranger with interest. Ze was young, dressed in the dark green of the fae regiment. The fae compound was deep within the great Hapi Forest. The location of compounds often dictated the color of uniforms. The faes were the sisters of butches: feminine people born with a masculine exterior. The fae warrior's skin and hair were deep black. Zir hair was tied with a green braid bearing the fae peacock feather emblem. Ze had a triangular-shaped face with a small nose and strong brows over dark brown eyes. Ze rode upright in the saddle, was of medium build, and muscular.

Efren dismounted, agitated. "This is Maryn, my cousin's partner. She is billeted here. By the luck of the Goddess, Maryn was posted as a bridge sentry."

Maryn swung a muscular thigh over her saddle and jumped down. She warmly greeted Skylar and Calida, but her broadest smile was for Florian. "Dear child, allow me to welcome you to our land. The leader does not speak for the fae. We embrace our own, no matter where they come from. I cannot imagine the hardship of your life. I wish you had grown here amongst us." Maryn was sincere and gentle.

Florian looked shyly at Maryn and then spontaneously hugged her.

When Bhaltair took their horses to graze and drink at the stream, Efren thrust a sheet of paper into Skylar's hand. It was a wanted bill offering a reward for the capture of two Albans and a butch warrior deserter. A crude drawing showed a masculine character in the butch warrior tan uniform, hiding beneath a hooded cloak, wearing a surly, sinister expression. Next to the warrior was a beautiful and fierce brown female with flowing dark hair and a long coat, holding the hand of a small, feminine child. The bad likenesses of Calida and Florian made them look both dangerous and calculating. Calida took the bill from Skylar's hand and laughed aloud.

"At least they captured your beauty," Maryn said.

"But not your bad temper at the cold," Skylar muttered, receiving a nudge to the ribs from Calida.

Efren remained serious. "There are guards on the bridge, both ends."

"But I come bearing gifts." Maryn pulled a pack from one of her saddle bags and drew out several wigs, shirts, skirts, breeches, and tunics of differing degrees of masculinity and femininity. "Might this be of use?" She showed Calida a long, blond wig.

Calida stared thoughtfully at the wanted bill in her hand. "I think I would do better to dress in a masculine way."

Maryn clapped her hands. "How ingenious."

It gave Skylar an idea. "And what if I were feminine?" She took the wig from Maryn and put it on her head.

Everyone laughed. Everyone except Bhaltair. He stared at Skylar in horror.

Maryn looked at Skylar, biting her lip. "I can help you make it look less like a bird's nest."

"It does not look that bad, does it?" Skylar laughed, trailing a long, golden lock between her fingers.

Bhaltair shook his head. Discomfort rose from him. Efren slipped her arm around Bhaltair's waist.

Florian took a tunic from the heap. "Do you think I should look male also?" He did not seem any more comfortable than Bhaltair.

"You do not have to," Skylar said. "That is an extremely poor likeness of you."

"No one will ask you to go against your true essence," Maryn said.

Florian held the tunic to zir chest. "But it would be safer if the bridge sentries see me as male?"

The adults nodded.

"Then, of course, I will do it."

"You are brave, Florian. You show great maturity," Bhaltair said quietly.

They dressed quickly. Calida hid her hair beneath a cap and tried to portray a masculine walk.

"You would do better to disguise yourself as a fae," Skylar quipped.

Efren rolled her eyes. "Ignore Skylar. Your natural gestures are fine. People are accepted for who they are here."

"Besides, we do not have a spare uniform." Maryn nudged Calida. "We would be proud to have you, but the femme regiment would protest fiercely."

Once disguised, they split into three groups: Bhaltair, Maryn, and Efren, who took all the horses and Kit, hidden in a large pack. Calida and Florian. And finally, Skylar, alone.

It was the best way to avoid arousing suspicion.

❖

Maryn, Bhaltair, and Efren had passed through the first guard post with ease. Skylar's throat was as dry as hay stalks as she watched Calida and Florian stand before two guards from the capital. None of the warriors had thought to mention that civil guards had been stationed here.

Skylar hung back, as agreed. She watched and waited, disturbed to see Calida and Florian a hair's breadth from the leader's guards.

But then they waved them on, and Skylar breathed again.

She set off toward a small sentry hut at the edge of the long, wooden bridge.

"Perhaps we should have questioned the butch warriors further," the older guard remarked to his fellow guard as Skylar approached.

"They looked nothing like the one we want. Do you even think Larkrye will be in uniform?" The second guard was younger, calmer, but equally aggressive.

"Who can say? She is arrogant, foolish, and dangerous enough to break the code. She could have brought damnation upon all our heads. I would very much like to be the one to arrest her."

Skylar slowed a few steps before the guards, her name and their words echoing in her ears. She swallowed, trying to effect a nonchalant expression. The older guard held up a hand, indicating she should stop. His eyes searched her face, taking in her clothing and the basket in her hand. He reached into the basket.

"Please do not damage the medicinal plants," Skylar said.

The guard's search became rougher. Then he withdrew his hand, frowning at her hair. Skylar tensed. The guard reached out to touch a strand. Skylar drew back angrily. "How dare you touch me without my consent?"

The guard grimaced, but his hand dropped to his side. "State your name and business in this region."

"Hera. Healer," Skylar gave her mother's name and profession. The roots, leaves, and berries in Skylar's basket lent truth to the lie.

"A healer, eh? I have a monstrous headache. Give me something for it." The second guard's tone was rude. Healers would help any who asked. Either both of these guards were unpleasant, or the leader encouraged their churlish behavior. She should change their name to the uncivil guard.

Skylar only had the few hedgerow plants Calida had thrust into the basket. Everyone knew rosehips were taken to shore off winter colds. She was tempted to give him dandelion leaves, commonly known as wet-the-bed. Instead, she reached for the orange marigold flowers. They were wound healers and would not cure his headache but would do him no harm, either. "Steep these in hot water and drink the tea," she said. "May I pass now?"

"You may not. What is the capital of Gaea?" The older guard blocked her path like a great, surly boulder.

"Civitas." Skylar's throat tightened. Even though the question was simple, it was hard not to fidget and sweat.

"When did work begin on the founders' memorial?"

Dates and information flew from Skylar's head. The herstory of the founders was taught in every Gaean school. Calida would not have been able to answer. Skylar cast her mind back to a dusty summer afternoon in the Elderwell village schoolyard. "It was in the twenty-second year, at the dark of the ninth moon."

The younger guard nodded. But the older one's eyes were fixed on Skylar's wig. "Your hair looks…strange." The guard stared into her face. She felt tendrils drifting at the corners of her mind and slammed a barrier around her thoughts. She slipped a hand into her pocket and groped for the hilt of her dagger. She did not want to kill him, but there were two of them. If she attacked, she'd better make the strike swift and fatal.

The guard moved closer still, and his fingers reached out again. She poured outrage into her expression. "I am a healer, permitted to travel freely from town to town. What is your name, civil guard?"

At last, the guard stepped aside with narrowed eyes and a frown. Skylar walked immediately forward. This, too, could be a test. She forced herself to walk slowly, even though she yearned to break into a run.

No bridge had ever seemed so long. Halfway across, Skylar let her basket drop. As she bent to retrieve it, she glanced back. The guards were watching her.

The sentry post on the other side of the bridge came into view. Calida, Florian, and the warriors were nowhere to be seen. That was something, at least.

Fortunately, the guards ahead were warriors from the general regiments. They were probably locals. Skylar felt someone reaching for her mind as she neared the post. The search was easily blocked. The behavior was unusual and unethical by Gaean standards.

Skylar stated her pretend name and reason for traveling to Hazelmere.

One sentry barely glanced at her. The other, the telepath, scrutinized her steadily for several long moments.

Then ze waved Skylar through.

She stepped from the bridge, deep in thought. Their situation was more precarious than she had thought. The leader was determined to pursue them. And, whatever her professed opinions on empathy and telepathy, she was prepared to defy Gaean laws to find them.

❖

The forest was wild and dense, as if people had no place there. Yet it teemed with life. Skylar felt the growth of plants, animals, and insects vibrating all around her. Stout oak dropped curling orange and yellow leaves at their feet. Mottled gray ash reached high above to create a fiery canopy that blocked the sky. Beech, rowan, lime, holly, and birch pressed into any space not claimed by the great trees. Ivy and brambles crept through the remaining ground, making it impassible on horseback and hard going on foot.

Sharp resin, sweet berries, and the musk of the forest floor filled the air. The day was dry, but they had walked since noon, and all they had found were more trees. Already, the light was beginning to fade, and they had no idea where Osheana's dwelling was.

Despite the pleasant temperature, Skylar shivered. She could not shake the feeling that the forest did not want them there. Something ominous pulsed through the low chatter of insect and bird.

They walked along a deer track in single file. Efren was at the front with her mare trailing behind. Calida followed, and then Florian leading their mounts. Maryn held the reins of the next two steeds so that Bhaltair could walk with his bow unhindered. Skylar brought up the rear. Kit, who usually disappeared to explore and hunt, kept strangely close, padding at Skylar's side.

No one spoke. The only sound apart from birds and insects was their soft footsteps. None of the horses whinnied or grunted, and even they trod lightly.

They passed a hazel heavy with nuts. The downy leaves were verdant, and the shells of the fruit a rich, ripe tan. The tree was ready to harvest, but something stopped Skylar from reaching to take the nuts. Skylar had a daft fancy the action might wake a forest guardian and bring a great force against them.

Bhaltair looked, but he, too, walked past the bounty. Bhaltair had the mindskill of intuition. He could not read people like an empath or telepath, but he sensed things, especially in times of need. Skylar noted that Bhaltair's hand clenched the bow tightly, and an arrow was ready in the other.

It grew darker. Perhaps clouds had covered the sky. It was impossible to see beyond the thick canopy. The trail narrowed as if the forest was linking arms against them. Both humans and horses picked their way carefully over trailing vine and arched rootstock. Florian stumbled. Maryn caught zir and pushed Florian gently upright. All without a word.

Skylar felt something watching and waiting, luring them in. It unnerved her, for she could not sense any life signs except for a family of squirrels and a few birds in the treetops.

So why did her heart race? And why was she compelled to grip the hilt of her knife?

Efren stopped. It had grown too dark to read the expression on her face, but Skylar sensed her concern. "I am lost. This trail has changed since I was last here. The forest has grown. I do not understand how growth this fast is possible, but grown it has."

Florian ran to Skylar. "There are beasts out there. They know we are here, and they are coming for us."

Skylar felt them then, too. Warm-blooded, four-legged predators. Hungry and intent. Hot breath hissed through jagged canines. Thick fur-coated muscular limbs ending with knife-sharp claws. They were kin, working as one.

Wolves.

Somewhere just beyond the trees, a howl rent the air.

Kit shot between Calida and Florian. Calida knelt to him, her hand on his neck. The horses began to shy and pull on their reins.

"Florian, calm the horses," Skylar said, turning to the adults. "Surround the child and the animals."

Maryn took torches from saddlebags. Her hands were steady as she struck flint and passed the heartening flames to Skylar and Efren. Bhaltair had nocked an arrow to his bow. Calida bore a knife in each hand. Skylar and Efren unsheathed swords. Maryn was ready with her flail. The adults stood in a circle around Florian, the horses, and Kit, facing the dark and silent web of trees.

A beast panted into the clearing, open-mouthed, and stopped ten steps from Skylar. Its eyes glowed in the torchlight. Skylar braced herself and took a step forward.

"No, keep tight. Hold the formation." Bhaltair was tense.

Skylar did not dare take her eyes away from the beast before her, yet she knew another wolf was poised before Bhaltair ready to spring. She felt them all around, ten or more. Twice their number.

Florian held on to Kit. Terror rose from both of them. It radiated outwards, and Skylar was sure the wolves had the scent of it.

"I feel these wolves are magical," Maryn spoke quietly as if a loud voice would provoke the creatures to attack.

"I feel it, too," Skylar grunted under her breath. "Where is your grandmother, Efren? Surely, Osheana can aid us."

"You are the only one who can reach her right now, Skylar. You'll need to be within a protective circle to do so. I have some of Iya's teaching. I can cast one," Efren whispered. "The four of us will mark the directions of air, water, fire, and earth. Go inside, Skylar, with Florian and the animals."

"I will not. We need all warriors to hold those wolves back. I will send my mind out and fight alongside you."

"No, Skylar," Bhaltair said firmly. "We must battle in the dark against beasts that see better than we do. Your attention will be split, and we risk Florian and Kit and the horses. Efren is right. Let her cast a circle. Your powers will be stronger within our protection. These beasts are formidable. I feel it."

Bhaltair's strategy and intuition could not be faulted. Skylar moved inward. Kit jumped into her arms, trembling. Florian was also scared, but ze held the reins of all the horses and soothed them in turn.

A wolf growled. The primal sound raked along Skylar's spine. She blocked it out and called to Osheana. She sent a picture of their group surrounded by the beasts.

The wolves closed in. Skylar tried to stay focused internally, but she felt their fury, their blood lust. They had the scent of the horses. The snarling grew louder, more furious. The pack leader barely contained the others. They were so driven by hunger. Skylar tried to push all that awareness aside. She flashed a beacon of images to any mind that could hear. Florian breathed hard and fast. The horses were half out of their wits with fear, and Florian was losing control of them.

Something new came through the forest. A great wind, a storm, a presence Skylar did not wish to battle. It was a power greater than any Skylar had felt before.

The wolves went silent.

No one moved. Not horse, not wolf, not even a leaf. Kit was rigid in Skylar's arms.

Then branches moved aside. Trees parted. A trail appeared where none had been, and on it, a figure stood.

"What is your business here?" The voice was old and loud, rich with witchcraft and ancient lore.

"We seek Osheana," Skylar said boldly. This was the crone or a guardian of hers. Who else could control wolves and wind?

"Iya?" Efren called.

For long moments, silence answered them. Then the figure spoke, "There is a reason my companions guard this forest from intruders. Fosterling, you are always welcome, but you know I do not invite others here."

Efren cleared her throat. "These are friends and siblings, Iya. They have need of your wisdom."

"We have met before, learned crone," Skylar spoke reverently in the manner due a powerful witch of Osheana's years. "Respectfully, wise one, when you sent your wolves, did you not know Efren was here?"

Osheana pushed back the hood of her cloak. The forest lightened as if clouds had unveiled the moon. The lines in Osheana's dark complexion were more plentiful, and the jet-black of her hair had given way to snowy white, but her back was straight, and her coal eyes burrowed as deeply into Skylar's soul as they always had.

"I receive thoughts, but I do not know others' feelings, nor wish to," Osheana said. "I only knew when you blasted your unwelcome message through my forest. How are you this age and so unruly, child of Hera?"

Skylar could not think of a suitable reply. Osheana's reputation was warranted. She was pricklier than a nest of briar and bramble.

"No matter. I do not care why. Follow me then, if you must. And Hera's child, keep your thoughts to yourself. I am old and easily disturbed by the babbling of others."

They followed Osheana in silence, the crone leading on a path that revealed itself only to her.

❖

For the first time in moons, Skylar slept past dawn.

She awoke alone. Osheana's cabin had only three rooms and a privy. Skylar found them all deserted.

In a clearing outside the cabin, sunshine played on a meadow parched from the summer and yet to drink from autumn's rains. Bhaltair and Maryn cleaned and sharpened weapons. Calida talked softly with Efren, Florian played with Kit, and Osheana sat in the shade of a beech tree on a stool with a raven on her arm.

Even though Skylar trod lightly onto the grass, Osheana turned her head as she approached.

"Good morning," Skylar said cordially.

"Morning broke some time hence," Osheana teased her rather than reprimanded. "Calida and Florian have been regaling me with tales of Alba. To my sadness, the country does not appear to have improved. You doubtless had many a snatched night's sleep."

Skylar's heart lifted. This strict but kind Osheana was the woman she remembered from childhood. She had made a fuss of Skylar and Cora. Skylar had not seen her since Cora's funeral.

"Assist me, child."

Florian looked up from rubbing Kit's belly and went to Osheana. His delightful massage interrupted, Kit narrowed his eyes and disappeared into the forest.

Florian stood a respectful distance from the bird with glossy dark plumage, a dagger beak, and coal-black eyes. Ze stretched out an arm, and the raven fluttered from Osheana to Florian. Florian smiled, biting zir lip. Skylar blinked. Florian's gestures were familiar to her now. It made the risk of losing zir, Goddess forbid, all the more poignant.

Osheana muttered to the raven. It faced her, tucking its head to one side. Suddenly, the bird took to the air. It flew across the clearing and flipped perfectly around.

"Hmm," Osheana grunted. "As I thought. You are not safe, even here. And you must train."

"Train?" Skylar asked, her sense of comfort evaporating in an instant.

"Your telempathy. That you are fully grown and still unruly is a grave omission. You bring danger to yourself and others."

"But my skills don't warrant training, do they? Hera said—"

"Do not quote your mother to me, child. Hera drowns her abilities with sleeping herbs. And as for your talents, why do you think you have cloistered yourself these years at Thale? Despite your skills in combat and leadership, you have seldom left the butch compound."

The words drove home. Before Captain Noro dispatched her to the earthquake region, Skylar had served on only a handful of missions outside the district. It had suited her to live among her bredren. Even so. "I learned to shield."

"Did you? Then why do you broadcast your every thought?"

Skylar started. She barriered her mind immediately.

"That is better," Osheana said wryly. "I will instruct you in proper shielding. You must always shield without effort, not just when you think of doing so. Hopefully, you will be a quick study, for then you should travel northwest."

"Northwest, Iya?" Efren asked.

"I think so. The scrying bowl will tell me more." Osheana removed the cover from a deep indigo dish at her feet. The stone was as dark as a moonless night. She placed it on her knee, poured water from a jug, and gazed into it.

Skylar felt tendrils from Osheana's mind reach out and slip into the swirling water.

Osheana inhaled sharply. Then, abruptly covered the bowl. "It is as it was several days past. I see bloodshed." She looked solemn. "It is inevitable if you confront the leader. But, perchance, if you go northwest, you can avoid it."

Skylar did not back down from a just fight. "You said 'perchance.' It is not certain then that we will be safe if we flee?"

Osheana rose stiffly, rubbing her knees. "Nothing is certain even for a soothsayer. Your choices determine your future, not the mist in my bowl."

Skylar did not want to risk the health or life of any of their party. The moons in Alba had shown Skylar what bloodshed meant. The lives taken weighed on her conscience. "Perhaps we travel on, then?" Skylar looked to Calida for her opinion.

"What is in the northwest?" Calida asked Osheana.

"Apart from rain and snow," Bhaltair said.

Calida's eyes widened in horror.

"The Witch Islands. Home to the most powerful collection of mystics in Gaea. If you can reach them, you will be safe. And your talents would be trained so that the three of you can be all you were meant to be."

Calida stared at Osheana in confusion. "What do you mean talents?"

Osheana placed her scrying bowl back onto the ground, then rubbed her hands together, massaging the backs of them. "The child has an affinity with beasts. I have a small measure of animal empathy, but yours, Florian, exceeds mine already. Do you link with all beasts or just the warm-blooded ones?"

Florian stirred. "All, I think. I connect with insects, birds, snakes, and frogs, as well as tame and wild creatures."

Calida blinked at zir in astonishment. "I did not know you spoke with creatures."

"I feared to tell you," Florian said. "In Alba, I was already marked as strange. And it was a comfort. I had friends who did not judge me."

"Florian's empathic with humans, too," Skylar said. The prejudice in Alba would have been searing.

Osheana nodded. "And you, mistress of the knives, are a weather witch and herbalist. Or you will be with proper instruction."

Calida looked about to laugh, but then her face grew thoughtful. "My mother was charged with witchcraft," she said after a time. "She was sent to a work camp in the south. Mama could grow anything. She knew when to water and when to hold back. She knew where to sow. We joked that the plants spoke to her."

"Perhaps they did. And who knows what you could be, daughter," Osheana said. "You three should leave on the morrow."

"I will come with you to ensure your safe passage," Efren said softly. "I have no desire to face Captain Noro." She grinned.

"Nor I." Bhaltair winced at the sound of the captain's name.

Maryn placed her hand on Florian's shoulder. "I will not turn my back on a fae child in danger. Plus, I am in no hurry to explain to my captain why I left my post on Hazelmere Bridge."

"Then, the die is cast. Go with the Goddess. Do what thy wilt and harm none," Osheana muttered.

Bhaltair pursed his lips. "I will harm none that do not attempt to harm me."

Osheana narrowed her eyes at this corruption of the witch oath.

"So mote it be," Skylar murmured.

Osheana nodded approval. "And blessed be you all."

Chapter Twelve

They climbed Morrigan's Pass, a two-day journey from Osheana's forest refuge. The grass and moss at the foot had given way to sheer rock, and the path had narrowed, forcing them to dismount and lead their horses. The few trees they encountered clung stubbornly to the mountain edge, bent to precarious angles by the constant wind. There was no shelter from its bitter chill. Calida pressed forward, drawing the hood of her cloak around her frozen ears. She glanced at the white clouds hanging ominously over them. Snow was on the way. She could not tell if it would arrive before nightfall. She hoped they would be across the pass and on the lower slopes by then.

It was true she could predict the weather, but could she command it as Osheana had hinted? Time and training would tell. Excitement stirred within her. There had been a time when she'd thirsted for knowledge and found great joy in learning. Was it possible that she could put *her* desires forward in this new country? She would endure great wastes of ice and snow for that.

Calida had made peace with Skylar's secret-keeping, though she had not told Skylar that yet. Gaea was such a different place. Over the last days, Calida had come to understand why Skylar had not been honest in Alba. Calida's attraction to Skylar was there, still burning away. But she was cautious about committing to deeper feelings. And that was all right. There would be many moons in the Witch Islands.

Maryn led their party, with Florian behind her. Efren followed, with Calida next and Bhaltair and Skylar at the back. Kit scampered alongside them. Even he, with his fur coat, wore a grimace.

Bhaltair stomped on the trail like an angry horse, spraying grit down the path. Calida was glad it was Skylar behind him and not her. She had no idea what had caused his bad temper. He was a fiery sort. She did not mind that, being quick-tempered herself. He was childishly competitive with Skylar, which Calida found amusing. But occasionally, he was churlish. Please, the heavens, this was not one of those days.

They rounded a corner, and the wind gusted so furiously that Florian shrank back. "Is it like this where we are going?" ze tentatively asked, holding on to Efren.

"Yes. If not worse," Bhaltair snapped.

Calida turned and threw him a look that would stop the mouth of anyone with sensitivity.

Unfortunately, Bhaltair had none. "If our weather displeases you, lady, you should have stayed where you were," he shot at her.

Calida caught her breath, furious. *He is young and arrogant. But he is Skylar's bredren.* She stared him down, but before she could speak, Bhaltair's fury turned to shame.

"Forgive me, Calida. I spoke out of turn."

Skylar tugged sharply on Bhaltair's sleeve. "You have been foul since the temperature dropped. You are no fonder of our northern climate than Calida is."

So that was the reason.

Bhaltair shook off Skylar's hand, but the eyes he raised to Calida were contrite. "It is true. I am not built for frozen lands."

"Why not go ahead, Calida, behind Maryn. And calm yourself, Bhaltair. It is difficult enough on this trail without your ill humor." Skylar sighed with infinite patience.

She would make a good leader. Calida glanced back at Skylar, cloistered within her warrior's cloak, smiling broadly at her despite the gusting wind. Even if the Witch Islands *were* cold and wet, it might not be so bad if Skylar were there. Calida knew some very good ways to keep them warm.

❖

They fell into silence. It was enough to concentrate on negotiating the rocky pass and to battle the wind.

Maryn and then Calida followed the winding trail as it turned under a ledge. A scattering of gravel fell onto the trail. Florian passed unawares, but Skylar looked up. An archer stood above, silhouetted against the sun. He loosed his bow. The arrow flew at Florian.

"Florian, get down," Skylar yelled, running forward. Even though there was no chance, no chance in all the world, she could reach the child before the flinthead pierced zir back.

But when she rounded the bend, it was not Florian lying bleeding on the ground but Efren. Above, the archer restrung his bow.

Skylar pulled her knife from her belt and threw it at him, shouting, "Hey," to pull his attention.

He turned into her knife, and the bow fell from his hands. He staggered out of sight. Bhaltair ran to Efren.

Calida pulled Florian into the mountainside, shielding zir with her back.

As Skylar ran past Maryn, she choked out, "We are under attack."

Skylar raced to the path above. The assassin had slumped onto a rock. He clasped the knife in his chest, too weak to pull it out. Blood stained his jerkin. His life force was draining away.

Skylar locked minds, not caring about invasion. *Who sent you?*

His dimming eyes fixed on hers. *The leader.*

Are there others with you?

The dying man's reply felt like "no," but he had gone, and Skylar could not be sure. She did not sense other strangers, but she had not felt this assassin lying in wait.

Maryn took Kit and scouted ahead.

Skylar walked back, reaching for Efren's life force. She barely felt the icy gusts, registering only that the wind had picked up. She could not feel Efren anywhere.

The arrow had been broken, and Efren turned onto her back. Her eyes were closed. Bhaltair knelt at Efren's side, his head bent as he wept on his lover's chest. Skylar let them be.

Instead, she gently pulled Florian from Calida's arms to hug zir close.

"Efren pushed me out of the way," ze whispered into her shoulder.

Skylar was numb. Efren was gone. Kind, gentle Efren. She was a warrior through and through. Steady. She had so much more to give, to experience, to share.

Skylar held Florian on that expanse of bare rock in the bitter wind and berated herself. Osheana had been right. She was untrained. If she had sensed the assassin, Efren might be alive.

Osheana. Skylar's spirits plummeted with the realization that she must be told. Though she was a seer. She may already know.

And then Skylar recalled with a terrible shiver the forecast of bloodshed in Osheana's scrying bowl.

❖

Osheana received them gravely. Calida wondered if she had foreseen their arrival and Efren's sad return.

Efren had been wrapped in cloth, placed in a hastily built drag sled, and towed faithfully by her horse. They had chosen the quickest, gentlest routes, ready to fight any that dared cross them.

There was a pyre in the clearing. The branches waited, laid together in layers, to make a last bed for Efren. Calida recognized the branches by their scent and bark: oak for comfort, willow for grief, and Hecate's tree, yew for protection and renewal.

Maryn took the horses behind Osheana's cabin to tether them away from the smoke and flame to come.

Bhaltair lifted Efren from the sled, carried her to the pyre, and laid her gently upon it. Osheana bent to rest her cheek on Efren's. And then she raised herself slowly, leaning heavily on her staff.

Skylar stood next to the pyre with a flaming torch. She looked at Osheana, who nodded, and Skylar passed the torch to Bhaltair. Four candles flickered inside clay pots. Calida knew from her mother's rituals they were placed in the four directions east, south, west, and north. The pyre was at their center.

Osheana walked a circle large enough to encompass all the humans and Kit, then stood before Efren.

"Mother, take my granddaughter into the air, let her rise in flame, flow within water, and grow again deep inside the earth. Your earth, your water, your air, your fire. Keep her for us until we meet again. Efren, you lived a good life. You were my fosterling granddaughter, my kin. I loved you all your life. May my love wrap around you now and carry you to a sweet, restful place." Osheana's voice was strong and steady. It resonated through the silent forest. Only the bow of Osheana's shoulders betrayed her grief.

"It is time, Bhaltair," she said.

Bhaltair put torch to wood. With a burst of flame, the pyre ignited. Bhaltair stepped back. The firelight reddened his flowing dark hair and brown skin. Calida was used to burials. She had a delirious moment of wanting to snatch Efren's body from the fire. But she calmed as the flames grew and the scents of herbs and oils filled the air.

Calida stood with her arms around Florian. *Oh, Efren, I would that you were here. You died to save my child. I can never repay what you did. But I can bear witness to your passing and lend my will to bring the people who did this to justice.*

Flecks of ash danced in the haze of fire. Gray smoke soared above the pyre, rising to meet the sky.

❖

Skylar turned over on her bedroll. Calida lay next to her, and she was glad of her presence. They, Florian and Kit, were squeezed into Osheana's workroom.

Bhaltair and Maryn had chosen to sleep outside beside the glowing coals of the pyre.

Skylar rolled this way and that, her thoughts turning as unrelentingly. What could she have done to prevent this horrible event? What if she had seen the assassin? What if she had scouted ahead of the main party? They should have had someone scouting ahead. Efren would still be alive. If she had ignored Kit's cry, if she had ignored her heart and come back to Gaea alone, if she had let her family be taken and returned…Efren would be here still.

Calida sighed deeply. She brushed Skylar's arm and rested her head on Skylar's chest. "This is a hard night," she murmured so quietly that Skylar hardly heard her. "She was special to you."

"We trained together." The other cadets underestimated Efren, as small and slight as she was. Not Skylar, because Skylar's empathy knew the power and determination inside her. "Efren was the best of my year in hand-to-hand combat. If the assassin had jumped her, we would not be mourning Efren now. I have always thought it is a coward's way to fire an arrow or, forgive me, Calida, to throw a knife. We who dare to take a life should witness firsthand the pain and suffering we cause."

Calida said nothing. Her chest rose and fell softly. Skylar held her, let the sweet scent of her soothe her soul, and wished with all her heart that things had turned out differently.

"I loved her deeply, mostly as a friend. We were better as friends. Our physical intimacy was an extension of training, of liking each other and respecting each other's skills. She was my very best friend." There were never enough words. Or words of the right kind. Not to explain grief nor death. Skylar knew the awful, terrible pain she felt at this moment would change. Efren's name would not always pierce her heart so. Eventually, her grief for Efren would be forged by pressure and time to stone. It would lodge in her heart beside the precious stone that was her love for Cora.

"I hope tomorrow brings peace for you, my darling." Calida entwined her fingers with Skylar's.

Her fingers were warm and strong and alive. That helped somehow, even while it did not.

❖

At dawn, Osheana appeared with a bowl of ashes. She had already daubed the skin beneath her eyes and streaked her cheeks. "We return to the mystery in the end," she said softly, anointing Skylar, Calida, and Florian in the same manner.

Today was the day to bury and scatter ashes, and then began the three-day wake. But Skylar had woken consumed with a restlessness that would not be eased.

She stepped out into the clearing to the rising sun. Maryn's and Bhaltair's bedding was gone. Kit sat guard by the dimly glowing fire. She felt a hand upon her shoulder and turned to find Osheana looking with narrowed eyes toward the forest. A moment later, Maryn and Bhaltair emerged carrying a pail of earth between them.

"He moves with haste, but it will not speed his healing," Osheana said.

Bhaltair walked with leaden limbs. Skylar felt his mind was elsewhere, somewhere protected, with his heart.

"Wise one," Skylar said. "I must take Calida, Florian, and Kit and go." She looked down at the lush green grass, knowing what she proposed was an insult. "We must not give the leader a chance to send another after us."

"I see. Well, Skylar, child of Hera, everything is changed now." Osheana beckoned to Maryn, Bhaltair, Calida, and Florian to come together. "There is no time for your training now. Once word begins to spread of my grandchild's death, the leader will commit further abuses to cover this one. That is the way of things when power and responsibility are held without honor or grace. The founders must lend our strength to your cause."

It was an audacious idea. But Osheana was powerful and learned. She had led the country in earlier, more perilous times. Skylar looked at Calida.

"You think this is the only way?" Calida asked.

"I do. First, we mourn Efren," Osheana continued. "Then we garner support. There will be no slipping away. We must bypass the leader and demand an audience with the council. Three days hence, we shall march on the capital together, gathering our numbers as we go."

CHAPTER THIRTEEN

By the time they reached the Shuimu River, their numbers had swelled to forty. People had come forth from villages and towns along the way to join them. Skylar was amazed so many were prepared to challenge the newly elected leader.

At a rest stop, some fifty leagues from Hazelmere, Skylar, Maryn, Calida, and Bhaltair debated how best to cross the tumultuous river.

"We are too great in numbers to pass over the bridge unchallenged," Bhaltair said. He had not been persuaded to take time to grieve nor to return to Thale. Skylar did not know if it was the best decision for Bhaltair, but she took comfort in his presence. It felt somehow as if Efren traveled with them, still.

"Indeed," Maryn drank heavily from her canteen, replenished with the fresh river water. She, too, had stayed. Seeking justice for Efren's murder was a strong motive for them both.

Skylar surveyed their group. They were mostly young, strong, and full of adventure, but some were seasoned retired warriors or mystics like Osheana.

Dust upon the road pointed to a rider. Skylar and everyone around her stood immediately. Bhaltair jumped onto his horse and galloped toward the rider.

Skylar turned to Maryn, who was halfway into her saddle. "Bhaltair must confer. He cannot act by himself like this."

"I agree," Maryn called, already riding after him.

Skylar sighed. "Something smolders within him. It makes him reckless."

Calida slipped her arm around Skylar's waist. "I see that. And you must decide, Skylar, do you lead this regiment or whatever we are? Because everyone looks to you. You are the Gaean wronged. I am Alban in everyone's eyes, and Florian is not yet an adult."

"I would prefer we were a council of five: Osheana, you, me, Maryn, and Bhaltair."

"Fine words, Skylar. I applaud them. We can proceed that way. But you should consider what happens if we come to battle. We will not have time for council meetings then."

What an alarming thought. They had been attacked, and Efren killed, but battle? In Gaea, against their own? They were forty already. It was conceivable their numbers would grow. Calida was right. They must discuss the possibility the leader would turn the civil guard upon them at the capital.

On the road, Maryn embraced the stranger, and then they turned their horses around. It seemed the tall, smiling, olive-skinned person of twenty years or so was an ally.

"My friend Kegan has come to join us," Maryn called when they drew nearer.

"Word has only reached me of your plight this day." Kegan jumped from his horse, ran to Skylar, and pulled her into a crushing embrace. "I rallied behind your cause immediately. And now I find my dear friend Maryn in your army. I am beyond excited. I believe I can be of immediate help, for there is a ford some ten leagues east. You can cross there and avoid Hazelmere altogether. I am afraid that area is closed to you since you deceived the guards there."

"How do they know we deceived them?" Skylar extracted herself diplomatically from Kegan's close and somewhat painful embrace.

His smile broadened. "News has spread of butch and fae warriors absconding from their regiments to join the great Skylar Larkrye. And who could blame them? Who would not want to save pitiful fugitives from the evil land across our border?"

Skylar dared not look at Calida, for she could feel the heat of her irritation. "I am not great, simply a person trying to do what is right."

"Indeed, indeed." Kegan's face attempted a solemn expression. It was a fair attempt save for the lips that twitched continually into a smile. "And that is how heroes are made."

Embarrassed, Skylar turned away to find Bhaltair staring at her solemnly. He rested a hand on her shoulder. "We all stand with Skylar, Calida, and Florian."

Kegan beamed. "Of course we do. The civil guard has taken command at Hazelmere. They are no longer expecting you to flee. They anticipate your march on Civitas."

"How is word traveling so fast?" Perhaps Skylar should have been pleased, but she found the information concerning.

"You have the old ones behind you, the first council. Their word carries great weight. Messengers ride from village to town— subtly, I might add. But still, someone was bound to tell the civil guard. Look at the followers you have already." Kegan's hand swept across the people assembled on the grassy riverbank. "Oh, my!" His eyes alighted on Florian, in deep conversation with a young butch of eighteen years with Kit beside them. The young butch stroked Kit's glossy coat.

"Is that the famed vultrix?" Kegan's voice rose in volume and pitch. "Come here, magical fox, if you please, I would know you."

Kit turned but made no move toward Kegan. Skylar was not particularly surprised at Kit's reluctance. He would not come to her when he was being deliciously cuddled by another.

Maryn laughed. "Not everyone falls in love with you at first sight."

Kegan grinned unperturbed. "I bring other news. There is a tavern in Millersford owned by the son of one of the first arrivals. They will support you there, and the inn is just a few leagues from the crossing."

It was an advantageous meeting indeed. Kegan was a welcome addition. Bhaltair rallied the group, and they set off east, now forty-one strong.

❖

They rode the two leagues to Millersford at nightfall. They had spent the afternoon getting everyone safely across the river and then set up camp a good distance outside the town.

On Kegan's suggestion, only Skylar, Calida, Bhaltair, and Maryn accompanied him to the Waterwheel Tavern. It was better, Kegan said, to meet the eager supporters discreetly as Millersford was a town of divisions stirred up by a new group called the Absolute.

"But who are they?" Skylar asked Kegan on her right. The exuberant fellow rode a little too closely for her liking. She was grateful for any supporter of their cause, but she did wish Kegan had more understanding of a warrior and their horse's need for space.

"A sect led by Emrick Blunt. They believe in the absolute right of Gaeans to preserve our border," Kegan said cheerfully.

"I have never heard of them. And they are strong in Millersford, you say?"

Kegan nodded.

"Word of the Absolutes came to Thale while you were away, Skylar," Bhaltair's voice sailed forward from behind. "They were not concerned with the border at that time. They preached about preserving Gaean values. We were called to a skirmish a moon or two ago on the High Road to Civitas."

"Blunt is from Civitas. He was a wealthy, influential merchant before he got his calling," Kegan said.

"They are a new cult then." Light flared ahead from the town gate torches. Skylar slowed her horse.

"New but powerful." Kegan slowed beside her. "I am afraid that your border crossing has boosted his recruitment a hundredfold or more. His sect believes the enchantment of the border is a divine right granted by the Goddess. Their ideas appeal to the devout as well as to the fearful."

"That is unfortunate," Maryn said, riding at the back of Kegan.

"Unfortunate but useful for the leader," Calida muttered. "There is something to be gained for this Emrick Blunt, I am sure. Power, perhaps. It seems to me Gaea and Alba have some things in common."

Kegan's face twisted. "Gaea is an entirely different place," he snapped.

As quickly as Skylar sensed his annoyance, it evaporated. "Well then," she said as they reached the town. "It is indeed wise to avoid these fanatics and speak discreetly with our allies."

"The streets are narrow. We must dismount," Kegan said.

Skylar did so, then led her horse through the gates.

"Goodness, my little friend, what are *you* doing here?" Maryn cried in amusement. She looked in her saddlebag, where a small, red, furry head with a sheepish expression peaked out.

Skylar lifted Kit into her arms. "I asked you to stay with Florian. Ze will be scared that you are missing." Kit gazed steadily back at her. Skylar shrugged and set him down.

They led their horses through quiet streets, Kegan at the head of their party. They passed houses and shops, dark save for a few flickering lanterns.

"This area, the streets around the Watermill Tavern, are disposed to your cause. The Absolutes hold sway on the other side of town." Kegan smiled. His teeth flashed in the scant moonlight. She was a quarter full and veiled behind wisps of cloud. Kegan walked confidently forward, pulling his horse. Skylar would have preferred to take a more measured, cautious pace, being a stranger to the town, but she deferred to Maryn's friend's familiarity.

A square lay ahead with the outline of a large building at its far edge.

"What was that?" Kegan whispered, staring into the gloom of a pitch-dark alley. "I thought I saw someone lurking there. I will investigate. Maryn, come with me." He grasped Skylar's arm. "Go forward. The inn is very close at the far side of the square."

Calida peered into the alley, knife in hand. "Is it wise to separate?"

Kegan laughed in a relaxed manner. "I am overcautious by nature. Go on to the inn. There are friends there. Maryn and I will join you in but a moment, I am sure."

"He has always been overcautious." Maryn rolled her eyes. "We will follow as soon as possible."

Skylar nodded. They hitched the horses to posts by a grassy area and walked on through the square.

The shadow of the inn loomed ahead. It was a two-story building large enough to accommodate many travelers. It was too dark to make out whether it was built of wood or stone. There was no torchlight flickering a welcome, no music or voices in hearty conversation, just a gentle babble from the stream that gave the Waterwheel its name.

Bhaltair halted several steps in front of the inn at the same moment as the hairs on Skylar's neck rose, and Kit flattened himself, peering toward the shadows.

Five hooded figures stepped from the gloom.

"Skylar Larkrye?" a deep voice asked.

The strangers carried double-edged axes. Skylar frowned. The labrys had a long association with lesbians. It was an unusual weapon for any group.

Calida reached inside her coat.

"Something's wrong," Bhaltair muttered, drawing his sword.

Skylar agreed. She unsheathed her sword and staff.

The strangers approached silently, spreading out to encircle them.

Skylar, Bhaltair, and Calida formed a triangle back to back. Kit took up a low growl.

"It is them. There's the witch fox." One of their number dashed forward, axe raised.

Bhaltair swung his sword to intercept the attacker.

Two ran at Skylar. She met the axe of the first with her sword. Metal clashed on metal, sending a jolt through her forearm. She twisted and thrust, forcing the axe away. Skylar spun backward and felt the second axe graze her right cheek, then a cry and a clang as that axe fell to the ground. She glanced back. Kit savaged the attacker's arm.

The first came at her again, and this time, his blow wrenched her sword from her hand. He swung the axe in an arc across her belly, meaning to gut her. She pushed her staff into the axe's path. It sliced the staff clean through.

She cast the pieces aside, bending for her sword. But the attacker kicked it away. It shot across the dirt into the shadows.

He raised his axe high with a grin.

You are never weaponless. Noro's voice rang in her ears. Skylar kicked out and swept her attacker's legs from under him, dodging the axe as it fell. Bhaltair leaped into the circle and ran the assailant through.

Calida battled the last antagonist across the square. They fought with daggers furiously and close. Blood ran from a long slash across Calida's shoulder.

Skylar picked up her sword and edged closer. She could find no gap in their close combat. No moment to swing at the foe without risk to Calida.

Calida turned, exposing her throat. The attacker's dagger swept toward it.

Calida blocked the blow with her forearm. Blood splurted as the knife sliced it open. And then the assailant crumpled, her mouth agape in a silent scream. Calida pulled her dagger from the attacker's chest and bent over, panting and clutching her arm.

Five opponents lay still on the ground. Kit huddled against Skylar's legs. As Skylar stared at the bodies, the clouds lifted. There were emblems on the cloaks. She bent to examine one. It was a single green leaf against a golden band. This was oft how the enchanted border was represented.

A figure ran toward them across the square. The three of them turned as one, weapons ready.

Maryn stared at the bodies. "I feared something like this. You are unharmed?"

"We need a healer for Calida." Skylar ignored the stinging cut on her cheek. "Do you think there is anyone in this town we can trust?"

"We cannot take the chance. Kegan betrayed us. As soon as I realized there was no one in that alley, I turned to leave, and he tried to stop me. When I pushed him aside, he ran away."

Bhaltair stepped close. "We must go. Townsfolk may appear at any moment."

They helped Calida back to the horses. Skylar pulled bandages from her saddlebags and quickly bound Calida's shoulder and arm. She bore the pain with barely a murmur.

As Maryn helped Calida onto her horse, Bhaltair bent to Kit.

"This little fellow helped me," he said, lifting him into his arms. Skylar smiled at the sight of them despite her concern for Calida.

They rode out of town, narrow streets or no, traveling as fast as Calida could bear. Her face was a mask of pain. Maryn's torment was of a different kind. After the night's events, it was clear they could not rely on old alliances.

Skylar rode back to camp, brooding on these new divisions and wondering what they meant for the future of their land.

❖

They proceeded ever closer to the capital. Calida had learned to endure much during her years of hardship in Alba, but after all the moons of rough travel, she began to long for a bed beneath her back and hot water to wash in. She stretched in the saddle, rubbing her back. Her forearm ached within its tight bandage. The attacker's knife had cut deep, leaving a jagged wound. Her right shoulder itched and chafed as the long slash mended. But there would be no inns. They all wished to reach Civitas quickly and without further skirmishes. The group, now more than sixty strong, had split into bands of ten so as not to draw attention. Some had been given the role of messenger. They visited towns along the way to walk the markets and sit in taverns, listening for information that they passed amongst the bands at the end of each day.

The news was mostly of ill feelings stirred up by the Absolute. Fortunately, the Gaeans likely to support the cult were too conservative to trust a faction the government had not endorsed. Calida yearned to reach the council. If they were as wise as Osheana believed them to be, surely they would find a peaceful resolution.

Calida, Skylar, Florian, and Kit traveled with seven others. For days, they had done nothing but ride, eat, sleep, rise from the stony ground, and do it all again.

As the sky began to glow with gold, Skylar called a halt beside a forest clearing.

Florian jumped down and immediately began assembling tents. Ze was the youngest of their band and yet worked eagerly alongside the adults. Florian was so efficient ze had been made tent leader to Calida's pride.

Calida dismounted more sedately, then set off with Skylar through the forest to search for firewood. She eased her shoulder and arm with gentle exercise as they walked, relishing a rare moment alone with Skylar. She kept an eye out for wood garlic and thyme for her wounds and for yarrow to mend the graze on Skylar's cheek.

Skylar seemed heavy in thought.

"You are quiet." Calida spotted a clump of white flowers bowing thirsty heads above broad, green leaves. She bent to pick a little of both.

Skylar scooped a thick branch from the ground. "I am taxed from the day, is all."

Calida straightened. "We are close to Civitas now, are we not? Are you worried?"

Skylar frowned. "I am apprehensive. Are you scared of what may come?"

Calida grunted. "I find no use for fear except to spur me on to fight."

"Spoken like a true warrior."

Calida searched Skylar's face for banter and found none. "I suppose I am one. Alba is a harsh drillmaster. I would have enjoyed learning at the hands of a mentor, though."

"You can. When we win our cause."

"I admire your confidence. As we draw near, I am not afraid, but I grow restless. It is a strange feeling."

"I understand. I pray the council will listen to us. I would avoid more bloodshed. I really would."

She felt a burst of warmth for Skylar. They had known each other such a short time, and yet their lives were so entwined. "You have given up much to be with us, Skylar."

Though Skylar's face was heavy with fatigue, her lips rallied into a smile.

Calida stretched out her hand. "I will be forever indebted to you for bringing us across the border, Skylar."

Skylar dropped the firewood to take Calida's hand. They stood with fingers interlinked. Their bodies leaned toward each other.

"Skylar. Skylar." Someone called at the camp insistently enough for their voice to carry into the forest.

They returned at once.

A messenger gulped water in front of the fire. Florian attended to the fellow's horse nearby. The steed was drenched with sweat, and the messenger flushed.

The rest of their band were gathered around him.

"What news?" Skylar cried.

He wiped his mouth with the back of his hand. "Ill tidings, Skylar. The leader has signed a treaty with the Absolute."

Skylar stiffened. "She aligns with those people? I can hardly believe it. What is the reaction in the town?"

The messenger's expression was grim. "The word spreads like wildfire, and the cult's numbers increase. They have coined a name for us: the challengers. And there is more. Emrick Blunt calls on his followers to march to Civitas to support the leader against us."

Skylar looked stunned. All the Gaeans did.

Calida did not react as they did. She did not have the same feelings for Gaea, not nearly yet. But this land was everything to Skylar. Calida slipped her arm through Skylar's.

Skylar needed Calida's support and give it she would. For she could no longer deny how deep her feelings for Skylar ran.

She took a moment to wonder at her audacity. How was it that suddenly she dared to dream? In the midst of uncertainty, with all that had come before, for the first time since the King's guards took Mama, she dared to indulge feelings she had always denied.

Whether that made her strong or weak, time would tell.

Chapter Fourteen

The challengers grouped together on a great hill in the center of Civitas. Festival Hill was a green area used by the capital's citizens for celebrations on high days and holidays. Its vast, level top made it a suitable campsite for their group of ninety.

They faced the old council building perched on the peak of Founders Hill opposite. It was the original seat of government, now occupied by the council. The imposing stone building was buttressed by a tall fence and parapets running the length and breadth of it. The defensible site and fortifications were necessary in the early days when the founders feared an Alban attack. By contrast, the leader building in the valley between the hills was a civic building accessible to the people of Civitas.

As tents were raised around them, cooking fires lit, and animals tethered to graze, Skylar met with Calida, Bhaltair, Maryn, and six founders.

Osheana addressed them. "The founders will speak with the council. They would not dare refuse us. Skylar should accompany us."

Bhaltair grunted. "Revered one, is that wise? Can you not see the civic guards in the valley below, barring the way to Founders Hill? Surely, you must take more than one warrior with you."

Lydia, a blind, light-skinned, white-haired crone standing beside Osheana, chuckled. She had two guides. A tawny owl who sat on her shoulder, and a golden wolf who kept vigil at her side.

"Child, we are witches and mages. Do not let our ages deceive you into thinking we cannot defend ourselves handsomely."

Murmurs of agreement passed between the founders. A brawny middle-aged man coughed to clear his throat. "And those of us without magic have fought in real battles, young warrior. We have seen bloodshed the like I hope you never will."

Bhaltair turned to Skylar with a questioning look under his furrowed brows.

Skylar clasped his shoulder. The noise of a camp at leisure was at her back: conversation, laughter, somebody playing the flute. "We are here in force, brother. Our presence on this hill will be noticed. We have no reason to believe the council will refuse to speak with us. Let us make a peaceful approach that gives no cause to be challenged."

"Well said, Skylar." Osheana shifted the dark purple shawl across her shoulders. "Then let us be on our way."

They descended the narrow trail on foot at a pace suitable for all of their number. Skylar's hand found the hilt of her sword. It was not the prospect of standing before the council that made her uneasy. It was the close monitoring of their approach by the civic guards at the bottom of Founders Hill. She liked even less the scurry of several guards into the leader building and the sudden appearance of another on horseback riding hard up the Founders Hill road.

She hurried to the front of their party to speak with Osheana.

"Perhaps we should take more warriors with us. I do not like the conduct of the guard."

Osheana turned to look. "I do not trust these civil guards either. They are too under the heel of the leader. Yet, we must make a peaceful approach. It is the only way the council will hear us."

Skylar ceded to Osheana's greater wisdom, though the feeling in her gut was not appeased.

When they crossed the valley and reached the base of Founders Hill, a squat and forbidding barrier barred the road. Twenty guards stood just as thickset and somber around it.

A civic carriage approached the other side of the barrier at an unhurried pace. The guard at the reins drew to a halt a few yards before the obstruction. The carriage door opened, and out stepped the leader. Skylar watched her walk calmly around the barrier, weaving through her guards, and wondered why she had ever been in awe of her. She thought of Efren lying still and bleeding, and hot rage coursed through her. Her fingers closed around her sword. She began to pull it from its sheath.

A hand pushed down on hers. Skylar blinked at Lydia in surprise.

"Not your finest idea," Lydia said so pleasantly she could have been proposing a picnic atop Festival Hill.

Osheana's tone was not sweet when she spoke to the leader. "We have nothing to say to you, Althea. We are here to speak to the council."

The leader took a slow breath, her face devoid of expression. "Unfortunately, the council has been called away to a matter of great importance."

"Pah!" Osheana spat the word out. "What can be more important than this?" She swept her hand toward the challengers on Festival Hill.

The leader followed Osheana's gaze. She stared at the tents and figures outlined against the low afternoon sun, and her composure faltered. "It is too late in the day for a conference, revered founders. Please honor me by meeting again at dawn. I am sure you and I can discuss the matter and reach a mutual agreement."

Osheana conferred with the founders in a tight group. Skylar stayed outside it to consider their options as a warrior.

Three more civic guards had casually joined their fellows at the barrier in the last moments, increasing their number to twenty-five. Forcing their way now would mean a bloodbath. It was unthinkable that the founders end their days here on the road to their very own hill.

Osheana beckoned Skylar over.

"We can break that matchstick and push past the leader's lackeys." The owl on Lydia's shoulder fluffed her feathers at her words. The wolf's breath was a low growl.

"To what end if the council members have deserted their building?" Osheana glared up at the council building.

"And they have. Indeed, none of the council are there," another founder, a powerful telepath, confirmed.

"If we must use force, we should forge a proper plan," Skylar suggested.

The founders nodded in agreement.

Osheana turned to the leader and raised her voice. "Ensure there are council members for us to speak with at dawn."

The leader smiled. "At dawn, then." She turned and walked back to her carriage.

She had thwarted their plan and somehow corrupted the council. But to what end? The challengers had the advantage of greater numbers. If she were sage, the leader would not force them to battle.

Being able to plot and plan, and manipulate certainly made the leader clever. It did not follow that it made her wise.

❖

Late into the night, restless and far from sleep, Skylar warmed her hands before the fire, looking across to Founders Hill.

Not long after sundown, an ant line of guards had trickled to and from the leader and council buildings. The leader prepared for something. Something beyond a conversation at dawn.

Founders Hill was eminently more defendable than the valley. A camp had sprung up in front of the council building. Light flickered from torches and cooking fires, and hazy smoke drifted upward. From the guards camped across the valley and the challengers at her back came the sound of stone sharpening steel as both camps prepared for battle.

Skylar sighed. She had never wanted it to come to this.

The challenger tents were crowded with warriors, farmers, carpenters, stone carvers, poets, many trades, all genders, and a bevy of hearts committed to their cause. Bellies were full. Shields had been polished. Scents drifted on the breeze of smoke and horses.

Someone else could not sleep—a lonely song carried from a resonant tenor who sang of hardship and hope.

The challengers would still parlay at dawn. There was a chance the leader merely prepared for betrayal on their part and would honor the agreement. Osheana had dispatched messenger birds to find the council. There was still a chance their original plan would prevail.

Something crept through a bush fifty paces away. A branch shifted, and a shape emerged. Four legs, a bushy tail, a black snout, and two pointy ears. The animal sniffed the ground and turned his head, sighting Skylar perfectly.

Kit.

He padded over and straight away nuzzled into her neck. She hugged him, not minding that he smelled of dirt, his last kill, and some musky thing he had rolled in. She chose not to think about what that might be.

"Well, I do not have to worry about you in battle," she told her friend. "You are a seasoned warrior. The best of your kind." Kit snuffled in her ear. She drew back to face him. "Promise me one thing. Protect Florian above all others."

Kit looked solemnly into her eyes and dipped his head.

Then, her body tingled at the welcome press of a hand on her shoulder. It was Calida. "Come in. Rest if not sleep. This brooding vigil will do no good."

Calida's gaze flicked to the hill opposite. She was too much a warrior not to take stock of what their future might hold. Then she beckoned toward their tent with a nod.

Skylar followed Calida inside. She was right. Whatever they did or did not do, the moon would complete her journey across the sky, marking time, and casting the die on all their fates.

❖

"Skylar, Calida, rouse yourselves."

Calida sat up in alarm, snatching the knife from under her pillow.

"Ill news." It was Maryn at the tent doorway. She sounded weary. "Come to the founders' area."

"What is it?" Skylar's voice was croaky with fatigue.

Moments before, they had been asleep, wrapped together in an embrace. Calida wanted nothing more than to slip under their blankets and curl against Skylar's warm body. Usually, she did not shy from meeting trouble face-on, preferably with a weapon in each hand. But tonight, she did not want to hear bad news. If talks failed in the morning, they would go into battle. What could be worse than that?

Skylar struck flint to tinder and lit the lamp. A flare of orange chased the shadows from Maryn's face. Her shoulders were slumped. Her eyes dull.

"Tell me." Skylar's body was tense.

Calida steeled her nerves. "Just say it, Maryn, whatever it is."

"The reserves have been drafted. They march through the night."

"They will be tired, at least, by the time they arrive." Calida began to pull on her breeches, tunic, and long coat. She checked it methodically for the knives sheathed within. Was there time to hide Florian in the city if a battle was inevitable? She paused, reluctant to even think it, but the words sprung to mind anyway. *And if it were unwinnable?*

Maryn bent as she stepped into the tent. "They are a league away. They will be here before dawn."

Calida froze. They had been outmaneuvered. "How many are in the reserves?"

Skylar slipped an arm through her tunic. "Two hundred or more." Her voice was steady.

Calida appraised her. Skylar was indeed worthy of her love. She remained calm and resolute in the face of bad tidings. Calida saw these qualities and wondered how bravery was born if not from oppression. Was that true courage? Not forged as a necessity from pain but crafted within the context of decency and hope?

"Well then." Calida reached deep within her stores of fortitude. "We had best go speak to the founders as instructed if we are to fashion a new battle plan."

Skylar smiled a sad half-smile, her eyes clear and bright, her face the most solemn Calida had seen it. But she clasped Calida's hand, and they followed Maryn to converse with the others.

❖

The morning was gray, and the clouds above heavy with sorrow at what must surely come. Their camp was hemmed in at the front and the rear.

If they had not claimed the hill, they would have been defeated. In front, the civil guard had fortified the valley. Behind them to the north stretched row upon row of the reserves.

The sun rose, brightening the sky, but it could not dispel its leaden shroud. There was a melancholy silence as Skylar, Calida, and Osheana descended Festival Hill bearing the banner of parlay.

The reduced group was Osheana's idea. They still hoped to spare the battle the leader clearly wanted. Florian remained behind, within the protection of the most powerful witches and mages. Maryn and Bhaltair stayed to lead their people should the parlay fail.

The civil guards were lined up with foot soldiers at the front, cavalry behind, and archers at the top of Founders Hill. Light glinted from their chest armor, swords, and shields. Some bore glaive spears, others carried axes. Horses whinnied and stamped their feet. Skylar swallowed, knowing the soldiers were primed to cut them down on their commander's signal. It took all her nerve to keep walking steadily forward.

The leader waited on a dais with Emrick Blunt at her side.

They halted ten steps from the first line of guards.

Osheana clapped her hands. A peeling sound soared past Skylar and up the slopes of both hills. When Osheana spoke, her voice was amplified.

"Althea, current leader of Gaea, you have divided our country with your actions. We, the founders, insist that you stand down your guards and the reserves, grant citizenship to Calida and Florian of Alba, and finally, that you take no action against the Gaeans who have supported their cause."

The leader radiated nonchalance and triumph. "Come now, surely, you are here to concede. You must see you are not in a position to make demands."

Osheana continued as if the leader had not spoken. "If you do as we ask, we will allow you to remain in post as leader of Gaea."

The leader laughed. Blunt laughed as well, glancing around him for witnesses to impress. How accurate Calida's assessment had been. This was a man who was a merchant just moons previously. Now, he was seated next to the highest position of power in Gaea, bar the council.

"Are your wits failing, revered founder?" Blunt dared to say. "I have followers in every village and town, loyal to the leader. You have nothing to bargain with except your reputation. And that you have sullied by aligning yourself with a lovesick warrior from the remote outpost of Thale and two Alban barbarians."

"Indeed," the leader said. "Now, hear me, Osheana, for this is the only bargain I will make. Concede. Give to me Larkrye and the two Albans, and I will not pursue the rest of your misguided brigade."

"Enough, Althea. You have misused your position. Our people know the founders stand against you. Your deeds will be judged." A slow thrum charged the air as Osheana's words echoed up and down the hills.

But the leader was beyond reason. Her eyes flashed with fury. "Arrest them."

Parlay had failed. It was time to play their remaining card. As guards moved toward them, Skylar tore the chain holding the bronze labyrinth on her neck and threw it at the leader's feet.

"I evoke the petitioner's right, one-on-one, in the way of our ancestors," she said. "The winner decides the outcome. I will accept a warrior of your choosing, or you may face me yourself." Skylar let the words fall away and felt no fear. The plan had come to her at the last moment, and it was right. It would prevent a battle. Every decision she had made since crossing the border had led here.

The leader stared at the intricate, inwardly winding circle lying in the dust before her and frowned. "We do not decide matters by petitioner's right anymore. The practice is from the days when we were as barbarous as Alba is still." She threw a look of disgust at Calida.

Osheana raised her staff. "The petitioner's right is in the statute books. It has never been repealed."

Blunt turned to the leader. For a moment, Skylar thought he meant to accept the challenge. "You cannot allow this upstart warrior to dictate the rules of war."

"I have no intention of doing so," the leader snapped in irritation.

"What do you know of war?" Skylar said to Blunt. "I have seen more combat, persecution, and atrocity in four moons than most Gaeans will ever see. And some of the persecution is at your hands, leader. Do not hide behind your office, face me in combat, or elect another to do so." A part of her was amazed at her daring. But the greater part had lost respect for the leader. She should have governed with grace and beauty. Instead, she had betrayed them.

As word passed from person to person, a cry of "petitioner's right" repeated up and down Festival Hill, and the leader paled. After deliberation, she said, "You are a trained warrior." She struggled to regain her composure. "Therefore, you should face a suitable opponent." She turned to the commander of the civil guard.

The commander was a bear of a man, tall and broad. He acknowledged the leader with a brisk dip of his head. He may be at the head of the guard, but he was no administrator. His skills were legendary.

He was the superior warrior, but Skylar did not let herself imagine any outcome but victory. "So be it."

Everyone moved back to their respective lines and silence fell. The significance of the moment weighed heavy on Skylar's shoulders. The petitioner's right had not been enacted in scores of years. Not in Skylar's lifetime had the outcome for a community rested in two warriors' hands.

Weapons ready, they faced each other. Then, the commander sprung. His broad sword raced toward her chest, and Skylar barely had time to raise her shield. The impact drove her backward. But she stayed her ground, cut up, pushed his sword away, and thrust forward.

His riposte almost battered the sword from her hand. The commander parried swiftly and hard. He was a master swordsman and ferociously strong. Forced back again, Skylar gritted her teeth and blocked with all her skill and might. His strategy was bombardment. She must find a gap in it.

She tried to deflect a fast diagonal cut and took a blow to the face from his shield instead. He advanced with a volley of thrusts. Her arms weakened. Her shield buckled. She would never win the combat like this. She blocked with her battered shield, and her wrist twisted on itself. She forced the pain away. She had to change tactics.

The commander was bigger, better, and he was crushing her. She must be lighter, swifter. Smarter.

She let her exhaustion show. Dangerously slackening her thrusts, she felt the commander's energy surge. She lunged at his chin to draw his attention. As he parried, Skylar dodged and slammed her shield into his left cheek.

He reeled backward. Skylar spun to the side and thrust at his ribs while placing her leg behind his knee. Dancing to avoid her sword, he tipped. His weight carried him to the ground.

Skylar stood over the commander and kicked his sword away. The point of hers rested atop his throat.

The commander took cautious breaths and met her eyes. "I concede." He was a seasoned warrior prepared to accept death in combat.

But Skylar did not want to take another life. Not when there was no need. "Rise, Commander."

She stepped away, relieved, joyous. She had gambled and won. They were free.

She turned, anticipating cheers of joy.

And was met with silence. There, in a semicircle between her and Festival Hill, stood her bredren. Florian, Calida, Osheana, Maryn, and Bhaltair.

Shackled, every one.

❖

Calida, Bhaltair, and Maryn stood apart from each other with manacled wrists, each guarded by a soldier bearing a raised sword. Florian was enchained, too. The sight was too sickening to comprehend. Skylar felt zir terror, even though ze stood bravely. And pushed to her knees—to her knees—was Osheana. She wore manacles twined with green stems. She had no plant lore, not really, but Skylar knew the herb threaded onto the iron cuffs must be dill. Its cultivation was banned in Gaea because it dampened magic.

It was an outrage. Osheana was ashen. She looked up with clenched teeth, holding her wrists away from her. Skylar sensed the contamination she endured.

Skylar turned to Festival Hill, where their supporters watched, frozen. She could command them to attack. By the time they poured down the hill, their leaders would be dead.

Althea stood with her fist curled around the phoenix head carved on top of her golden scepter. It was the symbol of her authority, and she raised it now.

"Skylar Larkrye," the leader was confident, buoyant even in her audacity. "You have committed grand treason. Together with revered founder Osheana, Bhaltair Eastwind of Thale, Maryn Ravenchild of the fae, Calida of Alba, and Florian of Alba. The sentence for your crimes is death by execution to be carried out immediately."

Skylar's fingers tightened around her sword, and her lips peeled back into a snarl. She would never accept this injustice. She quickly assessed Florian's and Calida's plights. There was no blade leveled at Florian yet. But if Skylar ran through the guard beside Calida, could Florian free zirself before ze were killed? Could Calida, with a blade already at her back? Her heart raced as she contemplated the unthinkable choice before her.

She could not even consider the fates of Osheana, Bhaltair, Maryn…

What she could do was insufficient, but do something she must.

"Drop your weapon, Skylar," the leader said. "And the child can live."

Skylar's teeth found her bottom lip. She bit down to not let her scorn for the leader ignite her face. She could not trust a word of truth to fall from the traitor's lips.

Kit, get ready to aid Florian, she signaled.

Skylar's eyes grazed Calida's, and she blinked once, an instant before meeting the leader's gaze.

Now.

A snarling ball of sinew and fur darted between guards to jump at the one holding Florian. At the same moment, Skylar whirled backward and knocked the sword from the hand of Calida's guard. It had barely clattered to the ground before Skylar was upon Florian's guard, her sword at his chest.

She forced him away from Florian and took stock. Calida's chained hands lay across her guard's throat. He grappled for the dagger at his belt, so she squeezed tighter. The guard's hands dropped to his side.

Maryn, Bhaltair, and Osheana were captive still but alive. "Release them all," she demanded.

The leader's voice came from her safe position behind Skylar. "Archers, stand ready," she called.

As civil archers marched to the front of the ranks, the commander sprang suddenly to life. To Skylar's surprise, he raised his hand. "Lieutenant Larkrye won the challenge. Do not commit this unlawful act. I command you to desist."

But the archers did not relax their bows. Nor did the guards holding Maryn, Bhaltair, and Osheana lay down their weapons. All looked beyond the commander to the leader.

Skylar would never have disobeyed Captain Noro. Althea had chosen her guards well.

"The laws of this land are *my* concern, Commander," the leader began but stopped when hoofbeats resounded through the valley.

A group of riders galloped fast toward them.

At the front was a tall man with flowing white hair. Behind him came six others. They were all elders dressed in white robes trimmed with purple, the ceremonial robes of the council. The riders looked trail-weary, agitated, and angry.

The front rider dismounted. He strode past the guards to Althea, unperturbed by the number of weapons drawn. His skin was pale, and his eyes were the piercing blue of an ice forest. His white robe fluttered in a wind that swept down from the north. When his gaze fell upon Osheana, his face flushed with fury. He unsheathed the dagger on his belt.

"Take your hand from the founder's shoulder," he ordered the guard behind Osheana. The guard obeyed immediately.

Osheana met his gaze. "Head counselor, I wondered when you might wake up to this obscene injustice."

The head counselor sliced away the dill bracelet and helped Osheana to her feet. "We were sent away, supposedly to an emergency. Your message found us at midnight." He turned to the guards. "Unchain these people," he commanded before fixing cold eyes on the leader. "It appears we have not been informed of many things, Althea."

The leader came forward hurriedly. "Head counselor, council members," she addressed the council with reverence. "We cannot all be present here in a battleground. Who would lead the country if we all fell? Please retire and allow me to calm this situation as I intended."

"Your time as leader is over, Althea. The council has spoken." The head counselor surveyed the challengers on Festival Hill. He stood for some time as if searching every face in the crowd. "And so have the people of Gaea. Hear me, one and all. There is no need for battle this day. Your cause is won."

His words were relayed along the ranks until a great cheer burst from the hill. Relief rolled across the leagues from the reserve guard and from many in the civil guard, too. Skylar sheathed her sword. She clasped Florian's hand and Calida's, guarding her injured wrist, and enveloped them both.

They stood in that close and weary embrace for a long time while shouts and songs of celebration rang out all around.

❖

Althea looked small on the defendant's dais in the council chamber. Just a short time ago, she had a regiment to defend her authority. Now, a guard stood on each side to ensure she did not abscond. Following the almost battle of Founders Hill, the council announced they would decide the leader's fate immediately.

The head counselor sat on the judge's platform, facing Althea. He tapped a small staff on the table in front of him. The sound reverberated through rows of tiered public seating packed with civilians and warriors. Skylar, Calida, and Florian sat together in one of the top tiers. Skylar's head was still swimming from the battle, but her attention was riveted to the proceedings.

When silence fell, the head counselor spoke. "You have been found guilty of two charges: murder and betrayal of the founding values of Gaea."

Althea stared ahead at the public seating, looking not at the counselor. "Whatever your findings, I have never betrayed my country. I did whatever was required to preserve our border security. Nothing is more important to me than protecting Gaean citizens from the tyranny of Alba. Today, we witness a trickle across our border that will end in a flood. With refugees will come criminals, spies, and agents of their king. Record my words and heed them well, for the decisions you make here will soon be judged and found wanting."

Murmurs of assent and disagreement spouted all around Skylar. She sat quietly and cradled her swollen, twisted wrist.

The head counselor indulged the public reaction momentarily before rapping his staff once more, bringing a hush to the room. "Althea Leewood, you will be confined for a minimum period of five years, with the term to commence immediately. In five years, the leader and council will consider your sentence. My recommendation is that a further term of fifteen years should be served. You will be escorted to the courthouse cells to await transfer to Nungal Prison. Guards, take the prisoner down."

Calida leaned closer to Skylar as the former leader walked from the chamber, her back ramrod stiff and her eyes blazing defiance.

When the doors closed behind her, the public seating area erupted with discussion and debate. Skylar rose and left the chamber with Calida and Florian at her side.

In the quiet of the large antechamber, she had just drawn a breath when Calida stiffened. Skylar followed her gaze to a warrior on duty at the entrance doors.

He was the civic guard who had held Florian. Calida's boots rapped across the tiled floor as she went over and tugged on his arm. "You." She poured seven hells' fury into the word.

He turned and looked abashed. "I followed orders. It was my duty."

"Well, guardsman, should you be ordered in the future to slay a child, I suggest you take the honorable course and resign your position."

The guard dropped his eyes.

Calida grunted and led Florian through the doors into the late afternoon sunshine.

"Come, you," she tossed back to Skylar. "You need knitbone on that wrist. Don't think I have not noticed how you nurse it. Plus, we all need a good meal. And I could do with a cup or three of wine."

Skylar chuckled. For a day that had started wretchedly, it looked to be ending favorably well.

❖

In the late afternoon of the following day, Calida relaxed on the terrace of their accommodation.

They had been billeted in a small house in the valley. The set of rooms was immensely comfortable, with bed chambers, a sitting area, and, best of all, the charming terrace with a view of the two hills.

She was content to do nothing but watch clouds drift by. With her face to the sun, the press of buildings and people eased away, and she could imagine riding across an open plain with the wind in her face as free as the sky above. She had never truly enjoyed living in Freymar. The great city of Civitas was even less to her liking.

She kept these thoughts to herself. At least, she hoped she did. Calida glanced at Skylar, who lounged in a chair opposite with her eyes closed. There was much to learn about in this new country, telempathy included. She thought about beginning a conversation and shrugged the idea away. Skylar looked so tranquil. Heaven knows they'd had few untroubled moments these past moons.

They were on their own. Maryn had taken Florian to meet with fae cadets stationed in the capital, and they would not return until late evening.

Skylar flicked open her eyes, smiled, and ignited a flame within Calida. The axe graze on Skylar's cheek had almost healed. She was valiant. Truly courageous. Deeper feelings stirred, and Calida realized she was in love. Now, that was a thought most definitely best kept private.

"Would you care to go for a run?" Skylar asked. "Or perhaps join me in weapons drill?"

Calida laughed. "No one could accuse you of idleness! Can you not enjoy a moment's peace?"

Skylar shrugged. "I am in the habit of training every day, lest my skills diminish."

"Very good, wise warrior. Are they all as conscientious at your butch compound?"

Skylar nodded. "Some more so. You have met Bhaltair, have you not?"

"Can I go there, to Thale, so I can see for myself?" Calida intended to tease, but now that the idea was out, it had its appeal.

Skylar narrowed her eyes. "It would not be allowed, which is a good thing. It would be annoying, not to mention a hazard, with all the butches mooning after you and getting in the way."

Calida threw her head back and laughed. It felt good. At last, there was nothing to fear. Nothing to hold back from.

Skylar gently pulled Calida to her. Calida met her lips. Nothing existed save the bump of her heart and their need for each other.

They drifted for many long moments. How long, Calida could not say, just that the sun faded on her face. She opened her eyes and found it shielded by a cloud.

Skylar followed her gaze. "Are you cold?" she murmured.

"Um-hum. But I have a remedy for that," Calida replied. She slipped her fingers through Skylar's and led her to the warmth of their rather grand, eminently comfortable bed chamber.

❖

"Will you return to Thale?" Bhaltair asked Skylar. He had stayed for the citizenship ceremony that day conducted by Osheana, interim leader of Gaea, and taken his leave immediately afterward.

Bhaltair had opted to lodge at the Civitas butch platoon barracks. Skylar went with him there to see him on his way. The building was smaller than Thale, but it felt familiar, awash as it was with tan uniforms. The sound of warriors at drill in the yard carried to the stables where they talked. Saddled and ready, Midnight nibbled patiently on the straw at his feet.

Skylar smiled a little sadly and shook her head. "I will miss the compound. The air is clean, and my bredren are there."

"I will miss *you*." Bhaltair reached for Skylar's hand in the Amazon clasp.

Skylar felt Efren's presence pass between them and was glad for it. "And I, you, Bhaltair. You are a brave and true warrior."

Bhaltair put an arm around Skylar's shoulders. He touched his cheek to hers. "I have grieving to do, brother. I know you do, too. One day, perhaps soon, I hope to see you again in happiness."

"Indeed. We will regale folk with tales of our adventures," Skylar said. "And drink much free ale in taverns. You will hit impossible targets with your arrows and spin your sword over your head in the style of your ancestors."

Bhaltair laughed. "I should do that before I drink the free ale."

"That would be best."

They drew apart, and Bhaltair led Midnight out to the gates. He mounted and rode away without looking back.

Skylar watched Bhaltair and Midnight upon the trail out of the city until there was nothing to see but the cloud of dust in their wake.

❖

In their comfortable rooms, Skylar enjoyed a hearty breakfast with Calida, Florian, and Kit. The sun fell across the dining table through large eastern windows, and a crisp breeze blew in from the door to the terrace. The season would turn soon, but here in the south of Gaea, it remained comparatively mild, even in winter.

Despite the magic of their union, Calida had slept fitfully beside Skylar. It seemed the abiding threat of the last moons had not released its claim on her. Or Skylar. She woke each morning with a hand reaching for the knife at her belt. It would likely be weeks before their uneasiness would fade.

Florian, by contrast, was as bright and cheerful as the morning. Ze filled zir plate with sweet rolls, heaping golden butter and purple boysenberry jam onto each one. Snuggled onto Skylar's lap, Kit was also content, taking tidbits of cold roast fowl from Skylar's fingers. He gobbled them down as if he had not eaten in days. Calida regarded them all with one eyebrow raised but said nothing.

Florian washed down a chunk of bread and jam with a swig of frothy milk. "Mama, what will we do now? Do you want to stay here in Civitas?"

"I'd rather move to the seventh frozen league of icy hell," Calida replied calmly.

"Are you sure? Do you not wish to consider the proposition awhile?" Skylar teased her.

Calida grimaced. "I am not fond of the noise or the crowds of cities. But it is not just for me to say. We must discuss what we do together."

"Is there a place you do wish to go, Mama?" Florian asked.

Calida wiped a smear of jam from Florian's robe. "The Witch Islands."

Skylar nearly choked on her tea. "You do know it is full of snow and ice?"

Calida laughed. "Indeed. I am aware." She rested a hand on Skylar's arm. It felt right there, warm and tingling with the current that sparked between them. "If I have magic within me, I want to explore it."

Skylar turned to Florian. "And what about you, child?"

"A child no longer," ze chided her. "In Alba, I would be an adult in six moons. I…" Florian swallowed, looking tentative. "I might like to become a fae cadet."

"You have the right to enlist now that you are a Gaean citizen." Skylar was proud of Florian. It was ridiculous, considering how short a time they had known each other. She had nothing to do with the fine person ze was. Her pride revealed the place Florian had in her heart.

"I felt content at the fae barracks. There were so many young people like me. A whole platoon, Mama, Skylar." Florian's eyes shone with the memory.

"So, you would be a warrior." Calida took up a small fruit knife and began to peel an orange.

"Skylar is one."

"And so is your mama. Not officially, perhaps, but what is a warrior, if not one who aids and protects and who is deadly when provoked?" Skylar grinned at Calida.

She dipped her eyes and continued to separate the peel from the fruit in one unbroken curl. "Am I to go to the Witch Islands alone, then?"

"Of course not," Skylar and Florian said together.

"I would know if I am an empath," Florian added. "Osheana says the mystics there are the most powerful in the land and will help us."

"And I can also benefit from magical learning, it seems," Skylar said. "But are you truly sure about traveling to the Witch Islands, Calida? It is a long journey, and the islands will be frozen in two moons. There are witches in warmer parts of Gaea."

"I *am* sure. Besides," Calida stroked the hairs on Skylar's arm, "are there not robes and strong butch arms to keep me warm?"

Skylar smiled. "It is settled, then."

Calida nodded. She turned to the view through the windows.

"We should leave soon. Before the mountains become impassable," Skylar said.

Calida did not reply.

"What is it?"

Calida met Skylar's eyes. "We are fortunate to be here, are we not, Florian?"

Florian nodded solemnly.

"Florian can be zir true gender. I can be my true self. But all is not entirely well in my heart, Skylar. My thoughts often fly to those like us in Alba. They have no idea there is a free land so close to them. Closed to them. And I think of my mama in prison there. I may never see her again."

Silence fell. Skylar felt sad, too. She had traveled through Alba and discovered how like Gaea it was. Aside from the tyranny, much united them. And all was not noble in Gaea. Althea sat in a gaol cell, but Efren was still gone.

"However, we must appreciate our good fortune," Calida's voice brightened.

"Indeed, Mama," Florian said.

"So I will allow myself this happiness." Calida pursed her lips. "And I'll fight anyone who tries to take it from me." She brandished the tiny fruit knife before her.

Skylar and Florian laughed, rousing Kit. He stretched and whined, jumped to the floor, and shook himself. He sniffed, then followed the breeze to the terrace door. He turned, looking back as if to say, *Why do you sit when the sun is bright and there is a garden to explore?*

Skylar rose. He was right. "Come, let us walk on the hills if you want space and air. Or into the alleyways of the old town, where there are trinkets to buy and delightful morsels to taste. Let us venture anew. Who knows what awaits our discovery?"

THE END

Glossary

Butch: a person proudly identifying as a masculine female. Can also be used for a person identifying as a masculine male.

Crone: a wise elder. Can be used for any gender.

Empathy: the ability to sense other people's feelings.

Fae: a person proudly identifying as a feminine male.

Femme: a feminine female, usually but not exclusively lesbian.

Healer: a person who uses plants to treat disease.

The leader: the elected ruler of Gaea.

Mage: a magical person.

Petitioner's right: a challenge to one-on-one combat upheld in Gaean law as a way to settle serious disputes. Combat may be to the death or not—the winner decides. Close combat weapons are allowed (no arrows, flails, crossbows, or knife throwing).

Protectorate: (Alba), a person with authority who works for local dignitaries (lords, mayors, etc). In status beneath a justice and above a bailiff.

Shielding: the practice of barrier-ing the mind for privacy or protection.

Spirit: the atmosphere around a person read by an empath. Their emotional core. Can be at the moment of the reading, or it may be their core emotional personality.

Telempathy/telempath: the ability to read minds/hear unshielded thoughts as well as feel other people's feelings.

Telepathy: the ability to read unshielded minds.

Vultrix: a sentient, magical fox. Has the ability to communicate telepathically.

Witch: a person who is trained in the use of spells, rituals, and other wiccan methods. Also one who possesses magic.

Witch Fox: Alban name for vultrix.

Ze/zir: neutral pronouns used in Gaea.

About the Author

Crin Claxton is the author of the butch/femme vampire novel *Scarlet Thirst*, the Supernatural Detective ghost mystery series, and *Across the Enchanted Border*, all five novels published by Bold Strokes Books.

The Supernatural Detective won an honorable mention in the Foreword Indie Fab book of the year awards (2013, Gay & Lesbian section) and was nominated for the American Library Association Over the Rainbow booklist (2013). *Death's Doorway* was an Indie Fab Award Finalist (2015) and won an honorable mention in the 2015 Rainbow Awards. *The Haunting of Oak Springs* was runner up in the Lesfic Bard Awards (2023, mystery section).

Crin is a proud butch lesbian. Ze is a lighting designer and production manager for theater. Crin lives in London with zir partner and child.

WWW.crinclaxton.net

Books Available from Bold Strokes Books

Across the Enchanted Border by Crin Claxton. Magic, telepathy, swordsmanship, tyranny, and tenderness abound in a tale of two lands separated by the enchanted border. (978-1-63679-804-2)

Deep Cover by Kara A. McLeod. Running from your problems by pretending to be someone else only works if the person you're pretending to be doesn't have even bigger problems. (978-1-63679-808-0)

Good Game by Suzanne Lenoir. Even though Lauren has sworn off dating gamers, it's becoming hard to resist the multifaceted Sam. An opposites attract lesbian romance. (978-1-63679-764-9)

Innocence of the Maiden by Ileandra Young. Three powerful women. Two covens at war. One horrifying murder. When mighty and powerful witches begin to butt heads, who out there is strong enough to mediate? (978-1-63679-765-6)

Protection in Paradise by Julia Underwood. When arson forces them together, the flames between chief of police Eve Maguire and librarian Shaye Hayden aren't that easy to extinguish. (978-1-63679-847-9)

Too Forward by Krystina Rivers. Just as professional basketball player Jane May's career finally starts heating up, a new relationship with her team's brand consultant could derail the success and happiness she's struggled so long to find. (978-1-63679-717-5)

Worth Waiting For by Kristin Keppler. For Peyton and Hanna, reliving the past is painful, but looking back might be the only way to move forward. (978-1-63679-773-1)

Flowers and Gemstones by Alaina Erdell. Caught between past loves and present secrets, Hannah and Vanessa must each decide if the other is worth making difficult changes for a shot at happiness. (978-1-63679-745-8)

Foul Play by Erin Kaste. Music librarian Kirsten Lindquist knows someone is stalking the symphony musicians, but can she prove that a string of murders and suspicious accidents are connected, all without becoming a victim herself? (978-1-63679-689-5)

Hollywood Hearts by Toni Logan. What happens when an A-list actress falls for a paparazzo, having no idea her love interest is the one responsible for the photos in a troublesome tabloid scandal targeting her? (978-1-63679-695-6)

Ride It Out by Jenna Jarvis. When the COVID-19 lockdown traps Mick and Katy in situations they'd convinced themselves were temporary, they're forced to face what they really want from their lives, and who they want to share them with. (978-1-63679-709-0)

Scarlet Love by Gun Brooke. Felicienne de Montagne is content with her hybrid flowers and greenhouses—until she finds adventurer Puck Aston on her doorstep and realizes nothing will ever be the same. (978-1-63679-721-2)

The Hard Stuff by Ana Hartnett. When Hannah, the sales manager for a big liquor brand, moves to Alexandra's hometown and rivals her local distillery, sparks of friction and attraction fly. It turns out the liquor is the least of the hard stuff. (978-1-63679-599-7)

The Hunter and Her Witch by Rachel Sullivan. When an ex-witch-hunter falls for a witch, buried pasts are unearthed, and love is placed on trial. (978-1-63679-830-1)

Trustfall by Patricia Evans. Devri and Shiv never expect their feelings for each other to linger, but sometimes what you've always wanted has a way of leading you to who you've always needed. (978-1-63679-705-2)

All For Her: Forbidden Romance Novellas by Gun Brooke, J.J. Hale, Aurora Rey. Explore the angst and excitement of forbidden love few would dare in this heart-stopping novella collection. (978-1-63679-713-7)

Finding Harmony by CF Frizzell. Rock star Harper Cushing has to rearrange her grandmother's future and sell the family store out from under her, but she reassesses everything because Gram's helper, Frankie, could be offering the harmony her heart has been missing. (978-1-63679-741-0)

Gaze by Kris Bryant. Love at first sight is for dreamers, but the more time Lucky and Brianna spend together, the more they realize the chemistry of a gaze can make anything possible. (978-1-63679-711-3)

Laying of Hands by Patricia Evans. The mysterious new writing instructor at camp makes Grace Waters brave enough to wonder what would happen if she dared to write her own story. (978-1-63679-782-3)

Seducing the Widow by Jane Walsh. Former rival debutantes have a second chance at love after fifteen years apart when a spinster persuades her ex-lover to help save her family business. (978-1-63679-747-2)

The Naked Truth by Sandy Lowe. How far are Rowan and Genevieve willing to go and how much will they risk to make their most captivating and forbidden fantasies a reality? (978-1-63679-426-6)

The Roommate by Claire Forsythe. Jess Black's boyfriend is handsome and successful. That's why it comes as a shock when she meets a woman on the train who makes her pulse race. (978-1-63679-757-1)

www.ingramcontent.com/pod-product-compliance
Ingram Content Group UK Ltd.
Pitfield, Milton Keynes, MK11 3LW, UK
UKHW040708110325
4939UKWH00018B/55